The *First* ONE

A NOVEL

TAWDRA KANDLE

The First One
Copyright © 2015 by Tawdra Kandle

Cover by L.P. Hidalgo of BookFabulous Designs
Proofreading by Kelly Baker
Formatting by Champagne Formats

Champagne
Formats

ISBN: 978-1-68230-193-7

Other Books by the Author

Dedication

To my daughters
Devyn Jeanne
Haley
Josephine
Cathryn Jill

With love

Chapter One

Flynn

MY EYES WERE BLEARY and dry as I sped along the two-lane road between newly plowed fields. I'd been back to Georgia twice over the past eight years, but never to this part of the state; I'd stuck to the high-rise buildings and traffic-clogged streets of Atlanta. It was safer that way.

But now here I was, hurtling straight back into the center of the town I'd run like hell to get away from. Straight back toward the girl I'd fought to erase from my mind and my heart.

I could almost feel her now, like there was some odd supernatural connection between us. I wasn't far from her family's farm. If I made a left at the next intersection, I could be pulling down the long driveway that led to the Reynolds' home within ten minutes.

No way was that going to happen. My plan for the next few days was simple: get in, do what I had to do and get out. I had a commitment in a week in Los Angeles, and I was going to be there.

But first I had to bury my father.

My hands tightened on the steering wheel. The shock was still there, along with a sharp, keening pain. His death had been so sudden that I couldn't quite wrap my mind around the finality. Part of me still expected to see him sitting on the porch when I drove up to the house, pipe in his hand. Mom never let him smoke it inside, so the porch was their compromise.

"That's what good marriage is built on, boy." He'd said it to me so often that I could hear his voice. "Compromise. It's about give and take, and often you think you're giving more than you take. But it all evens out."

If he were on the porch today when I climbed out of the car, he'd lift the pipe from his mouth, grin at me and call out, "Well, and if isn't Flynnigan Evans, come home at last."

He always called me that in playful moments, despite the fact that it wasn't my name. In fact, he'd used it so often during my early childhood that I'd given that as my real name to the kindergarten teacher, embarrassing my poor mother. Pop only chuckled and winked at me.

I couldn't quite believe he wouldn't be there today. Somewhere in the back of my mind, I'd expected that I'd come home at some point. It'd never been a clear plan, but I figured eventually, one day, I'd stop caring about Alison Reynolds and I'd feel comfortable returning to Burton. And when I thought about that vague day, Pop was always waiting on the porch.

I slowed and pulled the car to the narrow gravel shoulder of the road. Just ahead, a small green sign welcomed me to Burton, Georgia, population 2147. It'd been there, in its current incarnation, since my freshman year of high school. I remembered that because I'd been the back-up photographer for the school newspaper. Kyle Durham, who was a senior and the paper's main photographer, usually covered every event, but he'd just been diagnosed with mono—coincidentally, at the same time his best friend's girlfriend had come down with it, too. To say Kyle had his hands full at the moment was an understatement. But apparently his screwed-up life was about to become my opportunity. The newspaper advisor, Mr. Wilder, grabbed me in the hallway after school and told me to meet Rachel Thomas out front, because we had a story to cover.

I knew Rachel because she was a friend of my sister Maureen; she'd been the one to suggest I join the paper. But when I spotted the tall junior leaning against one of the thick cement columns, she wasn't alone. I recognized the pretty girl standing with her from my own class, but I couldn't quite remember her name. She'd gone to junior high out at regional, as did most of the kids who lived on farms surrounding Burton. When we'd started ninth grade, the small class I'd been part of since kindergarten had swelled to twice its size. I still hadn't learned most of the new names. This girl, though, was in chemistry and English with me, and I was pretty sure her name was Alice or Alicia. Something that began with an A, anyway.

She'd turned toward me, and for the first time, I looked at her. Really looked. Huge, gorgeous brown eyes gazed back at me, and I was gone.

"Hey, Flynn." Rachel pushed off the concrete. "We gotta cover the dedication of the new town sign. Try not to pass out from excitement." She glanced at the other girl. "Do you know Ali? Alison Reynolds, Flynn Evans. She's going to write the story. I'm just the wheels for this one."

Alison's perfect lips curved into a slight smile. "Yeah, Flynn and I have a couple of classes together."

They both looked at me as though they expected me to say something, but I could only manage a nod and a shrug as I followed them to Rachel's old Toyota.

The ride out to the edge of town was pretty uneventful, I thought, but I couldn't swear to it. I sat in the backseat, riveted to every move Ali made. Her light brown hair fell in silken curtains around her shoulders, and she frequently tucked it behind her ears. She never turned around to look at me, but when she faced Rachel, I was pretty sure she was glancing at me out of the corner of her eye. It made me feel funny each time I saw her in profile; my heart sped up, and my stomach clenched, like it did on the roller coaster at Six Flags. By the time we got to the spot where a couple of cars were pulled off to the shoulder next to the sign, I wasn't sure my hands would be steady enough to take the pictures.

The dedication was hardly world news. The mayor and a few members of the town council stood on the side of the road, while a police car diverted traffic, its light spinning in a silent whirl. I stood with Ali and Rachel as the mayor droned on, snapping pictures the old 35 millimeter camera Mr. Wilder insisted I had to use.

I didn't speak a word to either of the girls until we got back to the school, when Ali turned to me as I climbed out of the car.

"Do you want to work on the article together? You know, make sure it goes with the pictures you took?"

I managed to locate my voice. "Uh, yeah. Sure. I gotta develop them first, so maybe, uh, like Friday afternoon?" I knew I'd have to stay after school the next day to work in the darkroom, and I was still learning how to do that. It hadn't bothered me before that our advisor was making me learn how to use an old camera and film system, but now, I was cursing the fact that I didn't have the digital, where I'd be able to upload the pictures right away.

"That works for me. See you tomorrow." She flipped her hair back and shot me a brilliant smile. I managed not to trip over my own feet as I climbed out of the car.

Rachel leaned out her window. "Flynn, I'm dropping Ali

4

off at her house. I can give you a ride, too, if you want. I didn't even think of it until now."

I shook my head. "Thanks, but it's not far. I'll walk. See you later." I stood back as they pulled out. Once the car was out of sight, I hoisted my backpack over one shoulder and hit the sidewalk.

I'd made it part way home before a familiar blue Ford pulled up alongside me. "There you are, son. Thought I'd missed you."

I went around to the passenger side and climbed into the front seat. "Sorry, Pop. I told Reenie I had to stay after for newspaper."

"She told me, and so did Mr. Wilder, but I thought I'd come back and look for you. Save you a walk."

Since we lived in town, my sisters and I'd never ridden the bus. We either walked or, more often, caught rides with my dad. The drawbacks of having a parent teach at the same high school we attended were legion, but there were a few perks. This was one of them.

As we drove home, I slouched in my seat and stared straight ahead. From the corner of my eye, I caught my father watching me.

"So you had your first photojournalism job today, huh? How was it? Exciting as you thought?"

I rolled my eyes. "They dedicated the town's new welcome sign, Pop. It wasn't exactly dodging bullets on a battlefield."

"And may it never come to that." He shook his head. "But still, good for you. Get some decent shots?" My father was an amateur photographer who'd been the one to buy me my first camera and teach me the basics.

"I think so, but I won't know 'til I get them developed. I don't know why Mr. Wilder won't just let me use the digital. Or my own camera, at least, instead of that dinosaur."

"It's good for you to know how to handle film and learn

5

the old-fashioned way. That way you're prepared for anything."

I grunted, neither agreeing nor outright disagreeing. I kept seeing those brown eyes and the slow smile. *Alison Reynolds.* I said her name in my head, trying it out.

"Hey, Pop?" We were nearly home by the time I spoke again. "Do you remember when you met Mom?"

He grinned, his eyes crinkling at the sides. "Of course I do. Happiest day of my life. We were in college, and at a party. I was acting up, being wild, trying to get her attention because she'd caught my eye." He laughed. "I was not many years over here in this country at that point, you know, and not quite the confident man you see before you now. I tried to pull her into my foolishness, and she told me in no uncertain terms that she was having none of it. Said she wasn't interested in stupid little boys. I spent the next three months proving to her I could be more."

"*Three* months?" At the age of fourteen, that sounded like a lifetime.

"Yes, indeed. I got serious. Spent hours studying with her at the library, because that was the only place she'd agree to see me. No parties, no drinking . . . and finally, finally she agreed to go out with me. She made me work for it, your mother did." He grinned. "Still does."

"Why'd you do it? Why'd you go to all that trouble over a girl?" We'd turned into the driveway alongside our house, but neither of us made a move to get out, even after Pop turned off the car.

"Because I knew she was it for me. I didn't know if I'd be good enough for her, or if it would work out, but I knew I'd found the woman who was everything I'd ever wanted. She was worth the wait. Worth the work." He cocked his head at me. "This is an odd conversation for a Wednesday afternoon. Do you have your eye on a girl? Not Rachel Thomas, surely?"

I shook my head, trying not to grimace. Rachel was my

sister's friend, which made her off-limits, even if I were interested. "No."

"Hmmm." Pop shifted in the driver's seat. "Not going to tell me?"

"Not yet. Maybe it's nothing."

"All right then. I'm here when you need to talk." He opened the door and began to get out before pausing to look at me over his shoulder. "Keep in mind, you'd do well to find a girl like your mother. They don't come better than her."

I swallowed hard now, hearing his words echo. The sign still stood there, worn and weathered twelve years later. And here I sat, parked alongside the road, seeing ghosts of people who didn't exist anymore.

I gritted my teeth and took a deep breath. A few miles away, my mother and sisters were waiting for me. I had to pull my shit together.

It was time to go home.

Ali

W HEN I WAS A little girl, bored was a bad word in our family. If I ever dared to claim I had nothing to do, better believe my mother or my grandma found something for me, and it was never anything fun. I learned fast to occupy myself or suffer the consequences, usually in form of weeding a garden, shelling peas, peeling potatoes or putting labels on the jars of jam Grandma made.

Bored was not something I remembered being in the last decade or so. Having an eight-year old daughter, helping my brother run our family farm and the adjoining roadside produce stand . . . yeah, I was usually tired, overwhelmed, maybe anxious, but never bored.

At the moment, though, I was dangerously close.

We kept our farm stand, The Colonel's Last Stand—named for our several-times over great grandfather, Colonel Pierce Reynolds—open all year around, though we opened later and closed earlier in the winter. Now it was early spring, and none of our own crops were ready yet. We had some oranges and grapefruit up from Florida, but that wasn't exactly bringing in the crowds of shoppers. Business would begin picking up in another month, but for now, I had time to kill in the long gaps between customers.

This was new. Usually, I had my daughter Bridget hanging out with me at the stand, but she was spending this weekend at her best friend Katie's sleepover. I missed her happy chatter and smiling face. I'd already re-organized our shelves of non-perishables, dusted the tables, tidied up the cashier area . . . I sighed and wondered if I could justify closing up an hour early and heading home. My brother was more than likely out in the fields, and I might end up with the whole house to myself. The image of a frothy bubble bath popped into my mind, and I smiled. How long had it been since I'd had time for that? I couldn't even remember.

I'd just about talked myself into shutting down when I heard the familiar crunch of car tires on our gravel parking area. Stifling a groan—and watching my luxurious bath float away on one those shiny bubbles—I pasted a smile on my face and leaned out to see who'd stopped by.

My smile turned genuine when I recognized the sleek black Porsche. "Alex!" I darted out to meet him halfway across the small lot. "What're you doing here?"

His dark blond hair was perfectly styled, and his pale blue eyes twinkled at me. "Well, I just thought I'd stop at the best stand in Georgia and see what goodies you might have for me today. Plus get a hug from my best friend. What's doing, chick?"

I wrapped my arms around his neck, closing my eyes and breathing in his scent. "You always smell so expensive, Alex."

He laughed. "Darling girl, I *am* expensive." He tweaked my nose. "And you are adorable. Look at you, still rocking the pigtails."

I stuck out my tongue. "Did you come all the way from Atlanta just to make fun of me?"

"No, actually. I have some business in Savannah on Monday, and I thought I'd spend the weekend here with the folks before I go. I'm on my way to the farm now."

I tilted my head up at him, my eyes narrowing. "You've been spending an awful lot of time in Savannah in the last year. Something going on you want to share with the class?"

He flushed and looked over my shoulder. "Maybe."

"Oooooh, someone's got a boyfriend!" I sang the words.

Alex shook his head, but his mouth curved into a smile, almost as though he couldn't help himself. "Not quite. Not yet. But . . . maybe. Someday."

"I want to hear all the dirt." I took his hand and pulled him into the enclosed part of the stand. "Sit there."

Alex dropped into the folding chair we kept next to the register, and I hoisted myself onto the citrus display table, pushing a few bags of oranges out of the way first.

"There's not so much to tell. Not yet. I met him last year, when I came over for meetings. He's an art dealer with one of the galleries there. We hit it off, but he wasn't looking for a relationship. We were just friends. But we started chatting on line, and texting, and whenever someone had to take a meeting in Savannah, I volunteered." He shrugged. "Things are heating up a little, but we're both being . . . cautious. He got out of a long-term relationship a year ago, and it didn't end well."

"Awww . . ." I hugged my arms around my middle. "Romantic! What's his name?"

"Ah-ah-ah." Alex wagged his finger at me. "That falls under the category of me to know, you to find out. Maybe."

"Oh, come on. I won't tell anyone. I pinky swear." I held

up my little finger.

"Nope. I don't want to jinx it. But if anything gets more certain, you'll be the first person I call, okay?"

"Hmmm." I pouted. "Fine. And I want to meet him, too."

"So you can tell him all my deep, dark secrets? I don't think so."

"You're no fun at all."

"That's not what *he* says." Alex wiggled his eyebrows at me until I giggled. "So enough about boring old me. What's happening in the exciting metropolis that is Burton, Georgia?"

I lifted one shoulder. "Oh . . . you know. Same old. It's been slow here today, so I was just about to close up when you stopped. Nothing's really going on."

"And how about Sam and Meghan? Things still hot and heavy there?"

Almost involuntarily, I rolled my eyes. Alex narrowed his as he looked at me.

"Is that a yes or a no?"

I sighed. "It's a yes. As in . . . yes, they're still groping each other any time Bridget's out of range. PG kissing whenever she *is* around. It's disgusting." I couldn't help a smile, though. My big brother and the pretty art teacher from Florida had taken the long road to love, fighting their attraction to each other and then refusing to believe it meant anything more than a summer fling. No one was happier than me that they were officially together now.

"Isn't Meghan still in school?" Alex leaned an elbow against the counter.

"Yeah, technically. I mean, during the week, she lives in Savannah and goes to classes, and then she stays here with us from Friday night until Monday morning. But now that her roommate's moved, Sam worries about Meghan being alone in the big city. So she usually comes down here in the middle of the week, too. Oh, and Sam's gone up to stay with her a few times this winter, when nothing was going on with the farm."

"I'm glad for them." Alex tilted his head, studying me. "But . . . ?"

"But nothing. I'm happy for them, too. Thrilled."

"Oh, yeah, you sound it. I guess it's just you're worn out from turning somersaults in joy."

I laughed. "No, really. I am. I love Meghan like the sister I never had, and believe me, Sam's a much nicer person to live with these days."

"Getting laid regularly will do that for you." Alex nodded.

"I wouldn't know," I snorted. "Anyway, the point is, there's nothing I'd change. At the same time, though, I see the hand-writing on the wall. I know what's coming. Meghan graduates in May, and then she'll start working here in town full-time in the fall. Sam hasn't said anything, but he's got to be planning to pop the question soon. And even if he doesn't, she'll be living with us all the time. It's going to be an adjustment for me."

"Yeah, you've been queen bee of the farm for a long time now. I can't imagine it'll be easy to share that throne."

I swallowed over a sudden lump in my throat. "It's not about power or control. It's more . . . just a reminder that I don't actually have a place, you know? Sam would never kick me out of the house. Technically, it was left to both of us, but I know it's really his. I'm okay with that, but where do I go? Do I move into Grandma's bedroom and just settle into life as the old spinster aunt?"

Alex laughed. "First of all, you're not a spinster. You're a divorcee, and you have a kid. Second, you're not old. Third, why do you need to stay here? Maybe this is the push you need to finally move out. Find a place for you and the kidlet."

"It's a lot more complicated than that." I slid from the table and brushed off my butt. "Sam still needs me to help him run the farm and the stand. We're doing pretty well, but not good enough to support two households yet. To get my own place,

I'd need a job. And if I get a job, I can't help Sam. See what I mean? Complicated."

"Only if you let it be." Alex rubbed my shoulder. "Keep an open mind. Maybe something'll pop up. Someone who'd be willing to rent to you cheap. Are you really going to be comfortable living with Sam and Meghan after they get married and start popping out the bambinos?"

"No. But I'll burn that bridge when I get there."

"Hmmm." Alex studied me, and the gleam I caught in his eye sent a shiver down my spine.

"Hmmm what? I don't like the look you're giving me."

"Who, me?" He hooked a thumb at his chest and widened his eyes, trying to look innocent. "I was just thinking . . . that if you hooked a hottie and found your own HEA, maybe this wouldn't be so . . . what did you say? Complicated."

I patted his cheek. "You're so cute when you're delusional. Not going to happen, my friend. No hotties in the town of Burton. Well, one right now, standing in front of me, clearly." I amended my words in a hurry when Alex cocked one eyebrow at me. "But none who'd be interested in me."

"You have no idea, Ali Baba." The grin he shot me was so sweet, I didn't even swat him for using the nickname he'd given me when we were in grade school.

"Ha. How would you know, anyway? You don't even live here anymore."

"True, but I still keep my finger on the pulse, slow as it beats here in Hicksville. For instance, I happen to know that Mason Wallace is back in town."

I shook my head. "Of course you do. We were at his bar last summer, with Meghan."

"Right, but have you seen him? My mother tells me he's single again, and I can see the two of you together."

"Alex, he's single again because his wife died. And he has a kid. I doubt he's looking for a good time. Plus, he was in

Sam's class. He's old."

My friend rolled his eyes. "May I point out, my dear, that you too have a child? Maybe that's what makes it a good match. Yours, his . . ." He squinted. "And yours, take two."

"I'm not looking to be the next Brady bunch, thanks. I've got my hands full with Bridge. I don't need to deal with some guy's broken heart and his kid, too."

"Okay, fine. Well . . . there's got to be some decent talent in town." He stood, hooked an elbow around my neck and hauled me in for a quick hug. "Tell you what. Go out with me tonight. We'll get drinks and dance at Mason's bar, and you can flirt with the good old boys until you find one who lights your fire."

"Hmmm." I pursed my lips, considering. "I do happen to have a free night. Bridget's at her friend's house for the weekend. Meghan's on her way to the farm, and she promised to make dinner. I doubt she and Sam'd be unhappy if I gave them the house to themselves."

"Then it's a date. I'll pick you up at eight. Don't be late." Alex rubbed a knuckle on my hair. "See how I did that there, with the rhyming?"

"Yeah, real original, buddy." I pushed away from the table. "Okay, go home and see your mama. I need to get ready to close up. Text me tonight when you're heading my way."

"You got it." He blew me a kiss as he walked backward toward his car. "Dress slutty. Remember, you're looking for a man. You're on the prowl. You're—"

"Oh, get gone already, won't you?" I yelled. He was still laughing when he climbed into the Porsche and drove away.

I began to pull the covers over produce tables in preparation for closing up. It was still cool enough outside that we didn't have to move anything into refrigeration. Once the fruit was protected, I closed and locked the non-perishable cases, emptied the cash drawer and turned the key on the register.

Just before I was about to do my final walk-through—not

that I needed it, but because I knew my brother would ask if I did—I heard another car pulling up. Since I was out of sight of the parking area, I stomped my foot and growled.

"Shit and boiling bollocks. Can't these people come when I need them, not when I'm about to go home?"

"I heard that." Meghan's red head poked around the corner of the wall. "Lucky I'm not a paying customer."

I grinned. "Yup, and if you tell Sam what I said, I'll send Bridget in to have sleepovers with you every weekend."

Her eyes widened, and she clapped her hand over her heart. "As God is my witness, he'll never hear it from me."

"What, you don't like my kid? She adores her Auntie Megs."

"And I love her to pieces. But I have limited time with her uncle, and I like to make the best of it." A smile curled her lips, and I wondered what she might be remembering. Or maybe I didn't want to know.

"So what're you doing here? I thought you were heading right to the house to make dinner for us. My mouth's been watering all day, thinking about your burgers." Meghan's family owned and ran a beachfront restaurant in Florida, and I loved it when she made us their signature hamburgers.

"I'm on my way." The smile left her face, and she bit her lip. "I just wanted to talk to you by myself before tonight."

I leaned back against a covered table. "Oh, yeah? What's up?" My stomach turned a little; was this it? Was she going to tell me . . . she and Sam were getting married? No, I knew my brother; he'd definitely talk to me about that before he proposed. Or was she pregnant? My gaze dropped to her middle, still flat in her low-rise jeans.

"I stopped in town just now. Sam asked me to pick him up some part at Boomer's." Boomer was our local auto mechanic and one of my brother's best friends, even if he was a full generation older than us.

"Okay." I was mystified now. What could Boomer have to do with anything Meghan had to tell me?

"Ali . . ." She reached out and laid a hand on my arm. "Brice Evans died yesterday morning."

For a moment, I was confused. Brice Evans? No, I'd just seen him last week at the grocery store. I hadn't spoken to him, of course; the Evans family and I had operated on a strictly nod and fake smile basis for the past eight years. But he'd been there, looking the same as always. The same as he had when he'd taught my junior year history class in high school, and the same as when I'd seen him practically every day for four years. There was a time when I'd been like one of his daughters.

Meghan was continuing to speak, and I heard her vaguely over the buzzing in my ears. "Boomer said . . . it was sudden. Apparently he got up yesterday, went into the kitchen to get coffee and just . . . dropped. A heart attack, they think. He probably never knew it was happening."

"Oh, my God." I whispered the words, bracing my hand on the edge of the table as unexpected tears stung my eyes. "But . . . he was so young. I can't believe it."

"I know. Poor Reenie." Brice's younger daughter Maureen had been my best friend all through high school, but we hadn't spoken in over eight years. She and Meghan had gotten friendly last summer, although Meghan didn't say much about it, out of deference for my feelings, I suspected.

"I can't believe I didn't hear about it before now. Yesterday morning, you said?"

Meghan nodded. "Boomer said no one knew until early today. Mrs. Evans and the girls were at the hospital most of yesterday—they tried to resuscitate him, I guess. And then . . ." Her voice trailed off, and she glanced up at me with worry and sympathy in her green eyes. "They wanted to wait for . . . Flynn to get home."

I'd known it, realized the truth in some hidden part of my

brain, but hearing his name aloud jolted me. Of course he'd come home now. He'd return because he had to.

"He's here, then?" My voice was surprisingly steady.

"Boomer said he got in before lunch. He's with his family, at the house."

My body was stiff and my movements jerky as I nodded. "Okay." I swallowed hard. "I'm . . . I'm going to close up here and head for home. You coming?"

Meghan gripped my arm. "Ali . . . are you all right? I can't imagine how you must feel."

I forced a smile, as wooden as the ones I'd aimed at Brice Evans since the summer after senior year. "Yeah, I'm fine. I mean . . . it is what it is, right? I'm sorry for Reenie and Iona. I know what it's like—" My throat closed. "I need to go, Meg. I need to get home. Bridge—" *Shit.* She was staying in town, at Katie's house. I wanted her home, with me, away from where anyone—and by anyone, of course I meant Flynn—might see her.

Which was absolutely ridiculous. For eight years, my daughter had been living here, right outside Burton. She'd been going to school in town since she was five. In kindergarten and again this year, she'd shared a class with Graham Fowler, the son of Iona Evans Fowler . . . nephew of Flynn Evans . . . and while I'd been a little worried at first that someone might suspect the truth, when no one did, I'd relaxed.

But it was different now. Now her father was back in town.

Meghan stayed with me while I finished locking up, and she drove me to the house. Usually, I walked from the stand; cutting through the newly-planted fields and the budding groves of peach trees gave me a few minutes of peace and quiet between working the stand and dealing with bedlam at home. But today

I didn't hesitate when Meghan steered me into the passenger seat of her Corolla.

"Are you going to see him?"

I turned to look at her, frowning. I'd been wrapped up in my own spinning thoughts, forgetting she was even in the car. Which was really stupid, since she was the one driving it.

"See who? Oh, Flynn? No. No, I doubt it. I mean . . . I don't think he'd want to see me. And . . . his dad. That'll keep him busy. The funeral. And . . . everything." I sniffed. "And then there's the fact that he left me here, alone and pregnant, eight and a half years ago."

"But Ali, what about Bridget? Flynn's back in town. Aren't you going to tell him about her?"

"God, no." On that point, I was absolutely certain. "He won't be here long. Trust me, he'll get the hell out of town as soon as he can."

She was quiet for a minute, and then as we pulled into the long driveway that led to my house, she glanced at me sideways. "Ali, remember last summer? When I was leaving to go back to Florida, and Sam and I were . . . well, you remember. I believe your words to me were something like 'too stupid to see what was right in front of us'?"

I sighed. "Yes, of course." I had a feeling I knew where she was going with this.

"And I asked you what you'd do differently if you could go back to the day Flynn left. You said you'd leave with him. That not a day went by that you didn't regret letting him go."

"I know what I said, and I meant it. If I could go back to that day, I'd change what I did. But this isn't the same thing. It's nothing like the same thing. Because almost nine years have passed since he walked away from me, and a hell of a lot of stuff has happened. What do you think he'd say if I told him now that I had his baby and never let him know? You think he'd thank me for that?"

"If not now, when? When his mother passes and he comes back again? Or when Bridget graduates from high school and asks you why she's never met her dad? When is it the right time?"

I pressed my lips into a thin line and crossed my arms over my chest. "Not now. That's all I know." I turned in my seat and pointed at her as she parked the car. "And remember, you promised you wouldn't tell Sam."

Meghan looked miserable, her eyes stormy as she frowned. "I made that promise before Sam and I were . . . well, together. I haven't said anything to him because I promised you and it's never come up. And because you said you'd tell him yourself."

I unhooked my seat belt and reached for the door handle. "I will. But not now."

"Ali, please. Think about this. Flynn probably won't be here long, like you said, and you don't know when he might be back in town."

I twisted my face into a parody of a smile. "That's what I'm counting on." I opened the door and climbed out of the car, forcing myself to walk slowly and not look upset. My brother was weird; like most guys, he was clueless much of the time, but when I was trying to hide something, he suddenly morphed into a bloodhound.

He was sitting at the kitchen table when I stepped inside. When he looked up, his eyes were sparkling, and I laughed a little when his face fell.

"Don't worry, big brother, your sweetheart is right behind me. She drove me in from the stand."

Sam tipped his chair back, studying me. "You're back early. What's wrong?"

"We were slow all afternoon, and I decided to wrap up early. Why does something have to be wrong?"

The screen door behind me slammed as Meghan came in. She dropped her bag at my feet and skirted around me to get to Sam, whose chair legs clattered to rest on the floor again when he jumped up to meet her halfway. I rolled my eyes as he gripped her upper arms and brought his lips down to crush hers.

"Okay, guys. That's enough. Geez, you just saw each other Wednesday."

Sam released Meghan's arms, chaffing them a little as he smiled down at her. And then his smile faded. "What's wrong, babe?" He held her face in his hands, his thumbs brushing over her cheekbones.

"I stopped at Boomer's to pick up your whatchamacallit. And Boomer told me Brice Evans died yesterday."

My brother's eyes closed. "No. Oh, my God. What happened?"

Meghan told him the same thing she'd shared with me back at the stand. Sam didn't say anything, but I saw his Adam's apple bob as he swallowed. He'd known Mr. Evans as long as I had, though not quite as well; he hadn't dated the man's son for four years.

"Did Boomer say anything about Maureen and Iona?" He sat back down as Meghan turned to take her bag upstairs.

"Not really. Only that they were waiting to make arrangements until Flynn got here, and that he'd arrived this morning." Her eyes flitted to me, and then back to Sam. "Um, I'm going to take my stuff upstairs. I'll start dinner in a few minutes."

I pulled out the chair across from my brother, closing my eyes and letting my head drop back as I slouched.

"You okay?"

I opened one eye. "Yeah. Why wouldn't I be?"

He shrugged, careful not to look at me too closely. "I don't know. Your ex-boyfriend is back in town after eight years. His dad is dead. Thought you might, you know . . . need to talk."

I toed my sneaker off under the table and lifted my sock-covered foot to kick him in the knee. Not too hard; I wasn't trying to do damage, just get him to back off before I lost my shit right here in front of him.

"Ouch. What was that for?" He scowled at me, rubbing his leg.

"Man up. I barely touched you. And stop with the questions. I don't want to talk about this with you."

For a minute, Sam looked like he didn't know whether to be offended or relieved. Then his eyes narrowed. "You already talked to Meghan, didn't you?"

"We're girls, Sam. And she might be your snuggle bunny, but she's my best friend. Yeah, we talked. So you're off the hook. I promise, I'm not going to go nutso and chase after Flynn while he's in town. In fact, I'm going to do my damnedest to stay out of his way. I think that's the smartest for all of us."

"So you won't go . . . to the funeral? Or even just stop in and say hello? Ali, you practically lived at the man's house during high school. Between Reenie and you, and . . . well, you know. Seems like you should do something."

I shifted in my chair. "I've lived in the same town as Maureen without seeing her on purpose or talking to her beyond the bare essentials for a long time. Don't you think it would be a tad hypocritical to pretend we're best buds now?"

"It's what people do." Sam's eyebrows drew together. "You rise above old disagreements and offer comfort, right?"

"This is a little more complicated than Miss Peggy and Miss Alice fighting over their sweet potato recipe, Sam. Nothing good can come of me bringing up old hurts. It'd be more painful for everyone." I traced the grain of the table, staring at the ancient pattern. "Maybe later . . . I could see Maureen. When everything's over, and things are getting back to normal, I'll stop in and talk with her someday."

Sam grunted. "Make sure you do. It'd be good for you to be friends again. Pretty stupid to let high school crap get between you."

I nodded, but I didn't want to walk down that road. Not

now. "I thought that's why we kept Meghan, so she could be my friend. You know, so I could finally have the sister I always wanted."

He smirked. "Nah, we keep her for better reasons than that." One eyebrow quirked up suggestively.

I faked a gag. "You know, just because Bridget's not here doesn't mean y'all have to amp it up to an R rating. I'm still your baby sister. Your impressionable baby sister."

"Whatever you say." He stood up and flicked my nose as he passed. "I'm going upstairs now to, um . . . help Meghan unpack." He turned to wink at me. "You might want to stay down here. Sometimes she gets a little loud when she unpacks."

"Gross!" I threw my sneaker at his departing back. He only laughed.

I waited until his footsteps echoed at the top of the stairs, and then I reached for my phone. I had to cancel with Alex. I might've spent many years estranged from the Evans family, but it would be disrespectful to go out dancing when we'd just heard of Brice's death. And if there was one thing I knew, small towns like Burton had long memories. News of me partying would've gotten around to Maureen . . . and to Flynn. I might not want to see him, but I didn't want to rub that fact in his face. Once upon a time, we'd meant too much to each other. Once upon a time, Flynn Evans had been my whole world.

For a minute, I sat, staring down at the phone, remembering. I didn't let myself dwell, not often. Hardly ever, in fact. That stroll down memory lane was still too painful. But now his face was front and center in my mind, the way he'd looked that day twelve years ago when he'd first noticed me.

I'd been stupid crazy for Flynn Evans since the moment I'd seen him on the first day of high school. He was tall, with light brown hair that he wore a little long. But it was his eyes that had captured me right away: they were the most vivid blue, framed with long eyelashes I envied.

While he wasn't exactly skinny, neither was he bulked up, like some of the football players I'd seen around the school. When he leaned against a wall, bracing himself with one arm while he talked with a friend, the muscles in that arm sprang into definition, and my mouth watered. *Yum.*

I hadn't been able to help staring at him a little. I tried to be cool about it, sneaking a peek here and there, but it was hard to pull my gaze away. He didn't look my way, though, and that didn't surprise me. I'd spent most of my school years flying under the radar, never part of the popular crowd. I wasn't picked on or bullied; no one seemed to really notice me, unless it was as Sam's little sister.

"What're you looking at, Ali Baba?" Alex slid next to me as I lingered at my locker, quietly drooling over Flynn. Bumping his shoulder against mine, Alex followed the direction of my stare, took in the blush on my face and smirked. "Or should I say . . . who?"

"Nobody. Nothing. What?" I busied myself with my books. "I'm just thinking. About . . . chemistry. The class."

"Suuuure you are." Alex laughed. "Hmmm. Hey, I know that guy. He goes to my church. We've been in CCD together since we were little. His name's Flynn Evans."

"Really?" I tried to act as though I couldn't care less. "That's nice."

"Yeah, want me to introduce you? I can call him over." Alex opened his mouth, and I grabbed him by the shoulders.

"Are you out of your *mind?* Stop it." I hissed the words, my eyes wide.

He laughed. "Oh, girlfriend, how're you going to get the guy if you don't want him to notice you?"

I slumped back against my locker. "It'll happen magically. One day he'll look up and see me, and he'll realize that I'm everything he's ever wanted in a girlfriend."

"Uh huh. Well, when you get tired of waiting for fate to

take a hand, let me know, and I'll make the introductions." He patted my head in the patronizing way I hated. "Gotta run for Spanish. Hasta la vista, baby."

For three weeks, Alex teased, taunted and threatened. Every time we were together when Flynn passed by, Alex looked at me, eyebrows raised significantly. I wanted to murder him. At the same time, I was almost to the point of giving into him, because as far as Flynn Evans was concerned, I was totally invisible girl.

And then it happened.

I'd joined the newspaper at the beginning of the school year because I loved to write, and my parents were pushing extracurricular activities. It seemed like a good fit. I hadn't known Flynn was on staff, too, as a photographer, until our first staff meeting. Not that he'd seen me there; I'd cowered in the back and found the perfect angle to ogle him while still appearing to be looking up front at our advisor as he spoke.

Mr. Wilder had worked on a big paper in Richmond, Virginia, and he had definite ideas about how to run things, even at the high school level. He assigned all of us newbies to upper classmen who'd show us the ropes, take us along on stories they covered and teach us how to put together a tight article. He called it the Bee Helpful program, since the school paper was named the Burton Bee.

I was assigned to Rachel Thomas, a pretty junior with dark eyes and silky black hair. She was business-like but patient; I didn't have any delusions that we'd be best friends, but I figured I could count on her to answer any questions.

About a month into school, she came by my locker before school began.

"Hey, we've got an assignment for today. Wilder wants us to cover the dedication of the new town sign out on Highway 18. I'll drive. Are you cool to be a little late getting home?"

I nodded, making a mental note to find Sam and tell him

I wouldn't be riding home with him, unless he wanted to wait. And since it was harvest time out on our farm, hanging around after school ended wasn't an option. I'd have to see if my mom could run back into town to get me later.

As if reading my mind, Rachel added, "I can just drive you home after, if that makes it easier. That way, you don't have to scramble for a ride."

I smiled in gratitude. "That'd be great if you don't mind."

She nodded and turned to leave. "Meet me out front right after school. Bring your notebook."

At the end of the day, I hurried to my locker, traded out books and sprinted out to where Rachel lolled against one of the columns. One side of her mouth lifted when she spotted me.

"Slow down, don't kill yourself. We have to wait for the photographer." She rolled her eyes, and I frowned.

"Can't Kyle drive himself?" Like everyone else in the school, I knew Kyle Durham. He was a big shot, smart and athletic, and a gifted photographer to boot.

Rachel bared her teeth in a grim smile. "Didn't you hear? Kyle has mono."

"Oh." My mind reeled; I'd heard my parents teasing about mono being the kissing disease, but I knew it was fairly serious. "That sucks."

Rachel lifted one eyebrow. "Know what sucks worse? Lana Tyler has mono, too."

"Lana?" All the underclassman females in this small high school watched the intricacies of the romances between juniors and seniors as though it were a soap opera. "Isn't she dating Matt Gibbs?"

"Kyle's best friend? Uh, yeah." Rachel grinned. "You see the awkward? Anyway, the freshman photographer's covering today with us. Flynn's a good kid. His sister's a friend of mine. And their dad teaches history here."

I tried for an interested but unaffected expression, as

though all of this was new information to me. The last thing I needed was a reputation as a pathetic lovesick girl, which could happen if Rachel caught me mooning after Flynn.

"Oh, here he is. Hey, Flynn." Rachel straightened, smiling. "We gotta cover the dedication of the new town sign. Try not to pass out from excitement." She pointed at me. "Do you know Ali? Alison Reynolds, Flynn Evans. She's going to write the story. I'm just the wheels for this one."

My stomach felt as though it was going to flip right out of my body, and I was dizzy. Flynn turned those piercing blue eyes on me, and a spark zinged down my body, the same way it did when I inadvertently touched the live wire in the barn my dad always warned me not to get near. There was an echoing of the same shock and recognition in Flynn's eyes, and that warmed me to the core. It gave me the courage to smile at him.

"Yeah, Flynn and I have a couple of classes together." I was amazed at how calm my voice sounded.

He nodded, but he didn't speak. If Rachel noticed, she didn't give any indication as she gestured with us to follow her. I paused when we got her car, not sure where I should sit. But Flynn opened the passenger side door and climbed into the backseat.

I got in the car and half-turned in the seat. "You could've ridden shotgun. I don't mind the back."

Flynn lifted one shoulder. "Nah, I'm fine. Thanks."

He didn't speak again, not a word as Rachel pulled out of the lot, drove through town and out onto the highway. The two of us girls kept up a steady chatter, but I couldn't help sneaking a glance at him whenever I faced sideways.

The dedication was nothing more than a few old guys standing on the side of the road. I took notes on what was said during their speeches, while Rachel muttered her sarcastic take on the whole thing. Flynn stood near us, moving every now and then to get a better angle. The old 35 mm camera he used made loud clicks as he shot.

We piled back into the car when it was over, and just outside town, Rachel glanced at me. "So you've got this, right? I mean, it's pretty simple. And I don't want to dump it on you, but I've got three papers due next week, and I'm working on Mr. Gilbert's retirement interview for the paper."

"No, it's fine. I'll write it up and turn it in, unless you want to look the article over first."

Rachel shook her head. "No, I'm sure you'll do fine." Her lips curved, and she raised her voice just a little. "This is one of those stories where the pictures and the article have to jive. So you might want to see what Flynn comes up with before you turn it in."

I flushed, wondering what Rachel had seen in my face. But whether she meant to or not, she'd given me the opening I needed. I took a deep breath and turned around to face the backseat as her car bumped into the school parking lot.

"Do you want to work on the article together? You know, make sure it goes with the pictures you took?" My voice sounded smooth and didn't falter even once.

Flynn looked startled, but he nodded. "Uh, yeah. Sure. I gotta develop them first, so maybe, uh, like Friday afternoon?"

"That works." I managed to hold it together while Rachel offered Flynn a ride home and he turned her down. He stood back as we left the school again, and I kept my eyes off him with only the greatest restraint.

"So. How long have you been lusting after our boy Flynn?"

Shocked, I looked at Rachel with my mouth open. "Excuse me?"

"Oh, come on. I was a freshman once. And I fell hard for a senior. I know the signs."

I flopped back against the seat. "Oh, my God. Does everyone see it?"

Rachel laughed. "I doubt it. But you're braver than me. It

took me months to speak to my crush."

I ventured a glance at her. "How did it work out for you?"

"We're still together. He's at UGA, so I only get to see him about twice a month, which sucks, but we're making the distance thing work." She winked at me. "You should totally go for it, with Flynn. You two have chemistry. I think you could go the distance."

Thinking of her words now, as I stared at my phone, a deep sadness welled inside me. Everyone thought that Flynn and I would be together forever. But when it came down to hard choices, we'd both let each other down.

Which brought me back to Alex and canceling our plans for tonight. I texted my friend, fingers flying over the keys as I lapsed back into our old shorthand.

Did you hear?

His reply was swift. *Yeah, was just about to call you. I can't believe it.*

Me neither. Obviously tonight is off.

Of course. I'm sorry, Ali.

Yeah. I paused, not sure of what to say next. *He's back, you know. In town.*

Alex, who'd kept my secret so loyally, didn't need to ask who I meant.

Are you going to see him?

Not if I can help it.

I could practically hear the sigh that accompanied his next words.

Ali, think about it. Maybe it's time.

I gritted my teeth. Alex and Meghan were both singing the same song, even if I didn't want to listen.

Don't say anything. Please, Alex.

There was a long break before his next reply.

You know I won't. But you should.

Chapter Three

Flynn

"**H**ONEY, IT'S TIME TO go."

I jerked my eyes open. For a moment, I was confused; the living room hadn't really changed in the past ten years, other than the new sofa, upon which I was sprawled. But for a split second, I was lost, unsure about where I was. When it all flooded back over me, the pain was crushing.

I was back in Burton. I'd been here for five days, because my father was dead.

My mother stood in front of me in her dark green dress and shiny black heels, deep shadows under her eyes. One thin white hand clutched her small purse as she spoke.

"Flynn, the girls are ready. We need to leave."

I pushed myself up to sit straight, rubbing one hand over

my face. "Sorry. I guess I dozed off."

Mom reached out to brush my hair away from my eyes, a gesture so familiar that my heart clenched. "None of us have been sleeping very well. It's bound to catch up with us sooner or later."

"Yeah." I cleared my throat and stood. "Okay. Let's go." *And get it over with,* I wanted to add, but of course I didn't. It might've been true, but it wasn't what a son should be thinking before his father's funeral.

The reality was, I couldn't wait for this day to be done, yet at the same time, I dreaded it being over. I was tired of forcing the smiles, the small talk and the polite responses to expressions of sympathy. After today, I could hide. Or run away. Yeah, running away sounded good.

On the other hand, once today's service was behind us, it meant my family—or what was left of it—would have to figure out how to get on with the rest of our lives.

Maureen stood in front of the mirror in the front hall, her chin down on her chest as she struggled to force her curly black hair into an elastic band.

"Jesus Christ, why does my hair have to be such a freaking mess?" She muttered the words almost under her breath, but my mother never missed a trick.

"Maureen Ann, I won't have you talking the name of the Lord in vain, especially not on the day of your father's funeral."

Iona, standing by the door, rolled her eyes. "Because that's the part of the commandment Moses forgot to include on the stone tablet. 'Thou shalt not take the name of the Lord thy God in vain, particularly if you're on the way to your father's funeral'."

Maureen cut her eyes to our oldest sister and unsuccessfully bit back a bark of laughter that ended in a half-sob. "Je-geez Louise, we're making jokes about this. What's wrong with us?"

"That's a question I've been asking for many a year." Mom

shook her head.

"Nothing's wrong with us." Iona softened her words by reaching out to take our mother's hand in hers. "If Daddy were here, he'd be worst of all. Remember Granny Bea's memorial service? How much he made us kids giggle? You were so mad at him that day."

Mom brought her fingers to her mouth, pressing them to her lips, and tears filled her eyes. "I was. Oh, God forgive me, I was. If I could go back . . ."

"Mom, come on." Maureen pulled her into a tight hug. "Don't. Daddy knew how much you loved him. And you've got to hold it together, woman. If you lose it today, Iona and Flynn and I have no chance."

"Okay." My mother sucked in a long, shaky breath. "We need to leave. Everyone'll be coming, and we should be there." She patted Reenie's back and squeezed Iona's hand, and I fought against feeling like an outsider. As if she felt my pain, Mom glanced at me. "Flynn, you all right?"

"Sure." I stuck my hands in my pockets and jingled the keys. "I'll drive."

"Think you can remember how to get to the church?" Maureen poked me in the ribs.

"Does it matter? You're going to tell me how to go anyway."

"You're not wrong." My sister slid her arm through mine. "I know you've been gone a long time, but some things never change. Big sister always knows best."

We were all quiet on the ride to church. My mind was a jumble of everything that had happened over the past few days: visits to the funeral home, meeting with the priest who was doing the service today . . . the endless drop-in company as my mother's friends and my father's colleagues brought by casseroles, and plates of cookies, cakes and pies. Apparently death made the surviving family hungry.

Iona must've been thinking along the same lines. From the back seat, she leaned forward. "Did anyone remember to ditch Mrs. Shulman's tuna nastiness? I'd hate for it to be accidentally put out today with the other food."

Maureen wrinkled her nose and made a gagging noise. "Yeah, that sucker went down the glippety-glop last night. And it was followed by a whole box of baking soda, because it stunk up the whole dam—dang kitchen. Sorry, Ma."

My mother sighed. "She means well. They all mean well. Mrs. Schulman thinks all Catholics eat fish every Friday, so that's why she made the tuna. Bless her heart."

Iona snorted. "If the Pope had to eat that crap, he'd change the church laws, even about Fridays in Lent. Slow down, Flynn. The turn's coming up."

I bit back a retort. Yeah, I'd been away for a long time, but I'd been going to this church since I was born. I was pretty sure I knew the way.

"People are already here." My mother stared out the window at the cars that lined the curb in front of the large gray stone church.

"Father Collins promised to keep them outside until we . . . had some time to get settled." Maureen's eyes slid away, and we were all silent as I parked the car in the back of the church. I opened the door for my mother, and together we made our way inside. I brought up the rear, as dread threatened to choke me.

The sanctuary was empty, save for the open casket in front of the altar. My mother came to an abrupt halt just inside the doors, her hand still poised over the holy water chrism.

"Mrs. Evans." Mr. Hughes, the funeral director, hurried in from the door on the other side. "There's quite a line outside the church, which is of course so gratifying . . . Mr. Evans must've been very well-loved."

"He was." Iona spoke softly. "Everyone loved Daddy."

"We said a closed casket." Mom moved again, crossing

herself and stepping forward. "We were very clear. That's what Brice wanted. He always said he didn't want people gawking at him when he wasn't there to stare back."

"Of course, of course. We understand. But I thought perhaps before we opened the doors, we'd allow you a few moments alone. To say good-bye."

"We already said our good-byes." Mom stared down Mr. Hughes. He took a step back, and I pitied him for a minute; my mother had made many a lesser man cower with that look.

"Flynn hasn't." Maureen glanced at me. "He didn't get to . . . well. He wasn't at the hospital with us. Maybe he should have the chance."

Mom raised her eyebrows at me. "Flynn? Would you like a moment with your father before they—close things up and people come in?"

I opened my mouth to say no. I knew it wasn't him. I had no doubt my father was in the Great Beyond, sharing a cold one with St. Peter and cracking jokes with St. Patrick. But it struck me, in a painful, crushing blow, that this would be the last time I'd ever be able to see my dad's face. That face that had grinned at me as he teased my mom during hundreds of family dinners, had offered me steadfast encouragement at each turning point in my life, had shone with pride nearly every day of my life . . . I was never going to see it again.

"Yes." I nodded. "If it's okay."

"Of course it's okay, son." My mother patted my back. "Do you want me to come up with you?"

"No, I'll just be a minute." I leaned to kiss her cheek and turned to walk down the aisle.

The casket was a solid mahogany, the dark wood polished to a gleaming finish. The rolling cart upon which it sat was draped in black cloth, just in case anyone were to forget that we were here for a solemn occasion. I laid my hand on the closed part of the lid that covered my father from the waist down, and

I remembered the very first funeral I'd ever attended. It was one of my father's uncles who lived in Philadelphia, and I'd driven up north with him because my mother and the girls had something going on. A Girl Scout camping trip? Maybe.

At any rate, I couldn't have been more than seven or eight. I'd sat in the church next to my father among all these ancient Irish, women who smelled like mothballs and men whose noses were perpetually red. There was loud weeping, although, Pop had told me, Uncle Emond had been a hundred years old.

I'd stared at the coffin, suddenly terrified. Reenie had pestered me before we left, reminding me that I was going to be in a church with a *real dead body*. And that dead body was right there. I fidgeted as fear gripped me.

"D'you think he's wearin' pants?" Pop's brogue, which had softened over the years in this country, re-established itself whenever we were around his family. I turned wide eyes to look up at him.

"What do you mean?"

"They keep the lower lid closed, see, and I'm remembering old Uncle Emond didn't much like to wear clothes. Seems to me he'd rather go on to his reward minus his trousers. Dare me to peek?"

"Pop, no! You can't. Mom would have a fit." I might've been young, but I was old enough to realize my mother had a way of knowing everything, even from almost a thousand miles away.

Pop's shoulders shook with silent laughter. "You're not wrong, my boy. All right, then, we'll just have go without satisfying that particular bit of curiosity."

Now I smiled, thinking of that day and feeling my father's hand on my back. "Dare me to look, Pop?" I took a deep breath and forced my eyes to the opened lid.

His dark hair, threaded with silver, lay on the ridiculous white tufted pillow. Seriously, how stupid were we humans that we thought dead people needed to be comfortable? His eyes were closed, and they'd arranged his mouth in what I guessed they'd thought was a natural pose. But anyone who knew my dad would know that his lips were perpetually curved into a teasing half-smile, not bunched up like he'd tasted something sour.

His hands were folded piously across his chest, a white rosary threaded between his fingers. I ventured to touch his wrist where it showed below the cuff of his sports coat. But although it looked like my father's arm, it was not. The skin was icy against my fingertips and unnaturally firm. I recoiled, stifling a gag.

"Okay, then, Pop." I drew in a deep breath through my nose. The cloying scent of the flowers that covered the altar threatened my stomach again, but I clenched my jaw and ignored it. "Okay. So I know you're not really here, not in this box, but on the other hand, I can't see you missing out on a party like today. I just wanted to tell you . . . no one ever had a better father than I did. What I learned from you . . . how you raised us . . ." My throat closed again, but this time it had nothing to do with the flowers or the body in front of me. "Well, you did good, Pop. Someday I'm going to have a kid, and if I can be half the father you were, I'll be doing all right. I only wish I'd told you more. I wish I'd seen you more. I wish . . ." They were endless, the wishes and regrets, and when I glanced down, I was surprised to see splotches of wet on the edge of the white satin.

Behind me, the murmuring swelled, and I realized my time was dwindling. I looked down at his face one more time, and the tears in my eyes blurred my vision just enough that the contrived expression vanished, and for a flash of time, I could see him again, the grin, the twinkle and the light.

When I blinked, it was gone, and once again the cold body lay in front of me. I turned around and signaled to the funeral director.

"I'm ready. You can . . . close it."

My mother came up behind me, leaning against my shoulder. "Are you all right, sweetheart?"

I managed a crooked smile. "Of course. I've got all my best girls here to keep me in line. How could I not be?" I caught Mr. Hughes' eye and turned Mom, steering her away from the two men who were lowering the lid on the casket. "I think they're about to open the church doors. You okay?"

She inhaled once, closing her eyes, and nodded. "Yes. We'll get through this visitation, and then the Mass . . . and the wake. And then . . ." Her voice trailed off, and I knew what she was thinking. *Yes, and then what?* That was the million-dollar question.

My sisters joined us halfway up the aisle, and within a few moments, Mr. Hughes guided us back up front. Another man opened the doors and began to shepherd people toward us.

For two hours, we nodded, smiled, shook hands, hugged people we hardly knew and repeated the same words over and over.

"Thank you. Thank for you coming. We appreciate your kindness. Yes, we're hanging in there."

For me, of course, there were a few variations: "Yes, I got back into town about five days ago. No, I'm not sure how long I'm staying. Yes, it's been a long time."

At the start of the visitation, the people who passed through the line tended toward acquaintanceship: neighbors of my sister Iona and her husband, Maureen's patients—well, their owners, anyway; Reenie was a veterinarian—and other people who couldn't stay for the service. None of them spent more than a few minutes with us, expressing sympathy, offering condolences and getting the hell out. I didn't blame them. As time went on, more family members showed up, including my dad's brother and sister-in-law, who'd flown down from Philly, and of course my mother's parents, who lived only about an hour south of us on the Florida coast. These encounters were longer and more emotional.

Interspersed between the two ends of the spectrum were people I hadn't seen in years. Many of my father's co-workers at the high school were also my old teachers, and there was more than a few teary hugs.

"Flynn Evans. Look at you." Mrs. Pruitt had retired two years before, but she still managed to make me break out in a cold sweat with her snapping blue eyes. "You're the image of your father." She tugged a lace-edged hankie from her cleavage and dabbed at her nose. "God rest his soul."

I swallowed back a new wave of unmanly tears. "Thank you for coming, Mrs. Pruitt. You look great. How's retirement?"

She waved her hand in front of her face. "What's retirement? I'm still there at the high school, only now they call me a volunteer and don't pay me."

My father had told me that the administration had practically forced the English teacher out of her job after she turned seventy. I figured the volunteer role was probably some kind of compromise.

"How long are you planning to stay in town, Flynn? I'd love to hear about where-all you've been. I follow your pictures in the magazines. Makes me proud. I show them to my students and tell them, 'See what hard work gets you?'"

"Hard work, huh? Weren't you the teacher who told my parents I was lazy?"

Mrs. Pruitt rolled her eyes. "You *were*. Smart as whip, but didn't want to do the work unless it suited you. You remember when I assigned y'all *A Farewell To Arms* and you refused to read it?"

I did remember. Hemingway was never my favorite, and I'd tried to sweet-talk the teacher into letting me read Kerouc's *On The Road* instead. It hadn't gone over well.

"You'll be happy to know I did read it eventually. But I still don't much care for Papa."

"I'm proud of you, Flynn." She patted my cheek. "If you get a chance, stop in and see me before you leave."

"I'll try. And thanks for being here today, Mrs. Pruitt."

She touched her eyes with the handkerchief. "And where else would I be? Your daddy and I were buddies. I'm going to miss that man." She sniffled dangerously, and I prayed that she'd move on before the tears came.

Just before she stepped away, she turned back, her brow furrowed. "Flynn, have you been in touch with Alison yet?"

I froze. I knew this was bound to happen, and I'd have been lying if I'd said I hadn't been scanning the crowd, wondering if she'd come by. But no one had mentioned her name until now.

"Ah, no. I haven't, uh, seen her."

Mrs. Pruitt nodded, her face clouding. "I was very sorry when I heard the two of you didn't work out. As you can imagine, I saw a lot of high school romances in my time, and most of them I could tell weren't going to last. But after what that girl went through, and how you were always there for her . . . I thought maybe . . . well." She patted me again. "These things happen. I see her every now and then. Not often, since she doesn't come into town too much." She regarded me steadily. "Her little girl is very pretty. Quite a charmer, too."

That suffocating feeling was creeping back. "That's great." I glanced over my former teacher's shoulder, hoping she'd get the move-it-along message. The last thing I needed was to hear or think about—her.

"I'm sure I'll see you later." Mrs. Pruitt smiled a little as she moved past me. I caught Reenie's eye, and she hugged my arm.

"Hanging in okay, little brother?"

I covered her hand with my own. "Sure. How about you? Need anything? Water, tissues?"

She shook her head. "No, thanks, I'm—oh." She frowned, and I followed her gaze to the doorway of the church, where a tall man with brown hair had just come inside, holding the hand of a red-headed woman who was at least a foot shorter. Behind them, another man trailed. His dark blond hair was perfectly styled, and his clothes screamed that they had not come from any of the stores in Burton.

The first guy turned to speak to the second, and recognition sparked. *Sam Reynolds.* Older, a little more filled-out than when I'd seen him last, but no doubt it was him. I didn't know the woman whose hand he held, but the second man—yep, it was Alex Nelson. My eyes darted back to the door before I could stop them, but no one else followed them inside. Not her. She wasn't here.

Of course she wouldn't come. I'd left no doubt in her mind during our last conversation, when I'd laid down the ultimatum: leave Burton with me, or we were over. At the time, in the moment, I thought I'd meant it. A few months later, I hadn't been so sure, but by then, she'd apparently gotten over me, since it was about that time she'd married Craig Moss.

Reenie laid her cheek against my shoulder, bringing me back to the moment. "She's not with them. I didn't think she'd come."

"She was your best friend." I didn't try to hide the anger in my voice.

"She was yours, too. And your girlfriend. And . . ." Maureen raised one eyebrow. "More."

"That was a long time ago. Lot of water under the bridge."

Before she could answer, Sam was in front of us, his eyebrows drawn together and his mouth tight. I watched him embrace my mother, carefully, kiss Iona on the cheek—that's right, she'd been in his class—and then envelope Maureen in a hug.

"Reenie. I'm so sorry." He stood up again, looking down into her eyes. "Your dad . . . he was one of the best men I ever knew."

My sister, who thus far today had been stoic, bit her lip as tears slid down her cheek. "Thank you, Sam. Thanks for being here." She leaned to the side to take the hand of the red-haired woman next to Sam. "Meghan. Thank you. I'm so glad you came."

The younger woman had wide green eyes, which now swam with tears. "Maureen, I'm so sorry. I know . . . it's hard. If there's anything I can do . . ."

Reenie folded her into a hug. "You being here is enough. I can't tell you how much I appreciate it." She stood back and glanced up at me, just the slightest edge of trepidation in her eyes. "Flynn, you remember Sam, of course. And this is Meghan, his girlfriend."

"Meghan Hawthorne." She extended her hand. "I'm glad to meet you, although I'm sorry it's under these circumstances."

Before I could answer her, Sam was gripping my shoulder. "Flynn. I'm sorry, man. You doing okay?"

A world of memories crowded into my head as I looked at Sam Reynolds. When I first knew him, he was a senior in high school, the stereotypical big man on campus: captain of the football team, president of his class and destined for greatness. After I'd started dating Ali, Sam had morphed into the guy who gave me the stink eye every time I was at their house or whenever he caught us holding hands at school. The dude took protective big brother to the extreme.

And after their parents were killed, Sam Reynolds became the most important person in the world to my girlfriend. We'd had a talk about a month after the accident. Sam had just graduated from high school, and he was trying to figure out how to hang on to their family farm. He had a scholarship to UGA, but he was giving it up in order to stay home so that his little sister didn't have to move in with their grandparents.

"Listen, Evans. I see how you look at my sister. I get it that you two think you're in love. Whatever. I'm not going to say you are or you aren't. My parents—" His voice caught. The pain was still fresh. "They liked you. Said you were a good kid. Me, I don't have time to worry about you. From here on out, my number one priority is Ali. To keep both of us fed and clothed, I need to make this farm work. I can't be following you guys around, so I need you to man up and make sure my sister is protected and treated like the treasure she is. Be the shoulder she needs when she cries. Don't let anyone give her shit. Can you handle that?"

I'd swallowed hard and nodded, but it felt like a moment that needed more. "Yes, sir. Sam. I can do that. Ali, she's . . . I'll watch out for her. I promise, no one'll ever hurt her."

Sam had stared at me. It felt like he was seeing into my soul. "Good. Oh, and Evans." He laid one heavy hand on my shoulder. "If you turn out to be the one who hurts her, in any way, I'll tear off your balls and stuff them down your throat until you choke. Got it?"

Now as those same brown eyes fastened onto me, I remembered his words with sudden clarity. In the end, I *had* been the one who'd hurt his little sister. At least, it might look that way from a certain point of view. While he didn't exactly look like he was planning to rip off my balls today, it occurred to me that avoiding Sam Reynolds for the remainder of my stay in Burton might not be a bad idea.

"I'm doing okay." I finally answered his question. "Thanks for coming by." I shifted my gaze to his girlfriend. "And you, too. Nice to meet you. Thanks for being here for Maureen."

"Of course." Meghan stared at me, her eyes searching mine as though she were looking for something. It made me more than a little uncomfortable.

Before I could figure out how to move them along, Alex reached over Meghan to grab my hand. Sam and Meghan stepped out of the way, and Alex pulled me into a tight hug.

Real crying threatened me for the first time that day. I hadn't seen Alex in eight years, and I hadn't spoken to him in just as long. But at one time, this guy had been my closest friend after Ali.

"Been too long, buddy." His voice was a gruff whisper in my ear. "What the fuck's up with that?"

I couldn't help the grin that spread over my face. Once upon a time, Alex and I had been the cussing kings of Burton, Georgia. Of course, that was only when neither of our moms were in earshot. Or the nuns who taught our catechism class. After all, we'd been twelve. Together we'd mastered the casual use of the dreaded F word, even if we weren't entirely sure what it meant.

Only Alex would come to my dad's funeral and whisper that word in my ear.

"I don't know, dude. What the fuck're you still doing in Podunk?" I kept my words low. His mom wasn't nearby, but mine sure was. And cursing in church wasn't a line I was willing to let her hear me cross.

"I'm not usually." Alex stood back, his face growing somber. "I live in Atlanta. But I was back visiting my parents when I heard. So I just stayed." He blinked rapidly and licked his lips. "I didn't know if you'd want to see me or not, but I couldn't let you go through this without at least telling you . . . you know, I'm sorry. Like you haven't heard it a thousand times today already."

"Maybe so, but I didn't hear it from you yet. Thanks, Alex. It means more than you know." I flicked a glance over his shoulder. It lasted less than a second, but he never missed a trick.

"She's not coming." Sympathy and something else—could it be frustration?—filled his eyes. "I think she wanted to, but . . . she didn't want to make it worse today for you."

Like anything or anyone could do that. "Probably a good idea. No drama. And it's been a long time."

"Are you going to be in town a little while? Maybe you could talk to her. Like you said, it's been a long time."

I shook my head. "I'm leaving as soon as I can get out. I have a commitment on the west coast."

Alex raised one eyebrow, mocking. "Well, excuse us, Mr. Big Shot. We wouldn't want you to hang around here longer than you had to. It's not like you've been gone for fucking ever . . . or wait a minute, yes, you have."

I opened my mouth to answer, but before I could, Iona tapped my arm. "It's just about time to begin the service. Mr. Hughes is going to ask everyone to sit down."

Alex punched my arm, near the shoulder. "I'll see you later, bud." His eyes met mine again. "I'll be right here. Hang in there."

"Flynn. Oh, look at you. You look so dashing."

I glanced up from the plate of macaroni and cheese, potato salad and coleslaw as a pair of thin arms wrapped around my shoulders. The gray-haired woman leaning over me was nearly as familiar as my own mother.

"Mrs. Nelson." I moved my plate to a nearby tray and reached up to hug Alex's mother. "I hoped I'd get to see you."

She sat down next to me on the same flowered sofa where I'd dozed earlier. Our house was full to bursting with guests, and seats were at a premium. "I'm so sorry about your father. And I'm even more sorry that it took something like this to bring you back to town."

I winced. Mrs. Nelson never did mince words. And there was nothing like the plain, hard truth from someone I knew and respected to bring me to my knees.

"It's not like I didn't see my dad in all this time." I hunched my shoulders. "He and my mom came to visit me a lot. So did

Iona and Maureen. We met whenever I was in the area." I heard the defensive tone and hated it. The decisions I'd made all these years . . . yeah, some of them were impulsive, some of them weren't my best ideas. But I hadn't abandoned my family. Only the town that I'd seen as holding me back.

And the girl who wouldn't go with me.

I pushed the thought to the back of my mind as Mrs. Nelson sighed. "I understand what it's like to want to see the world. I was young once. You know Alex went away to college, and he's lived in Atlanta since. But he comes home to see his father and me." Her eyes gleamed for a moment. "Now recently, he's been back pretty often, and I'm not stupid. I know there's another reason. Not even worrying about Ali could bring him to Burton that often."

I tried not to react to her name, but the woman sitting next to me never missed a trick. I remembered that Alex used to call her old Eagle Eyes. She shook her head.

"Have you been to see her? I didn't notice her at the church."

"No. I haven't been anywhere but with my mom and the girls. And I don't think she came today. But there were a lot of people." There was no way I would've missed her if she had. I made a stab at sounding nonchalant. "Been a lot of years since I've seen Ali. I'm sure she had better things to do than come to a funeral."

"Alex said she didn't come because she didn't think you'd want her here. And you think she didn't come because she didn't want to. Y'all both need to grow up and remember what good friends you were before."

I rubbed my forehead where a sudden headache had blossomed. I heard myself asking the question I hadn't dared to mention to my mother or sisters. "How is she?"

Mrs. Nelson didn't exhibit any surprise. "She's good. I see her quite a bit, either at the stand or just around the farm."

44

She smiled. "Bridget is crazy for horses, so she talks either her mother or Sam into bringing her over to our place to visit ours. And Meghan, of course, she takes her on tromps around the woods and fields to sketch."

I frowned. "Bridget?"

"Yes, that's Ali's little girl." She cut me a sideways glance. "You knew about her, didn't you?"

"I . . ." In theory, yeah. Maureen had mentioned the baby to me in the casual way my mother and sisters had of keeping me up-to-date on anything Ali-related without making a big deal of it. I'd been numb to the news at that point; the bigger hurt had come months before, when the girl I thought I'd love forever had married another guy and then announced her pregnancy. By the time their baby actually came, I'd shut away that part of my past. I didn't think I'd ever heard her name. Odd . . . Bridget was my grandmother's name. It wasn't used very often anymore. I wondered what had inspired Ali to give her daughter that name.

"She's a doll, that one is. Smart as a whip and pretty, too." Mrs. Nelson went on as though I'd answered. "Ali's a wonderful mama. And to think she'd done it all by herself."

I thought I might've detected a hint of censure in her voice, which was also weird. Before I could say anything else, she kept talking.

"She and Sam work themselves ragged on that farm. But we're all so proud of them. You remember they'd leased parcels out to a bunch of us after their parents died, but they've been taking them back, little by little. I expect this year, Sam'll farm the land we've been keeping for them. Their mama and daddy would be proud. Those two sacrificed so much to make it all happen."

As one of the sacrifices, I wasn't sure I could jump up and join the applause. I might've said something to that effect, but Alex appeared at that point and sat down on my other side.

"Mom, are you torturing Flynn?" He winked at me. "Cut him some slack."

His mother spread her hands wide, lifting her shoulders. "I don't know what you're talking about, Alex." She patted my knee. "We're just catching up."

"Watch it, woman. I'm hip to your jive. I heard you." He mock glared at her and then turned to me. "Flynn, the service was beautiful. Your eulogy . . ." He thumped one hand to his heart. "Your dad would be proud."

"Thanks." I picked up my plate again and scooped some potato salad onto my fork, keeping my eyes down so I didn't have to look at my friend. Holding it together while speaking had taken everything I had. Talking about it after might just break me. "So how long do you think people will stay?"

"Depends. A bunch will eat and run, and then you'll have those who just hang around, wanting to keep talking." Mrs. Nelson paused. "Speaking of hanging around, how long are you in town?"

"Subtle, Mom." Alex rolled his eyes.

"I'm hitting the road the day after tomorrow. At least that's the plan." I stabbed one more piece of macaroni and set down my plate again. "I'm supposed to shoot a piece in Los Angeles for an interview with the senator from New Mexico who's rumored to be a presidential candidate in the next election." I was just trying to explain, not brag, but Mrs. Nelson tilted her head at me, and I knew I was screwed.

"Excuse *us*. You haven't darkened the doorway of your own hometown in over eight years, and now you want to bury your father and then run off again? Have you thought about what that'll do to your poor mother, not to mention Iona and Maureen? You'll break their hearts all over again."

"Mom, seriously, maybe you should—" Alex looked from me to his mother, his face getting red.

"No, sir." She held up one pink-nailed finger into her son's face. "You just hush up, Alexander. I'm talking to Flynn. Now, your mother will never ask you to stay, because mothers don't do that, but she needs you here. You can tell that senator to take one of those—what do you call them, the self-pictures."

"God, Mom. They're called selfies. And you need to leave Flynn alone. He's a grown-up, remember? He knows what he's doing."

Mrs. Nelson stood up, leaning on my shoulder as she did. "I've said my piece. Now I'm going to see about helping with clean up. Alex, are you riding home with me, or with Sam and Meghan?"

Alex shrugged. "I think they left a few minutes ago. Meghan said something about needing to get back to Savannah for class tomorrow. I'll just wait for you." He was silent while his mother gathered our plates and hustled off to the kitchen, and then he turned to me. "Sorry about that. She means well."

I leaned back, resting my head on the sofa cushion and closing my eyes. "I know she does. It's just that . . . being back here reminds me why I left. I feel like I'm smothered, you know?"

Alex laughed softly. "Do I ever. Why do you think I maintain a nice distance by living in Atlanta?"

I slit my eyes open. "Your mom said you've been visiting a lot more recently. Seems to think there's a reason why."

"Does she?" He lifted his hands in a faux-innocent gesture. "Maybe, maybe not. Maybe I just enjoy seeing my parents and hanging with Ali." He squeezed his eyes shut. "Sorry."

"For mentioning her name? Don't be. I know she's your friend." I hesitated. The wound was still tender, so I plunged ahead, getting all the pain out of the way at once by repeating the question I'd asked his mother. "How is she?"

"Do you really want to know?"

I shook my head and then nodded. "No. But yeah. I mean . . . do I want to hear that she's never gotten over me and spits on the ground when she hears my name? Maybe. Or maybe it's better to hear that she never mentions my name and doesn't think about me at all. That I was just some guy she dated back in high school, and I never cross her mind."

Alex blew out a sigh. "The truth, if you want it, is a little of both. She doesn't mention your name. Neither do I, at least not in front of her. If someone else does . . ." He rubbed the back of his neck. "It still hurts her. She hasn't forgotten you, Flynn. But I hadn't heard her say your name for a long time, not until she was talking to Meghan last year about old times. We were at The Road Block—"

"The Road Block?" I cocked my head.

"Yeah, remember Mason Wallace? He graduated with Iona and Sam, left town to work in the music business?"

When I nodded, Alex went on. "He did well, made a lot of money repping acts in Nashville. I guess he worked for an agency and then started his own up. Got married, had a kid and then the wife died. So he moved back here, to have family nearby to help out, and wouldn't you know, turns out his mom has cancer. Anyway, he bought some land off Highway 44 and opened a bar. It's got a big dance floor, and he uses his old connections to bring in some pretty good bands. Up and comers, he says."

"And you were there with . . . ?" I wasn't ready to say her name yet.

"With Ali and Meghan last summer. Ali'd had a few beers, and she started talking about the old days after Trent hit on Meghan."

"Trent Wagner? He's still around?"

Alex grinned. "You know it. Still the same old dog. Hits on anything with boobs, and still has the rep for lovin' and leavin.' Anyway, Ali started talking about how we'd all hang out back in high school, and she mentioned you. First time in years."

I clenched my jaw. "Doesn't surprise me. She didn't waste

any time starting up with Craig after I left." I glanced at my friend. "I always knew he had the hots for her. He was just too scared of me to act on it."

Alex quirked an eyebrow. "Or maybe he didn't want to hit on his friend's girlfriend. Ever think of that? Plus, come on. Everyone knew Ali only ever saw you. When the two of you were together, it was like no one else existed." He gave me a small shove in the ribs. "Believe me, I had a front row seat to the Flynn and Ali show. If I hadn't been gay, I probably wouldn't have been able to take it."

I scowled at him. "Yeah, well . . . it turned out to be more show than reality."

"What're you talking about?" Alex wrinkled his forehead. "You think Ali wasn't really in love with you?"

"When it came down to going with me or staying with her brother, we saw who was more important. And the fact that she got married and popped out a kid before we'd been broken up for a year tells us all something about how she felt, doesn't it?"

Alex stared at me, unblinking. "Flynn, man, I love you like the brother I never had, but you're goddamn fool."

Before I could ask him what he meant, he pushed off the sofa and stood up. "I'm sorry about your dad. And it was good to see you, even under these circumstances." He looked at me, and I saw hurt in his eyes. "You know, when you left Burton, you didn't just leave the town. You pretty much shook off all of us. Maybe you need to think about that before you start making judgment calls on how people reacted."

He pivoted and stalked into the kitchen. I closed my eyes again and wished my father were alive. And that I was any place in the world other than Burton, Georgia.

Ali

W E ONLY HAD THREE customers at the stand the entire day of Brice Evans' funeral. I sat there until about two in the afternoon, when I couldn't stand it anymore. Bridget's bus wouldn't drop her off until four, but I needed to be back home for my own sanity.

I trudged back to the house through the fields, not seeing anything that I passed. Instead, my mind kept up a running film of the Evans family, what they were going through today, all the while remembering the awful day we'd officially said good-bye to my own parents. I'd been just about to turn fifteen, at the end of my freshman year. Flynn and I'd been dating, official girl-friend/boyfriend, for about six months.

Our relationship had begun slowly, evolving from two people who'd discovered they liked to hang out together into a real friendship. By Thanksgiving of our freshman year, we were talking for hours on the phone every night, and no one had been surprised when Flynn asked me to be his date to the school's annual Christmas dance. But he was careful with me; we didn't touch beyond what was required for dancing, although I often caught him staring at my lips. When he left me at my front door that night with a chaste kiss on the cheek, I'd stomped into the house and called Alex.

"I think he's gay." I shimmied out of the strapless black dress I'd been sure would entice Flynn into kissing me. *Really* kissing me. Maybe even . . . more.

Alex sighed on the other end of the phone. "Ali, he's not gay. Believe me, I'd know. He's just . . . waiting. I think he wants to make sure you're okay with it. He told me how much he likes you. He doesn't want to rush you into anything you're not ready for."

I fell onto the bed with a frustrated groan. "Oh, I'm ready. Believe me, I'm real ready. If I'm any more ready, I might just implode."

"Whoa there, little miss hot-to-trot. Stop and think. Trust me when I say holding back isn't easy for our boy, either. And I doubt he's going to be able to do it much longer. But you should be flattered, because he really likes you. That's why he's waiting."

So I'd swallowed my tenuously-banked passion and smiled at Flynn at school, sat on my hands when we were studying together in my living room, and gritted my teeth when we went to the movies and sat side-by-side without touching.

The day before Christmas break began, Flynn asked me to walk home with him after school, so he could give me my Christmas present. He promised his mom would drive me out to the farm afterward, and once I'd cleared it with Sam, I slung my backpack over my shoulder and met Flynn at his locker.

"Ready?" He picked up his own bag and then reached over to mine. "Here, let me take that."

I felt a delicious thrill as his hand lifted the strap from my back. And then I nearly passed out with happiness when he extended his hand to me. "Let's go."

I slid my hand into his, and he laced our fingers together, squeezing for just a minute as he gazed down at me.

We walked to his house through the unusually cold December air. This part of Georgia didn't usually get a real cold snap until late January. But I didn't feel anything except the warmth of Flynn's hand against mine the whole way. We talked a little, mostly about what we wanted to do over break. There were a couple of movies Flynn wanted to see, and I'd talked Sam into driving Alex, Flynn and me into Savannah one day to see the lights and do some real shopping.

Once we got to his house, Flynn gave me a pretty gold necklace, a delicate chain from which dangled a small A. I wore it every day for four years, and I still had it, up in my jewelry box. But my real gift that day was his hand in mine as we walked.

The day after Christmas, Flynn asked me to go with him to Cary Maynard's New Year's Eve party. He'd held my hand the entire night, and when the clock struck midnight, Flynn Evans finally, finally kissed me.

It was worth waiting for. Totally worth it.

Over the next six months, Flynn and I were together almost constantly, or at least as constantly as our parents and school would allow. We didn't move beyond kissing and hand-holding, since private time was hard to come by. But our kissing had gotten more involved and creative, and every now and then, his hand strayed somewhere in the vicinity of my boob. But never for long, and never close enough.

That May, my parents celebrated their twentieth wedding anniversary. They decided to drive over to Gatlinburg for a week, just the two of them, so my grandparents came up from Florida to stay with Sam and me. My brother'd groused that he didn't need a babysitter, but my mom pacified him, saying Gram and Grampy were coming so that he didn't have to keep his eye on me the entire time. She winked at me behind his back, though, so I knew the truth.

I actually didn't mind having my grandparents stay with us. They liked Flynn, and as long as we didn't interrupt their afternoon talk shows, we could sit out on the porch as long as we liked, which is why we were the first ones to see the police car pull up that day.

I knew all the local cops. There weren't many, and in a town the size of Burton, there wasn't much turnover. This was not someone I knew, and as I sat up, in the porch swing, pushing against Flynn's chest, I realized it was a state police car.

My first thought was Sam, who'd stayed in town that afternoon to work on a group project. But as soon as the first trooper spoke, I knew. I just knew.

"Is this the home of Joseph and Elizabeth Reynolds?"

I couldn't speak. My mouth moved, but no sound came out. Flynn took my hand, tight, and spoke for me. Through a loud ringing in my ear, I heard him say that yes, this was their home. My grandfather opened the door and stepped out, and after that, I didn't remember anything. For the next week, everything was hazy and painful and too loud, and the only constant was Flynn holding my hand. He never left my side. At night, he slept next to me on my bed, waking to hold me when the nightmares made me scream.

The day of their funeral, that horrible, surreal day, Flynn sat with us in the church. At the end, when I began to cry hysterically, he pulled my face into his shoulder and whispered into my ear.

"Shhh, baby. Ali. It's okay. I'm here. I'll never leave you."

Remembering that time still cut deep. And I felt not a little guilty that I hadn't had the courage to go to Flynn's father's service today. No matter what had happened in the intervening years, nothing could erase my gratitude to him for his support during the darkest days of my life.

I got home, not surprised to see that Sam and Meghan were still out. I thought about taking that elusive bubble bath, but I was too restless. I wandered around the house, picking up dirty socks from Bridget's floor, putting away the few dishes that were in the sink. But everything was too silent and too empty. It made me uneasy and antsy. I almost wished I'd stayed back at the stand.

I heard the slam of a car door and hurried into the kitchen. When the screen door opened, Meghan stepped inside, her face pinched. Sam was right behind her.

"How was it?" I knew it was a terrible thing to ask, but I couldn't stop myself.

Meghan just shook her head and walked through the kitchen. I listened to the sound of her climbing the steps and glanced at my brother, one eyebrow raised.

Sam dropped into a chair at the kitchen table. "It was hard on her. You know, it's only been a few years since her dad, and it's still tough on her."

I sat down, too. "I'm sorry. Was . . . was it very emotional?"

"It was a funeral, Ali. Yeah, it was emotional." He ran one hand through his hair until it stood on end. "He was looking for you. Flynn was."

Panic and something akin to hope flared inside me. "He was? How do know?"

"He kept looking over my shoulder, at the door. Like he was waiting for someone else."

"How do you know it was me? Maybe . . . it was another classmate. Someone from his family. Or did you ever think, maybe he's got a girlfriend and she was supposed to be there today?"

Sam rolled his eyes. "For God's sake, Ali. I could tell. He looked at me, saw Alex and right away, he starts staring at the door. Like he's just willing you to come through it."

Unexpected tears filled my eyes. "It was better for me not to go. Trust me."

"See, I don't get that." Sam leaned forward, resting his elbow on the table. "I remember the two of you back in high school. You were tighter than any other couple I'd ever seen. One time . . ." He rubbed his forehead and sighed. "It was the year after . . . the accident. I was coming around from the fields, and you two were on the front porch, sitting in the swing."

I groaned and covered my face. "Oh, God, Sam, I hope this isn't what I think it is."

He shook his head. "No, Ali. Believe me, if I'd caught you doing that, I wouldn't have waited ten years to let you know. You were just cuddling, or whatever. Sitting close together. You didn't see me, but I could hear you talking, and it hit me that you guys reminded me of Mom and Dad. How many times did we see them doing the same thing, just talking and you know, *being* together. I thought, wow, those two really are going to go the distance."

"Yeah, well, we all were wrong about that, weren't we? I don't see what that has to do with today."

"It has everything to do with today." Sam studied me, his eyes narrow. "Why did you and Flynn fight on graduation night?"

My mouth dropped open. "Aren't you, like, nine years too late to ask that question?"

"Probably. At the time, I figured it was just something that you two would work out. And you were doing that girl-crying thing. I didn't know how to deal with it." His mouth twisted. "If I'd had Meghan around in those days, maybe she could've helped."

I smirked. "If I were a really cruel sister, I'd point out that your girlfriend was only thirteen at that time. I somehow doubt she'd have been much help."

Sam shuddered. "You really are cruel. The last thing I want to think about is Meghan being almost ten years younger than me. Anyway, you're changing the subject. The point is, I never really knew why you and Flynn fought. Maybe if I'd been a better brother, gotten involved, things might've turned out different."

I reached across the table and laid my hand on his arm. "Let me put your mind at ease. There was nothing you could've done to make things turn out different for Flynn and me. He gave me an ultimatum. I didn't like it. He left. End of story."

"What kind of ultimatum?" He tugged at the dark tie around his neck. My brother was so not the suit and tie type.

I waved my hand. "Doesn't matter. I don't want to talk about it anymore."

"Ali." Sam sat back, studying his hands. "Were you . . . were you seeing someone else behind Flynn's back? Is that the ultimatum he gave you—give up Craig or he was leaving?"

"What the hell are you talking about? How could you think that about me?"

Sam's eyes were clouded, his face filled with misery. "I don't want to think it. I didn't want to think it at the time. But Flynn left, and two months later you were marrying Craig. And then you were pregnant. It was awful sudden, Ali. You can't blame me for wondering."

I couldn't answer him. It'd never occurred to me that Sam might think I'd been cheating on Flynn. Looking back, I could see his point. At the time, though, Id been so preoccupied with my own misery that I'd never considered how it might look to my brother. I'd been grateful that he accepted what I told him without question.

"Why didn't you ask me about this before now?" I kept my voice low.

"I guess . . . it was easier not to wonder. I told myself you were grown up and you knew what you were doing." He hesitated for a minute before lifting his eyes to mine. "I even thought once or twice that maybe . . . maybe Bridget was Flynn's. But then I knew you'd never do that to him. You couldn't deny him his own child."

I felt the blood drain from my face, and my chest tightened. I bit down on my lip, just to keep from crying. I couldn't speak, but tears welled up and ran down my cheeks.

"Oh, no." Sam whispered the words, and I saw the reflection of my own agony in his face. "Ali. You wouldn't. All this time . . . and you never told him? You never told *me?* How could you do that?"

I couldn't answer him over the lump in my throat. I only shook my head.

"Alison." He dropped his forehead onto the heels of his hands. "God. I can't even . . . what kind of idiot did you take me for? Why didn't you tell me? We could've dealt with it together."

"*She.* Not an it. Bridget was my baby. She's my child. Don't talk about her like she was a problem we could've solved." Bitterness tinged my words. Yeah, maybe I still had some lingering resentment over how alone I'd felt in those days. Alone by my own choice, but I remembered how many time I'd wished Sam would figure it out.

"When I said 'it,' I meant the situation, not Bridge. God, Ali, you know I love that kid. I wouldn't change anything about having her in my life. But I can't believe you'd intentionally keep Flynn from knowing about her. He deserved to know. He still does."

I choked back another sob. "But he'd left me, Sam. He'd walked away from me, when he promised he'd never leave me alone. If I'd told him I was pregnant, he'd have come back. But it wouldn't have been for me. It would've been because he felt obligation. All Flynn ever wanted was to get out of here. You know that. He couldn't wait to leave."

Sam stood up and stalked across the kitchen. "And you didn't think about that before you got pregnant? Before you—he—" My brother couldn't get out the words.

"I thought I was going with him." I finally voiced the words I'd avoided. "We'd planned . . . we were going to leave town together."

Sam turned on me, brows drawn together. "Really? When was that decided? I don't remember discussing it with you."

I folded my hands on the table, squeezing them tight. "We were going to talk to you after graduation. I wasn't going to just leave."

"So what changed?" Sam braced his hands on the back of the kitchen chair across from me.

I swallowed hard. "I decided I didn't want to leave Burton." It wasn't the complete truth, but it was as close to it as I was getting.

Sam stared down me, unblinking. "So you changed your mind about leaving. But you could've changed it back once you found out you were pregnant."

"By then he'd left me. I was miserable and freaking out, but Craig was there, and he offered . . . well, he said he'd marry me and be the baby's father. We'd been hanging out already, and I know now it sounds dumb, but I thought . . . why not? He was so excited, and I figured it might work."

"It *might* work." Sam slammed his hand down onto the table, and I jumped a mile. "God, Ali, when did you become such an idiot? Where did I go wrong, that you thought it was okay to fuck with people's lives, so long as you didn't have to be inconvenienced?" He was yelling now, and I cowered, burying my face in my arms.

"Sam." A soft voice in the doorway pulled our attention away from each other. Meghan had changed into jeans and one of Sam's flannel shirts. Her hair was down around her drawn face as she glanced from my brother to me.

"Meghan." He crossed the room to pull her into his arms. "I thought you were going to get a nap before you went back to Savannah."

She laid her cheek against his chest for a moment, and a surge of jealousy shot through me. I wanted that. I wanted that security, that comfort. It was killing me that I'd never have it with the one person I needed.

"I was lying down, but I could hear you arguing." She looked at me around his shoulder. "Sam, you need to cut Ali a break. Don't yell. Let's just sit down and talk about this calmly."

"But you don't know—" He began to speak, and then realization dawned in his eyes. "You do know. You knew already, didn't you?"

"Sam, don't blame Meghan." I couldn't let my crap get between my brother and the love of his life. "I told her last summer, before the two of you were together. I begged her not to tell you, and I promised I would. It's all my fault."

Sam studied her, his fingers gripping her chin. He closed his eyes and leaned his forehead into hers for a moment before he looked at me again. "God, Ali. I'm beginning to feel like I don't even know you. So not only did you lie to me for years, you pulled Meghan into it, too. You put her in a rotten position."

"I'm sorry." I wiped at my cheeks. "I'm sorry, Sam. And Meghan. I didn't mean to screw everything up. I just wanted to protect Bridget."

A loud creaking outside drew our attention away from the tension in the room. Meghan pushed her hair away from her face and glanced at me. "That's the bus. Bridget can't come into this, not right now. How about I take her into town and get some ice cream while you two settle down? Work this out."

I nodded. "Thank you, Meghan. That would be great. I really appreciate it." I paused for a beat, and then added, "You'll keep her away from the Evans' house, right? Just in case."

Sam snorted, but Meghan ignored him. "I'll do my best. But Ali, you need to make this right. I know it's going to be hard, and painful, but you've got to do it."

I didn't answer, and she sighed as she stood on her toes to kiss Sam. He caught her arm and pulled her tighter.

"Are you sure about this? I thought you were heading back to the city tonight."

She touched his cheek. "I think I'll wait until tomorrow. I don't have anything pressing back there tonight, and maybe I can help out a little." She kissed him and went out the front door.

"She's right, you know." Sam leaned against the archway that led from the living room into the kitchen. "You need to tell Flynn the truth. Now. Before he leaves town again."

My stomach clenched. "But what if he tries to take Bridget away from me? Sam, I'll die. I can't lose her. She's my life."

My brother pressed his lips together. "Yeah, I know. But you should've thought about that before you kept her from her dad all these years."

When I began to sob in earnest, Sam relented, sighing and pulling up a chair next to me. "Come on, Ali. This is Flynn. He'd never take her away from you. But he deserves to know the truth, and he definitely needs to get to know his daughter. If I ever found out I had a kid and the mother hadn't told me, I'd be furious about the time I didn't get. But more than that, I'd want to make sure I didn't miss anything else in her life."

"Sam." I managed to speak somehow. "But what if he hates me? What if Flynn . . . despises me?"

He slowly shook his head. "I don't know, Ali. I guess you take it one step at a time and hope for the best." He wrapped his arm around my shoulders and drew me tight to his side. "But I promise we'll get through it together, no matter what happens.

Okay? I'm here for you." He tilted my chin up until my teary eyes met his. "I always have been. Don't forget it."

Chapter Five

Flynn

"**H**EY, REENIE, YOU SEEN my gray sweatshirt?" I stood at the bottom of the steps and yelled upstairs. A wave of déjà vu swept over me. It felt like I'd never left home, with my sister stealing my clothes.

"No, you big doofus. You left it on the chair in the kitchen and I hung it up in your closet. You know, like, where the clothes live."

I bit back a smartass retort. I was mature. I wasn't the little brother. I didn't have to sink to her level. "Thanks, Maureen." I took the steps two at a time, and like I'd done my whole life, when I got to the top, I gripped the newel post and swung around into my bedroom door. Only today, I nearly toppled over my mother, who was in the hall, carrying a basket of dirty clothes.

"Watch it, kid. You're not one of the Flying Wallengos. And you're old enough to know better." She fastened me with a quelling look, one eyebrow raised. I dropped a kiss on her cheek before I slid into my room.

"Sorry, Ma. Old habit." I paused, glancing at her over my shoulder. "You need help with that laundry?"

"No, thanks." She propped the basket on her hip and leaned against my door jam, studying me. "So. Are you . . ." She licked her lips, and I realized she was nervous about something. "Have you thought about how long you're staying? In town, I mean."

I stuck my hands in the front pockets of my jeans. "Uh, well." I cleared my throat. "I have a job in Los Angeles. Tomorrow. I thought I'd drive into Savannah tomorrow morning, drop off the rental car and catch a flight to Atlanta to make my connection. With the time difference, I can still make it on time."

My mother pressed her lips together. "Oh. Okay. I guess . . . I didn't realize you had to leave so soon. I was hoping . . ." She let her voice trailed off, and then she shook her head. "No, it's fine." She forced a smile. "Make sure you give me any of your clothes you need washed. I don't want you going across the country with dirty laundry."

"Mom, listen." I grabbed her wrist. "I've just got to do this one job, and then I'll come back. I know we have a lot of stuff to work out, and I'm not going to dump it on you and the girls. I'll be back. But I can't miss this shoot. It's been in the works for months, and it's a huge deal."

"I understand, honey." She patted my cheek. "You have to do what you have to do. You know your father always said that we had to respect your schedule and understand that you're just not like the rest of us."

I bristled, clenching my jaw. "What's that supposed to mean? Not like the rest of you? I'm the thing that doesn't fit in?"

"No, sweetie, of course not. I just mean, you have other

priorities. We understand that." She turned to leave, and as I listened to her footsteps going downstairs, I dropped back onto my bed with a long, exasperated sigh. My mother had a way of making feel like I was ten years old again, on the verge of making a decision that would disappoint her, even as she assured me that she'd keep loving me no matter what. It was a gift.

"Hey." Maureen leaned against the door frame, taking Mom's place. "You okay?"

"Yeah. Just trying to figure out what Mom wants, what she needs from me, and how to make it all work." I threw my arm over my eyes. "I think she wants me to be here longer, but she won't say it. She just talks in circles until I can't figure out if I'm doing what she wants or letting her down. Again."

Reenie snorted. "The woman has mad talent when it comes to guilt trips and making you wonder which idea is yours and which is hers. So what's the situation this time?"

"I told Mom I need to fly to LA tomorrow. I have this shoot—"

"Yeah, yeah, we all know about the shoot. Presidential candidate, yada, yada. So what's the big deal? Go, do your thing."

I knew she was trying to make me feel better, but it still stung. "You don't want me to stay?"

She threw up her hands. "God, Flynn. There's no winning with you, is there? If we want you to stay, we're being needy and smothering you. If we say you can go, we don't need you. Figure out your shit, dude. You're worse than a thirteen year-old girl."

I flipped her off, lifting my arm without moving the rest of my body from the bed. "You have no idea, Reen. You don't know what it's like to be the one who moves away. I feel like if I don't get out of here, I'm going to explode. But at the same time, I feel like if I leave, I'm abandoning all of you. And when I realize y'all don't need me, it feels . . . like I'm not part of the family anymore. Like you all moved on without me, and I'm just the stranger who breezes in and out."

Maureen came into the room and sank onto the bed next to me. "Okay, first of all. . wow. I'm starting to think Iona and I ruined you when we used to dress you up like a pretty, pretty princess when you were little. Because do you know how many times you just the word *feel?* Like, seven."

I bared my teeth at her. "Bite me."

"Yeah, well, no thanks. Anyway, just a little reminder that you, brother dear, are the one who made the decision to move away. You couldn't wait to shake us loose. We all love you, but there're still consequences. You're part of us. You always will be. But when you don't live here every day, you're not part of our lives in the same way. That's just how it works. And you have to understand that having you here has been huge for Mom. But she's afraid to lean on you too much, because she knows you won't be around for the long haul."

Stung, I sat up. "That's bullshit. I've always been here for Mom. I'm only a phone call away. She knows she can count on me."

Maureen lifted her shoulders. "Sometimes a phone call is too far away. She—" Her ass buzzed, and she swore under her breath. "Shit, what now?" Leaning forward, she pulled the phone out of her back pocket and frowned at the screen. She swiped one finger over the bottom and leaned back on her elbow. "Hey, Meghan. What's up?"

I could only hear the low sound of the voice on the other end of the phone. My sister's expression changed from curiosity to puzzlement before she finally said, "Sure, that's fine. About twenty minutes? We can do that. No problem. See you then. Bye." She ended the call and tossed down her cell.

I raised one eyebrow. "What was that all about?"

Maureen shook her head. "I'm not really sure. Meghan— she's Sam Reynolds' girlfriend, you met her yesterday—asked if she could stop by to see me before she heads back to Savannah. Which is not so weird, but she asked if you were around." She fastened me with a suspicious look. "What did you do?"

"Nothing. I didn't even talk to her at the church beyond the basics. Who is she, anyway? I don't remember her from high school."

"You wouldn't. She's not from Burton."

I clapped my hand to my heart and feigned an attack. "What? Sam's dating someone who isn't a fromer? How the hell did that happen? I didn't think the guy could leave the boundaries of town without combusting."

"Stop." Reenie swatted my head. "Meghan came to Burton last summer to teach art to the elementary kids. She's in art school in Savannah, and she was part of this volunteer program. Sam and Ali put her up while she was here, and I guess one thing led to another . . ." Her voice trailed off.

"Hmm." I grunted as I sat up. "She's a little young for old Sam, isn't she?"

My sister kicked at my legs. "Watch it, bub. Remember Sam and Iona are only a year older than me."

"I know." I nodded, putting on an expression of regret, my mouth pressed into a faux grimace. "Do you still have all your own teeth, by the way? And is that arthritis cream I smell?" I sniffed the air.

"You're such a brat. What time do you leave tomorrow?" She scooted to the edge of the bed. "And how fast can I get you gone?"

"Thanks, sis. Feeling the love." I picked up my hooded sweatshirt and pulled it over my head before I stood up.

"Where're you going?" She rose, too, and put her hands on her hips. "I told Meghan you'd be around."

"I'm going for a walk. I just want to get out and breathe a little. I'm used to being by myself all the time, and y'all have been up my ass for almost a week. I need a break."

"Hey, do you know that's the second time in the last few

minutes you've said *y'all?*" She grinned and poked me in the ribs. "Look at that! There's still some country left in my citified brother."

"Oh, for God's sake." I rolled my eyes. "Just because I don't go around chewing and spitting in overalls and a ball cap doesn't mean I've forgotten my roots." I tapped her nose. "I'll see you in a little bit."

"Fine, go off and leave me." She folded her arms over her chest, pouting in true-Reenie fashion.

"Hey, she's your friend. And Mom's here." I tromped down the stairs, Maureen trailing after me. I paused at the bottom and yelled toward the back of the house. "Ma, I'm going for a walk. That okay?"

Her voice floated out of the laundry room. "Sure, honey. I'm running out to the grocery store. I'll be back in a little while. You be careful."

My sister giggled. "You know, she tells me to be careful every time I leave the house, even if I'm just going to work. I think she's afraid if she doesn't one of us'll forget and do something wild."

I smiled. "See, that's one of those things you don't appreciate, but I do. No one tells me to be careful unless I'm on the phone with Mom. It makes me feel good." I waited for her to tease me for being a mama's boy, but she only hugged herself and nodded.

"I get that. I mean, I joke about it, but especially right now . . . believe me, I'm big on appreciating everything and not taking anything for granted." She reached up to hug my neck, quick and hard. "And Flynn, don't ever think we don't miss you. Or that we don't need you. We're strong, Ma and Iona and me, and we'll make it. But we still love you and miss you and need you, all the time. When you're gone, it always feels like something's missing. I'm glad you're here, now."

I coughed, covering up the lump in my throat. "Yeah,

thanks. But I'm still not staying here while Meghan visits."

She shoved against me. "Jerk."

"But you love me anyway." I swung the door open and turned to go outside, but I stopped abruptly, my heart suddenly pounding and blood rushing in my ears.

Ali Reynolds stared up at me, face pinched and pale. She licked her lips and spoke.

"Hello, Flynn. Could I come in? We need to talk."

I didn't remember moving from the door to the living room, but we were there. I sat on the sofa, hands clenched at my sides. Meghan perched on the edge of the armchair in the corner, leaning forward with her elbows on her knees. Her eyes never left Ali, who was across the room on the loveseat. I didn't want to look at her, but at the same time, my eyes kept straying in her direction.

Nine years. I couldn't believe it had been nearly that long since I'd laid eyes on the girl I'd promised to love forever. Part of me wanted to pretend no time at all had come between us; I wanted to hold her tight, kiss those full lips until her eyes went soft and hazy. Talk to her for hours about everything I'd seen and done while we'd been apart.

But another part of me was still wounded, and even glancing her way hurt so damned much that I wanted to hit something. I wanted to yell at her the same way I had the last day we'd fought. I wanted to shake her until her eyes rolled back, ask her how the hell she could've married Craig. I wanted to know why she hadn't trusted me and why she hadn't chosen me.

Next to me on the sofa, Maureen cleared her throat. "Meghan, I'm sorry. I don't want to be rude to you, and I'm sure you mean well, but this . . . this isn't cool. You're not from here, and you don't know the history. The last thing my brother needs right now is this kind of drama." She looked at the other two girls. "In case you forgot, we just buried our father yesterday."

I didn't know Meghan at all, but I couldn't miss the misery on her face. "I know, Maureen, and believe me, I'm so sorry. If this could've waited, we wouldn't be here. But we weren't sure how much longer Flynn would be in town, and we couldn't put it off anymore." She turned back to the other side of the room. "Right, Ali?"

Ali lifted her hand and tucked a strand of her light brown hair behind her ear. I knew that gesture so well. She ducked her head down, and I saw her lips were curled tightly over her teeth. She stared at a spot in the middle of room, not looking at me. She hadn't acknowledged me at all since I'd stood back to let her in the house.

But now she lifted her face, slowly, to gaze at my sister. "Maureen, I'm really sorry, but could you please give Flynn and me a little privacy?"

Reenie began to protest. "Ali, seriously? Come on. We're not in high school anymore. If you have something to say to my brother—"

"Maureen, please." Meghan rose from her chair, her eyes pleading with my sister. "Let's just give them a minute."

"I'm okay, Reen." I tried for a half-smile. "You can go. We won't be long."

Still, she hesitated a minute before sighing and turning to leave. I couldn't see the look she shot Ali as she passed her chair, but judging by the way the younger woman cringed, it must've been a doozy.

I heard Meghan suggest that they sit out on the back porch, and within a few minutes, their voices had faded. I leaned back on the sofa, my arms along the back of the cushions as I leveled a steady gaze at Ali. "Okay. So we're alone. What's up?

What's so important that you had to lie to my sister to get in the house? What do you have to say that you couldn't in the past nine years?"

A little bit of mad sparked in her eyes. "Oh, yeah, it was *so* easy to get in touch with you. You know, I can't remember why I haven't seen you in nine years. Wait a minute, yes, I do. Because you *left*. You left *me*."

I tamped down the flare of hurt and guilt. "No, I left Burton. I didn't leave you. At least, I didn't want to. I wanted you with me, remember? I wanted what our plan always was. You're the one who threw it away. Let's not re-write history, sweetheart." I spit out the last word, leaving no doubt that it wasn't an endearment.

"I didn't—" Ali began, and then she stopped, closed her eyes and took a deep breath. I could see the rise and fall of her chest under the long-sleeved cotton shirt she wore, and damn my soul, I still wanted her.

"I didn't come here to fight with you, or to rehash old crap. That was a long time ago. I don't blame you for anything."

I cocked one eyebrow at her. "Generous of you."

She looked as though she wanted to rise to the bait but thought better of it. "I need to tell you what happened . . . after. And before I say anything, Flynn—" Hearing her speak my name made my heart thud in a weird way. Maybe Maureen was right. I was becoming a girl. "I want you to know that I'm sorry. I did the best I could under the circumstances. And maybe I was wrong, and maybe I was stupid. And maybe you'll hate me. But I'd like you to keep in mind that I was only eighteen, and I was trying to figure things out on my own."

A mix of unease and misgiving trickled down my spine. "Are you talking about Craig? Is that what this is? You want to explain to me why you married one of my friends as soon as I was out of sight? Fine. I'd like to hear this." I crossed my arms over my chest and leaned back.

Ali had gone even paler. Distractedly, I noticed how thin she was now, and I recalled Mrs. Nelson telling me how hard she and Sam had been working on the farm. With no little effort, I pulled my attention back to what she was saying.

"I know how it looks. Believe me, it wasn't an easy decision. I . . . after you left, Flynn, I lost it. I couldn't get out of bed, and I cried all the time." She flicked a glance up at me and swallowed hard. "I thought my life was over. Making that decision was the hardest thing I'd ever done. I know you couldn't understand it then, but I just couldn't abandon Sam. Not when he'd given up everything to stay on the farm and make it work."

"Yeah, I get it. You made a choice, and I wasn't it." I'd thought I'd gotten over this a long time ago. The hurt gripping me now said otherwise.

"It wasn't that. You wouldn't even consider any other options. I had to leave with you, or we were through. You made it impossible." She shook her head. "But that's not why I'm here. I just . . . I was so sad. And Craig was there at a time when I honestly didn't know what I was going to do."

I couldn't sit still another minute. I stood up and stalked back and forth across the living room. "If that's why you came today, to make yourself feel better about marrying him, then you can just get the hell out. I don't care why you did it. You couldn't even wait a few months, talk to me, see if we could work things out. Nope, you moved right on, with one of my friends." I stopped pacing as my anger built. Leaning over her, I braced my hands on either side of her so that I was in her face as I spoke, my voice low. "Were you sleeping with him even before I left? Were you *fucking* my friend? Maybe that's what made it so easy to let me go. You knew you already had my replacement warmed up and ready to roll."

Her brown eyes were wide and filled with tears, but her words dripped with bitterness. "How can you say that? How can you think it? You know there was never anyone for me but you. I loved you from the time I was fourteen until—" Her gaze skittered away from mine, and she clamped her mouth shut.

"Oh, really? Then you want to explain why it was so easy to jump into marriage after I left?"

Ali pushed forward until her nose was nearly touching mine. I straightened, unsettled by how damn much I wanted to kiss her when my face was that close to hers. She grabbed my arm to keep me from moving away and spoke in a furious whisper.

"Because I was pregnant with your baby, you son of a bitch."

Chapter
Six

Ali

MY GRANDMA USED TO talk about people who went white as a ghost, and when I was little, I liked to imagine what that looked like. I never saw it actually happen until I told Flynn that he was a father.

I stayed quiet for a full moment after the words flew out of my mouth. I hadn't meant to say it so abruptly; over the past twenty-four hours, I'd rehearsed over and over in my head how I'd say it. I planned to be calm and matter-of-fact and contrite. But I'd forgotten how much fire this man stirred in me. He could make me so mad that I wanted to scream. And at this moment, despite how my heart was pounding in trepidation, my hands itched to grab his face and kiss him senseless.

Now, though, I just stayed perfectly still, waiting for him to process what I'd said. I watched as disbelief morphed to shock which gave way to realization and . . . yep, we were back to shock.

"You had my baby?" He spoke so quietly that I had to lean forward again to hear him clearly. "You were pregnant, and you never told me."

This was the part I'd been dreading. I had to try to explain something that I didn't quite understand myself: how I'd justified keeping Bridget a secret from her father.

"I didn't know when you left. I think . . . I'm pretty sure it happened the night before graduation."

Flynn's eyes dropped, and I wondered if he remembered that night as vividly as I did. It'd been our last night together, but at the time, we thought we were one the cusp of the greatest adventure of our lives.

"When did you find out? That you were pregnant?" He spoke in even, quiet words.

I caught the corner of my lip between my teeth. "About a month after you left. I didn't even think of it, and I was so . . . well, like I said before. It was really a bad time." I pushed that memory away. "By the time it dawned on me . . . and I took a test . . . I was over eight weeks along."

Flynn nodded, as though I'd just given him a weather report. "And once you knew, it never occurred to you to call me? Just a head's up? You know, 'Hey, Flynn, what's new with you? Oh, by the way, I'm having your baby.'"

"You weren't here." I covered my face with my hands. "You were gone, and you'd told me that night that nothing or no one was going to hold you back. When I asked you to stay with me, you told me that if you did, you'd end up hating me. Resenting me. So strangely enough, the idea of asking you to come back was not very appealing."

He exhaled a long breath, moving back away from me. "God, Ali. You knew I was mad that night. I didn't mean all that. I was—" He ran his hand through his hair. "I was hurt."

"Yeah, well, you sounded dead serious to me." I slumped in the overstuffed chair. "Tell me something, Flynn. And be brutally honest. If I had gotten in touch with you and said I was pregnant, what would you've done?"

His eyes shifted to the floor. "I'd have come home. I would've been here for you. And no way would I'd have let Craig Fucking Moss raise my child."

"Really?" I hugged my arms around my ribs. "And just what would you've done then? Gone to school, when you hadn't applied anywhere? Moved in with Sam and me at the farm, gotten a job?" I laughed, dry and mirthless. "You would've hated that. And pretty soon, you'd have hated *me*. So tell me how much better everything would be now if I'd told you I was pregnant. Like it or not, Flynn, I did you a favor. I gave you the freedom to find what you were looking for."

"You took the decision away from me by never letting me know." His anger was palpable, and I grit my teeth, curling back into the chair.

"Flynn, I get it that you're furious with me. I understand that. I know this is shock, but can't we—"

"You fucking bitch."

I jerked my head around to where Maureen stood in the doorway to the living room, her hands fisted at her side and her eyes blazing. Behind her, Meghan bit her lip, meeting my eyes helplessly. We'd agreed she would break the news to Maureen while I faced Flynn. Clearly it hadn't gone well for either of us.

"How could you do that to him? How could you not tell *us?* My God, Ali, I was your best friend. We told each other everything, and you couldn't tell me you were having my brother's baby? What the hell's wrong with you?"

Flynn stepped toward her, with his hands palm out. "Reenie, I've got this. It's not your battle."

"Bullshit. She was my friend, Flynn. For all these years

I've been living in this town with her, while it turns out I have niece right here, going to school with Graham." She swung back to face me. "You kept her from her family. My father died never knowing he had another grandchild. And you let it happen."

Tears stung my eyes. "I never meant to keep her from you. But telling you would be the same as telling Flynn, and . . ." I gripped the arms of the chair, digging my fingers into the rough fabric. "As I told him, I didn't know what to do. I was alone, except for Sam, and I just couldn't lay that on him. He had so much weight on his shoulders already."

"We would've been happy to share the burden." Reenie's mad had given way to hurt. "Mom and Dad, Iona and me . . . we would've been here for you."

"I think maybe instead of rehashing what happened back then, we should let Ali and Flynn figure out what they're going to do from here on out." Meghan stood behind Maureen.

Flynn sat down again across from me, on the sofa. "I want to see her. Does she know about me? Does she think Craig is her father?"

I shook my head. "She doesn't really know anything. Bridget never knew Craig, because he left when she was an infant. I've never mentioned him to her. She asked me about her father a few years back, and I told her . . ." I took a deep breath. "I told her that her father loved her very much, but that he couldn't be with us. I never gave her anyone's name."

He nodded once, short and curt. "So you tell her now that I'm here. And I'll come out to see her." He narrowed his eyes at me. "Today. I want this to happen now."

"How do you think she's going to take it?" Maureen glanced at me. "Should you have someone there? Like a professional?"

"Bridget is one of the most well-adjusted kids I've ever met." Meghan dared a smile. "I think if you're honest with her, and keep it simple, she'll be fine." She paused, as though debating whether or not to go on. "I understand it hurts you both that you didn't know Bridget was part of you. But I want you to know that this child is loved, and she's happy. Sam is an amazing uncle, and Ali . . . she's like super-mom. Bridge is smart and funny and respectful . . . she's already a talented artist." Meghan turned to Maureen. "She probably got it from your dad, like you told me last summer. Didn't you say he used to be a mason?"

Reenie nodded. "Yeah, when he first came over to this country, and then during the summers after he started teaching. He made the prettiest fireplaces and stone walls." She sniffled, making me wonder if she was choking back sobs.

"Okay." I stood up, looping my purse over my shoulder. "So the first step is telling Bridget." I twisted the strap of the bag around my fingers. "I'll call you when we're ready for you to come over."

"Don't drag your feet on this." If there was a subtle threat in Flynn's words, I chose to ignore it. "I've already been robbed of eight years with my daughter. I don't want to miss anymore." He dug into the back pocket of his jeans and pulling out a brown leather wallet, slid out a white business card. "My number's on there."

"I don't want you to miss any more, either. Believe it or not, Flynn, I want my daughter to know her father." I was surprised to realize it was true. Now that the hardest part was over, I was relieved and ready to move on.

For a moment, we all stood awkwardly, staring at each other. There wasn't anything to say, and yet just walking out the door felt wrong. I could tell Meghan was itching to go; she'd missed another day of classes today in order to come here with me, and now she wanted to get back to Sam.

I glanced at Flynn. "I know this is going to take a while to digest. I understand that you're angry and hurt. I hope that we can get past it and . . ." I tried to think of what I wanted to say. "Parent our child together. If that's what you want."

I didn't know what I expected from him. Maybe on some level I hoped he'd take two steps closer and pull me into his arms. Not anything lusty or leading to a declaration of life-long love, but maybe just comfort. Understanding.

Instead he raised one eyebrow. "I'll be waiting for that call."

Sam was sitting on the front porch when we got home. Meghan and I pulled around to the back door and walked through the house to find him.

Meghan opened the screen door and went straight for the swing, sitting down next to my brother and curling her body into him. He pulled her close and kissed the top of her head, glancing up at me. "So how'd it go?"

I dropped into a wicker chair. "It went. I told him. He hates me. So does Maureen." I leaned my forehead into my hand and massaged. I had a wicked headache brewing there. "I have to talk to Bridge when she gets home, then he's coming over to see her."

"That's fast." Sam rubbed the side of Meghan's arm and then tilted her chin up with one finger. "You okay?"

"Maureen is so mad at me." Her voice was muffled against his arm. "She asked me how I could keep something like that from her."

"It wasn't your fault." I was so tired, so completely ex-hausted. And the fun wasn't quite over yet today. "If I hadn't told you last year, you wouldn't have known either. All of this comes down to me, and the decisions I made." I nudged Meghan's knee with the tip of my shoe. "Don't sweat it, kiddo. Reenie'll come around. She gets mad fast but never holds a grudge. It's the Irish, I think."

"That's why she didn't talk to you for almost nine years?"

Ouch. "That was as much me as her. I think she started to thaw toward me after Craig left town, but I never let her. I was afraid if I did, I'd end up telling her the truth." A loud whoosh of air brakes signaled the arrival of Bridget's bus. My stomach tumbled. "Guess it's time to face the music. Again."

"Ali, do you want to talk to her alone? Sam and I can go upstairs."

I shook my head. "If it's all the same, I'd rather you stay. I'm going to need all the help I can get."

Within a few minutes, my beautiful daughter came bounding up the long driveway. Her dark curls bounced on top of her backpack, and her red sneakers kicked up a cloud of dirt behind her. My heart swelled; this child was the love of my life, the one shining gift in decades of loss and pain. There wasn't a blessed thing I wouldn't do for her.

She began calling me as soon as she spotted us on the porch. "Mommy! Maisie invited me to her birthday party next month and it's going to be in Savannah at the pirate restaurant where you went with Uncle Sam and Aunt Meghan last year and we're gong to walk around and maybe even see ghosts." She finished in a burst of breath as she climbed the steps to the porch. "I can go, right? Please?"

I pulled her up onto my lap, remembering with a pang when she'd fit so easily under my chin, tucked in a ball. Now her arms and legs were becoming gangly, and her face was losing some of the sweet baby chub. My little one was growing up. And now I had to learn how to share her.

"We'll talk about it, sugar, okay?" I stroked back her hair. "Listen, do you want a snack? Some milk and some of those yummy peanut butter cookies Aunt Meghan made?"

"Yes, please!" She made to wriggle off my lap, but I held on, glancing at Meghan. She nodded and pushed off Sam's chest.

"Why don't you stay out here with your mom, and I'll bring all of us a snack? Babe, you want milk or coffee?"

"There's still some in the pot from earlier. I can just heat that up." He began to rise, but Meghan gently pushed him back.

"No, you stay out here with the girls." She leaned down to kiss his cheek, causing my daughter to fake gag.

Meghan tugged on one of her curls as she passed. "Watch it there, Miss Bridget, or I'll sit on his *lap* when I come back out."

"No!" Bridge clutched her throat and pretended to pass out.

"All right, Sarah Heartburn." My brother shifted, making the swing screech. "So tell us what else happened today besides Maisie's party invite. How did the math test go?"

"Good. I think I got it all right." Bridget slid off my lap onto the porch floor and shrugged off her backpack. Unzipping it, she pulled out her folder. "No homework this weekend 'cause we all turned in our projects this week."

"Sounds good." I opened the folder and flipped through the papers without really seeing them. Meghan backed through the door carrying a tray with cups and a plate of cookies.

After she'd passed around the goodies, I leaned down to squeeze my daughter's shoulder. "Hey, sweetie, I need to talk to you."

"Uh huh." She broke her cookie in half and dipped into her milk.

I took a deep breath. "I want to tell you about your father."

"Okay." She didn't even look up at me, absorbed in her snack.

"Bridge. This is kind of important. Your dad's here. He wants to see you."

Now she did turn her head to look at me. "Here? At the farm?"

"No, in town." I paused. "Do you want to see him?"

Bridget stretched out her legs. "Yeah. Is he nice?"

I quirked one eyebrow. *Well, that remains to be seen.* "Of course he is. He's very nice, and he has a wonderful family." I hesitated a minute and then added, "You know Graham Fowler? From your class? Your father is his uncle. Which makes Graham your cousin."

Her mouth dropped open. "I have a *cousin?*" She spoke with breathless surprise. "What else do I have?"

Sam turned a laugh into a cough, and I shot him a warning look. "Well, you have two other aunts. And a grandmother."

"A grandma?" Bridget's eyes shone. "So next time it's Grandparents Day at school, can I bring my grandma?"

The excitement in her face made my heart drop. I'd never realized how much my daughter had felt she was missing, how much I'd denied her by keeping the truth from both Flynn and her.

"Well, honey, we can ask."

"Cool. When is my dad coming over?"

It was, apparently, as easy as that. "I have to call him. You're ready to see him now? Today?"

"Uh huh." Bridget stuffed the last cookie into her mouth and then talked around it. "Uncle Sam, do you know my dad?"

Sam's eyes widened and his mouth dropped. "Uh . . . yeah, I do. At least, I knew him before, when he lived in Burton."

"Is he nice? Do you like him?"

Sam glanced at me. A mix of expressions crossed his face. "Yes. Yes, he's very nice. He's a good man, and you should be proud to have him as your father. He loves you very much." My brother grinned at me, and I knew he meant to be encouraging. "But you have lots of people who love you. Your mom, of course, who's been here for you every single day of your life, and Aunt Meghan, who's the coolest aunt ever—" He winked at his girlfriend, who rolled her eyes. "And me. I've loved you since the day you were born. Even though you screamed at night and kept me awake when you were a baby."

I stood up. "True that. Okay, let me make this call. And then someone's going to get me some more cookies, since some little piggy ate them all up." I tickled Bridget under her arm as I walked past, dialing Flynn's number to the sweet accompaniment of my daughter's laughter.

Flynn

THE LAST TIME I'D driven down this driveway, I was eighteen years old and thought I had life by the balls. I remembered that day with crystal-clear high-def precision: we'd graduated earlier in the day, and I was meeting Ali at the farm so we could talk to Sam, let him know that we were leaving town. Together. Thanks to our newspaper advisor, Mr. Wilder, I'd secured an internship with a photographer in New York, and we'd planned that Ali would go to college up there. We'd both work part-time, and that combined with the money I'd been saving would see us through until I starting making money by taking pictures.

I was walking on air that day as I'd pulled my old Chevy Chevette around to the back of the house, like I always did. I took the steps to the kitchen door in one leap and gave a cursory knock before I threw open the screen and went into the kitchen. When I spotted Ali sitting at the table, the grin on my face got even bigger and brighter . . . until I got a good look at her face.

My world started to crumble to pieces at that moment.

Today, though . . . today was different. Today I drove my Audi A7—okay, yeah, it was a rental, but I could've had one of my own, if I ever stayed in one place long enough to need a car. And today I wasn't nervous about the idea of talking to Sam Reynolds. I wasn't that boy anymore, the one who was stupid in love with a pretty girl. Now I was a man who knew love like that didn't last.

The old farmhouse was right in front of me as I rounded the last bend in the driveway. Ali was sitting there on the porch, curled up in a chair I was pretty sure had been there when we were in high school. It was a weird kind of been-there, done that; I couldn't count how many times my girl had been waiting for me, right in that chair, when I'd come by on a weeknight for a study date. She'd wave and blow me a kiss as I drove up, and then meet me at my car, throwing her arms around me as soon as I climbed out of the driver's seat. I could almost feel the sweetness of her body pressed against me, soft and promising, and her scent filling my senses.

With no little effort, I pushed that image from my head, reminding myself that the same girl who'd greeted me with such love had broken my heart and denied me my own child. That was what I had to keep front and center. I couldn't let her get under my skin again. Not ever.

I pulled up to the side of the house and turned off the car. I got out and slammed the door, hesitating just a minute to make sure I was ready. I needed to keep it all together and remember I was here for Bridget. For my daughter.

Fuck. I had a daughter. It'd been hitting me today, over and over. Like someone had taken the life I thought I had all figured out and turned it upside down. Funny how just one small piece of information could do that. Yesterday, I'd been Flynn Evans, photo-journalist. Well-known in certain circles, with my name mentioned among the up-and-comers in my field. Opportunities coming out my ears. As footloose and fancy-free as a guy could be in the early twenty-first century.

Today, I was a father. The word still felt foreign. I didn't know how to deal with kids. Shit, half the time I could barely stand to be around my nephew Graham. And a girl? How the hell was I going to talk to her? What did I have to say to an eight-year old female?

"Flynn?" Ali had come down off the porch and stood leaning about the brick balustrade alongside the steps. "You okay?"

I straightened up. "Yeah. Just making sure the car's locked." I angled my body slightly and pulled the clicker out of my pocket.

Ali raised one eyebrow. "I think it's safe out here. No one's going to bother your car."

"Just habit, I guess." I managed a tight-lipped smile. "I'm used to living in the city, where you lock anything you want to see again."

"Oh, sure." She nodded, but I was fairly certain she wasn't buying my excuse. Whatever. I didn't have to justify my actions to Ali Reynolds. "Well, you don't have to be nervous, you know. Bridget's really excited to meet you."

"I'm not nervous." I frowned. "Why would I be?"

Ali crossed her arms, throwing her boobs into prominence. *Damn.* Some part of me wondered if she'd done it on purpose. I'd always been a sucker for this girl's rack. I dragged my eyes back up to her face as she spoke.

"I don't know, Flynn. I thought maybe today's been a tad traumatic for you. It wouldn't be unusual for any guy to be a little on edge." She pushed off the wall and pivoted to climb up the porch steps. "But clearly you've got it all under control.

Come on in. Bridge is upstairs."

I followed her, pointedly not looking at her perfect little ass swaying inside her tight faded jeans. "Uh, Ali." I coughed, trying to clear out the crack in my voice. "How did it go when you told her about me? Was she okay?"

Ali stopped just before opening the screen door. She looked back at me, studying my face as though trying to decide how much to tell me. "She was fine. Actually, she was . . . really great. Just a warning, though she's thrilled with the idea of having a grandmother. And a cousin. So I hope you're planning to tell the rest of your family about the new addition, because it'd crush her to find out she can't meet them."

I nodded. "No worries on that front. I told Mom before I came over here. And Reenie told Iona."

Panic flittered across her face. "Do they hate me, too?" She spoke low, worry in her voice.

I sighed and rubbed my chin. "No. Mom was . . . surprised. And I think a little sad that she didn't know until now. But she's happy about it. She said a new grandchild is always reason for celebrating, and I'm pretty sure by the time I left, she was getting excited about buying Bridget clothes."

Ali smiled a little. "Good luck with that. This kid lives in jeans and sneakers. But maybe a grandma would be able to change her mind." She reached for the door handle but paused again before opening it. "What about Iona?"

I shifted my weight from one foot to the other. "She told Maureen that she'd suspected it for a while, but she figured that there was no way you wouldn't tell me. Or Reenie, at least. I think she's happy Graham'll finally have another kid in the family, so close to his own age."

"Yeah, they're only a few months apart." This time, she opened the door and went inside, holding it for me as I came behind.

The living room hadn't changed, not one bit. The sofa was

the same faded rose pink, the area rug the same worn green. I almost expected to run into my old self, perched on the edge of the checked wing chair, waiting for Ali to be ready for a date.

Instead, she stood at the bottom of the steps, one hand on the newel post as she called upstairs. "Bridget! Come on down, honey."

Loud scrambling footsteps echoed above us, and within a few seconds, a dark-haired tornado raced down. She came to a screeching halt at the bottom of the stairs, breathing hard and staring up me. And just like that, I was looking down into my daughter's face.

Her eyes were the first things I saw. They were wide and brown, the exact same color and shape of Ali's. Her nose was a cute little button, and I realized it reminded me of Maureen's. Perfect rosebud lips were slightly parted, and then they curved into a grin, and my breath stopped.

My daughter had my dad's smile, the mischievous curl of the mouth and the answering twinkle in her eye. I never thought I'd see it again, and yet . . . here it was.

Without thinking about it, I knelt down next to her. "Hi, Bridget. I'm . . . Flynn." I'd planned to say Dad, but at the last minute, I chickened out. I didn't want to force anything before she was ready. "You're incredibly beautiful, you know that?"

She cocked her head at me, so reminiscent of her mother. "Yeah, I know." Oh my God, this kid had attitude and confidence. I loved it.

"Do you want to come sit down and talk a little?" I motioned toward the sofa, unsure of what else to say.

"Why don't you go out onto the porch?" Ali spoke, and I looked up at her. I'd nearly forgotten she was standing there. "It's a beautiful afternoon."

"Okay." Bridget started toward the door, and then she stopped and stretched out her hand to me. "Come on."

I let her lead me out the door and to the swing. Ali leaned

out, holding onto the screen.

"Flynn, do you want anything to eat or drink? Bridge already had her afternoon snack, but there're are few peanut butter cookies left."

"I'm okay, thanks." I couldn't think about eating right now. Not with my stomach up around my throat.

Ali nodded and began to close the door. Panic gripped me. "Hey, aren't you . . . coming out with us?"

She stood there for a minute, her eyes steady on mine. "No. I think you've got this." Her gaze flickered to our daughter. *Our daughter.* "Besides, I think you two have a lot of catching up to do." She ducked back inside, shutting the door quietly.

Bridget climbed up onto the swing, and I sat down in the wicker chair with chipping paint, the same place Ali'd been sitting when I pulled up. It was still warm from her body. I ignored the feeling it gave me and attempted to strike up a conversation with my daughter.

"So." *Yeah, that was an auspicious start.* "Bridget, your mom said she. . told you about me."

She nodded. "Mommy said you were in town. Where've you been? Why weren't you in town until now?"

Okay, so we're going straight for the essay questions. "Well, uh, I travel all over the world. I take pictures for magazines, and I have to go to where the news is."

Bridget blinked. "Most of my friends at school have dads who live in their house. Or somewhere around here. Except Bella, and her dad left last year." She raised her foot up to the swing, bending her knee and wrapped her arms around it. "Were you here when I was a baby?"

I shook my head. "No, I wasn't. Believe me, if I'd been here then, I never would've left."

"Why weren't you here? Why don't you live with Mommy and me?" She scratched at the side of her leg.

"Um. I didn't know you were my little girl, Bridget. I . . ."

This was a pivotal moment. I wasn't sure how to answer her, but I knew I had to tread carefully. "When your mom found out you were on the way, I'd already left Burton. And . . ." The image of Ali's face as she'd described our last fight flashed across my memory with a stab of regret. "Your mom couldn't get in touch with me, to tell me that you were coming. That was my fault. Because I'm the one who left her. But you have to know, Bridget, that if I'd known about you, I would've been back here. Nothing could've kept me from you."

She bit her lip, a small frown between those deep eyes. "Are you going to live with Mommy and me now? And Uncle Sam and Aunt Meghan?"

I blew out a breath, rubbing my knee. "No, I'm not. I'm not married to your mom, and . . . yeah. Listen, Bridget, your mom and I've got a lot to talk about and figure out. For me, the most important thing was to meet you and let you meet me. Now that we've done that, we can see what happens next."

"Are you going away again?" There was just a little tremor in that voice, and again, I was back with Ali, seeing her eyes filled with tears and her voice heavy with pain as she asked me a similar question. *Are you going to leave me?*

I'd been wrestling with this since Ali had left my mom's house this morning. A big part of me wanted to jump that plane in Savannah and head for Los Angeles. I could go back to being the Flynn Evans who didn't have a kid: I could forget all about Burton, Georgia and brown-eyed women who could still make me a little crazy. But on the other hand, I knew leaving wasn't going to fix this problem. I had to figure out what my life was going to look like, now that I was a father.

And having seen her, I was sure leaving was out of the question. At least leaving tomorrow was.

"Not right away." I finally answered her. "And if I do have to go someplace else, I'll be back. I promise. I know you just met me, but I really want to be your dad."

The wrinkles between her eyes smoothed out. "Can I call you Daddy?"

Another piece of my heart broke off and flew into this kid's hands. "Nothing would make me happier." I ventured out a hand to touch her curls. "I don't have any practice in being a daddy, but if you have a little patience with me, I think we can make it work."

There was that grin again. I couldn't help smiling back when I saw it. "I've never had a daddy, but I always wanted one." She fiddled with the lace of her sneaker. "Mom said I have a grandma now, too. And Graham is my cousin." She twisted her face. "He's a crazy boy. My teacher says he's wild."

I laughed. "Yeah, he is. I think it's possible that kid's a little spoiled. Maybe you can help straighten him out."

She brightened. "Can I beat him up? Mom never lets me hit anyone."

"Ahhh . . ." *Okay, I see how this game is going to play.* "Remember how I said I didn't know much about being a dad? Well, I'm pretty sure your mom knows best about this kind of stuff, so let's just say for the time being, if she gives you a rule, same goes for me. Got it?"

She sighed and nodded. "I was afraid of that. But it's okay." She pursed her lips, like she was thinking hard, and then glanced up at me. "Do I get to see my grandma?"

"Oh, yeah, that's a given." I tapped her nose. "Your grandma is just itching to see you. If it's okay with your mom, maybe you can come visit sometime this weekend."

"Really?" Her small face shone, and I thought I'd do just about anything to keep that joy alive in this kid. Forever. "What about a grandpa? Do I have one of those, too?"

I closed my eyes. Here was the bitter that came along with the sweet. "You do, honey, but . . ." *Shit, what did she know about death?* How was I supposed to explain it to her? The last thing I wanted to do was to screw up her little psyche. I decided honesty was best. "Your grandpa went to heaven. Just last week. And I got to tell you, it makes me really sad, because he would've loved you to pieces. He was the coolest grandpa ever." I swallowed over the lump in my throat. "You would've loved him, too. You have his smile."

"I do?" Her mouth curved, proving again what I'd just told her.

"Yeah, you do. It makes me really happy, because I thought I'd lost that smile forever. And now, I get to see it on you." I remembered something Meghan had said earlier, at my mom's house. "I hear you're quite the artist. So was your grandpa."

Bridget jumped up from the swing. "He was? Did he draw? I can draw and paint. Aunt Meghan is my art teacher, and sometimes we go out in the woods or over to Farmer Fred's and I draw his horses."

I couldn't resist anymore. I reached across and drew her closer to me, boosting her onto my lap, sensitive to the slightest resistance so that I could let her go if I were jumping the fence. But she snuggled right onto me, taking one of my hands in both of hers. *Oh, I was so wrapped around this kid already. Gone. Sunk.*

"Grandpa Brice used to draw funny pictures for me when I was a little boy." I hadn't thought about that for years. "But most of his art was in bricks and stone. See, he was born in a country called Ireland—"

"I know where that is. It's part of the British Isles, across the Atlantic. It's very green, and leprechauns comes from there."

Yeah, my kid was a total genius. "Wow, you're smart. I'm not sure I knew where Ireland was when I was eight, and my family came from there. Anyway, when he lived in Ireland, Grandpa trained to be a mason. He built beautiful walls for people, or paths for their gardens, or he made them fireplaces. When he came to America, he kept doing that, but he also went to college. He learned how to be a teacher, and he taught history at the high school, right here in Burton."

"Aunt Meghan's a teacher. Or she's gonna be one, after she graduates." Bridget nodded. "But she's teaches art." She twisted to look up into my face. "Do you want to see my drawings? Uncle Sam got me a portfolio for Christmas, and all of them are in there. It's up in my room."

"Of course I do." I let her pull me to my feet and back into the house. Ali was sitting on the sofa, on the other side of the window, her face wet with tears that she was trying to wipe away.

I came to a halt, staring at her. Emotion swirled inside of me, and for the first time today, I looked at this woman not as my old girlfriend, not as the person who'd betrayed me on some level, but as the mother of my child. The woman who'd raised this magical little girl who was already deep into my heart and soul.

I stopped Bridget and stooped down again. "Honey, why don't you run up to your room and get your drawings? I'll wait right here. I just want to talk to your mom for a minute."

She nodded and was gone in a flash, tearing up the steps like a bright little comet. I turned to go into the living room, sitting down next to Ali, just close enough that I could smell her hair. *God, it smelled the same as it did when we were in high school.* Lilacs and jasmine. I had to steel myself not to reach out and wrap one silky strand around my finger.

"Hey." As opening lines went, it wasn't inspired. "So . . . I just wanted to say . . . she's a great kid. I mean, I know I just met her, but she was easy to talk to, and she's smart and funny."

Ali lifted her eyes to mine. "She's amazing. Every day, she does something or says something that makes me think . . . wow, how did someone like her come from me?" She smiled a little. "I mean, from us."

I nodded. "Yeah. But I get that it's you. You're the one who's been putting in the time with her. You made her who she is. So, thanks."

She shrugged, but I saw her face pink a little. "I heard what you said to her. Sorry, I was totally eavesdropping. I'd apologize for that, but Bridget's my daughter, and I needed to make sure she was okay. Getting a father all of a sudden—I wanted to know she was handling it."

An hour ago, I might've been offended and pissed. But now that I knew my daughter, I completely understood. I would've done the same thing in her position. Protecting her was our number one priority. *Ours.*

"So I wanted to say . . . thank you. For what you said to her, when she asked you why you didn't live with us, why she'd never met you until now. You could've told her the truth, and I wouldn't blame you. But you didn't. You let her believe it was all on your shoulders. I can't tell you how much that means to me. I was so afraid." She took a deep breath. "I didn't realize how scared I was. I was terrified to tell you, but losing Bridget's love and respect would've killed me."

"I don't want to take her away from you, Ali. I'm still not sure how I feel about what happened back then, about how you handled it, but I know we need to move forward. My mom said something to me this afternoon. She said if I get stuck resenting the past, I'll risk ruining the present and losing the future. I don't want to do that."

Ali cast her eyes down, staring at her hands as they lay in her lap. "Your mother was always one of the best people I ever knew. I've missed her all these years." She sniffled long, dabbing at her nose with a disintegrating tissue. "I missed them all. You know, after you left, Maureen was still okay with me. She was still my friend, at least until Craig started hanging around."

That name brought back the resentment. I understood, to a certain extent, why Ali hadn't told me she was pregnant. I still didn't get why she'd turned to a guy who was supposed to have been my friend. That was going to take some time.

Before I could ask her about him, Bridget ran back down the steps and leaped onto the sofa between us. "I couldn't decide which ones to bring down, and I only wanted to show you my best."

"Hey, no fair." I brushed the back of my fingers over her cheek. "I want to see them all."

"I will, but I wanted you to see my best first." She grinned, and then her smile faded as she saw her mother's face. "Mommy, what's wrong? Why're you crying?"

"Oh, I'm fine, baby. These are happy tears. I'm so glad your daddy is here with us."

"Me, too." She reached out her small hand to touch my knee and the other to take her mother's hand. "Even if my daddy can't live here, I'm glad we're a family."

A family. I met Ali's eyes, and I saw thinly-veiled panic there before it melted into something that might have been close to hope.

Chapter
Eight

Ali

CHANGE HAD NEVER BEEN my friend. When I was little, it took me weeks to adjust to the twice-a-year daylight savings time shift. And when I left home to live with Craig after we got married, I almost lost my mind. I hated being out of my routine and having to establish a new one.

Once Bridget and I had moved home, I'd quickly established a schedule and my own way of doing things. I'd reorganized the kitchen in my new role as woman of the house, and I'd laid down ground rules for Sam about helping me keep things clean and running smoothly. For the last seven years, our lives had remained essentially the same, with just a few tweaks in the schedule when Bridge started school.

Of course, a couple of things had changed when Meghan

became a permanent part of our world, but even so, she'd been careful to adapt to our home and rules. I liked the fact that she cooked for us occasionally, that she took her turn at the dishes and helped with Bridget. As long as she didn't rock my boat, I wasn't going to complain. Sure, as I'd told Alex, sometimes I worried about what would happen when she and Sam made it all official, but I'd figure that out when it happened.

At the moment, I had a more pressing concern. When he'd left the farm on Friday afternoon, just before dinner, Flynn had suggested that we work out a schedule for him to see Bridget. He'd also asked if he could take her to meet his mother over the weekend. I couldn't say no, of course, and I didn't want to; Bridget was ecstatic about the plan, and I loved Cory Evans. She'd been good to me when I was dating Flynn, even stepping in to mother me once in a while. I remembered when it came time for our junior prom. There was no question that Flynn and I would go, but I was secretly dreading it. All my friends were talking about picking out gowns with their mothers, pretending to complain all the while I could tell they loved it. I knew Sam and I didn't have the money for a fancy new dress. We were doing okay, thanks to help and guidance from the Guild, a group of local businessmen who'd taken Sam under their collective wing. But doing okay didn't extend to trips to Savannah for gown shopping, even if I'd wanted to go by myself.

About a month before the dance, Cory had stopped me as I was leaving her house after a study date with Flynn.

"Ali, honey, could I have a quick word with you?" She flicked a glance to her son. "Flynn, run out and warm up the car."

He wrinkled up his brow. "It's not that cold, Mom."

"Do it anyway, and don't argue with your mother."

Flynn was smart enough to obey, and with a shrug, he headed through the front door. My heart was pounding: I couldn't imagine why his mother wanted to talk to me alone.

Remembering what had happened down at the river two weeks before—Flynn and I had finally gone all the way—made me feel guilty as hell. *Did she know? How could she?*

Cory pointed to a stool at her kitchen breakfast bar. "Sit down, sweetie." Once I'd boosted myself onto the chair, she leaned her elbows on the granite countertop. "Listen, Ali, I don't want to overstep my bounds here. I know I'm not your mom, but I can imagine how much you miss her. And I was just thinking today that maybe you might want to go shopping with me for your prom gown. We could drive into Savannah if you like."

My breath caught. "Really? Oh, wow, that would be . . ." Suddenly I remembered that the money for my dress was tied up on our fields, in the onions and peaches and what-all Sam had growing. My smile faded. "That would be great, but I'm not sure I can. I was just going to check out the thrift store in Farleyville."

She nodded. "That's perfectly okay, if that's what you want. I'd still like to go with you."

So that Saturday, Cory picked me up out at the farm, and we drove to the thrift store. I'd heard stories of almost-new gowns, beautiful dresses for just a few dollars. But apparently we were too late for those, since the only possibilities on the racks were tired old bridesmaids' gowns or worn dresses that were several sizes too big for me. I flipped through the hangers one more time as desperation stiffened my shoulders.

"Ali, there's nothing." Cory put one soft hand on my back. "Honey, hear me out. Let's just go into the city for kicks and see what we see. Sometimes they have amazing sales, and who knows . . . you might find something."

Since she was driving—and since I recognized the determined gleam in her eyes, as I'd seen it often enough in her son's—I really didn't have a choice. And once I'd spotted the silvery-blue strapless gown with the soft lace overlay, I was a goner. When I checked the price tag, I nearly died. But Cory only covered my hand with hers.

"Ali, please. Let me do this for you." She drew in a shaky breath. "When your mama died, I just felt so . . . helpless. There was nothing I could do for you and Sam, other than cook you some meals and try to be there for you if you needed me. But this is something I could do, on behalf of your mother. I want to think that if it'd been Brice and me who weren't here anymore, your parents would be good to him. I can't take her place, but I can make sure you have the perfect dress to wear to your prom. Please?"

I couldn't say no. And when I saw the look on Flynn's face the night of prom, I was glad I hadn't.

So I had no qualms about Bridget hanging out with her grandmother. It was just the idea of sharing my daughter's time with her father from now on that made my stomach clench. I was used to being the only parent, the one authority and the one who called all the shots. Sam had always been there as my back-up, to make sure Bridge knew she wasn't going to get away with any nonsense. But he deferred to me as the one who made the rules and was the final say in my child's life. Having to adjust to sharing wasn't going to be easy.

Flynn was very business-like when he called me on Saturday morning. I'd just gotten to the stand and was unlocking the register when my phone rang.

"Hey, Ali. It's Flynn."

I had a dizzying flash of déjà vu and had to swallow hard before I answered. How many times had I answered his calls with anticipation and a swell of happiness? Too many to count. But now everything was different.

"Hey, Flynn. What's up?" Silently I congratulated myself on sounding grown up and smooth. I could do this.

"I just wanted to let you know . . . I canceled my flight for today and backed out of the job I had in Los Angeles. I'm going to stay in Burton for the time being."

I couldn't tell whether he wanted me to apologize for screwing up his life or acknowledge that he was doing the right thing. I decided to go with a little of both.

"I'm sorry you had to change your plans. But I know Bridget's going to be so happy to have the time to get to know you." I paused before adding, "And I'm sure you're going to be glad to have the time with her, too."

"Definitely. It wasn't even a question." He sounded sure, and that made me feel a little less guilty. "I just had to make sure someone else could take the job. Otherwise I'd have flown out there, taken the photos and then come right back. But it works better this way."

"Okay, that's great. Bridget said something about meeting your mom this weekend?"

"I was hoping we could do that. If it works for you, maybe I could pick her up tomorrow morning. My mom's doing a big family dinner in the afternoon, but I thought if Bridge comes early, they can get some time together, and then she can meet everyone else. What do you think?"

What I thought was lost in the pure panic over the idea of my daughter being thrown into a situation I couldn't control. What if they didn't like her? What if Graham was mean to her? What if Iona and Maureen took out their anger at me on their newly discovered niece?

It only took a fraction of a second before I realized how crazy that was. I'd known the Evans girls for a long time, and they'd never been anything but kind to me. Maureen and I'd been as close as sisters for several years. They'd welcome Bridget into the family, and the worst thing that would happen was she'd be spoiled rotten.

"I think that sounds wonderful. Bridget's going to be in seventh heaven." I tamped down my own misgivings and tried to sound like I meant it. "What time do you want me to have her ready?"

"Is ten too early?"

I laughed. "May I remind you, we live on a farm. Early is never a problem. She'll be all set."

"Cool. So I was thinking, maybe we could come up with a regular schedule for me to see her. I could pick her up from school some days, or if you were okay with it, she could spend the night at my mom's with us."

Panic filled me. "But she takes the bus to school." It sounded stupid to my own ears, but I couldn't stop the words from tumbling out.

Flynn's voice took on a patient tone. "I'm sure we can work out something where I pick her up or drop her off. By the way, how come Bridget goes to the elementary school in Burton? I thought she'd be at the regional one."

"They re-districted everything a few years back. We're right on the line, so we were given the option of sending her to either school. I thought it would be easier for her to be with the same kids all the way through, rather than making the transition at high school like Sam and I had to."

"That makes sense. And it makes it easier for me, too. What would you think of me picking her up Tuesdays from school and then having her over night? And maybe one day a weekend?"

"I . . ." I bit my lip. "Yeah, I guess that works. I'll have to go into the school and make sure you're added as a parent. They're very strict now about who's allowed to pick them up, you know." This was going to mean telling other people the truth. I didn't know why this hadn't occurred to me before now, but for some reason, I'd thought I could keep the whole situation quiet, just between Flynn and his family and me. But once I told the school, the news would run through town like a wild fire. *Great.*

"Can you do that on Monday? The sooner, the better. That

way if I ever need to get her, it won't be a problem. Right?"

"Sure." I couldn't say anything more over the lump in my throat.

"Are you okay?" Flynn sounded cautious. "You sound . . . weird."

"No, I'm fine." I rolled my shoulders and closed my eyes. Honesty would be best here, I decided. "You just have to understand, Flynn, that right or wrong, I've been Bridget's one and only parent her whole life. Getting used to sharing that responsibility might take me a little time. I've only been away from her overnight a few times in her entire life. The furthest and longest I've been apart from her was when she stayed at Katie's last fall while I went to Savannah with Sam and Meghan. This is very new for me."

He was quiet for a minute. "I can understand that. And if I'm moving too fast for you, just tell me, and we can talk about it. But I'm trying to catch up on eight years of missing out. I don't want to lose another second with her. Especially if I'm going to have go away again."

"How long do you think you'll be in town?" I wasn't sure I wanted to know the answer.

He blew out a long breath. "Not sure. I was planning to be state side for a while anyway, even before . . . well, before everything changed. I'll have to go back to work eventually, but it isn't pressing, unless a really incredible opportunity comes along." He paused for a moment. "But no matter what, I'll be back. I'm planning to make Burton my center of operations from now on."

"Oh." I wasn't sure how I felt about that. I'd gotten used to a life that didn't include Flynn Evans. Having him in town full time had the potential to turn my world upside down. "Won't that be a big change for you?"

"Yeah, it'll be an adjustment, but it makes sense. Mom's going to need some help, and I want to be here for Bridget."

"Do you have an apartment in New York?" I'd always pictured him living in one of those lofts I'd seen in sitcoms, something spacious and modern, with a deli on the corner and a view of Central Park. Having never left the great state of Georgia, I relied heavily on television and movies for my information on the world at large.

"I have one that I've been renting from a friend of a friend. Actually, I move quite a bit, even in the city. All my shit that I can't take with me on the road, I keep in two big rubber totes in whatever apartment I'm currently using. If I need to vacate before I can get back there, I have a friend who swings by, picks them up and moves them to the next place."

"Geez. That's . . . wow. I just can't imagine not having a steady place I could come back to, even if I were traveling most of the time."

Flynn was quiet for a beat. "I guess I lost the taste for a home after I left Burton. At least, home the way you're thinking of it. At this point, I take everything I need with me. Traveling light isn't a bad thing."

"I guess not. It hasn't really been an option for me for a long time. Maybe ever. I'm one of those people who comes with baggage." At some point, we'd stopped talking about apartments and homes. We'd veered into dangerous territory, where I felt like I might be walking close to quicksand.

"I'm going to say something, but I don't want you to think I'm trying to blame you for anything again. I just want to say that if I'd known . . . God, Ali. I would've been there every step along the way. You wouldn't have had to do it all alone. Even if we couldn't work things out between us, I would never have abandoned you."

I closed my eyes and leaned my forehead against the heel of my hand. "I think on some level, I knew that. But I couldn't let myself really believe it. So many times I came close to calling you . . ." A particular memory burned against my mind for a nanosecond. I winced and pushed it away. "I was so afraid. I kept the possibility of you as my last resort. But at the same time, I was terrified of what would happen if I did call you and you didn't come. Or refused to believe me. Or said you didn't care. If that had happened, I'd have truly felt like I was on my own."

Flynn sighed. "I wish I could go back and change what happened, Ali. We can't do that, but I promise, from here on out, we're a team."

It'd made me glow, that promise. Sharing my daughter—*our* daughter—was going to take some getting used to, but the idea of not shouldering the entire job of parenting her made me a little giddy. I loved being a mom. I adored Bridget beyond the telling of it. But having another person to help me make decisions and take some of the responsibility was something I'd scarcely dared to dream I'd ever have.

Keeping that in mind, I made it through the next day, when Flynn came by to take Bridget to his mother's house. She was excited, hopping first on one foot and then the other as we waited on the front porch.

"Do you think they'll like me?" Her sudden question was the first indication that she might've been more nervous than she let on.

"Oh, sugar, they'll adore you. How could they not? You're the prettiest, smartest, most talented little girl who ever walked God's green earth. You just remember that. And remember, too, that you're a Reynolds. So you hold your head high."

Bridget glanced up at me, mid-hop. "Am I still a Reynolds? Even though my daddy has a different name?"

Crud. I hadn't expected this issue to pop up so soon. "Well, honey, legally you don't have your daddy's name." I bit my lip. Bridget's name, on her birth certificate, was Moss, and Craig was listed as her father. When I'd registered her for school, though, I'd asked that they list her as Reynolds, since it was my last name. I'd never gotten around to changing my name on anything legal after Craig and I'd gotten married, and we hadn't been together long enough for it to matter. "Not yet, anyway. We'll see what your dad wants to do, okay?"

"Okay." She frowned. "But will I still be a Reynolds even if I have a different name?"

"Always, sweetie pie. You're part of me, and you're part of Uncle Sam, and we're both Reynolds. Nothing can change that."

I heard a car on the gravel of our driveway, and a moment later, Flynn's gray sedan appeared. I didn't know much about luxury cars, but I knew this was one. He opened the door and stepped out, and I tried not to stare. It was warmer today than it had been the last week, and Flynn was wearing faded jeans that fit his fine ass to perfection. And the blue T-shirt on top hugged his broad chest, showing off arms that had taken on quite a bit of muscle definition since he was eighteen. My mouth went dry. *Hot damn.*

Flynn grinned up at us. Well, mostly at Bridget, but I was claiming some of that smile, too.

"Morning, ladies." He stopped at the bottom of the steps and stuck his thumbs into the front pockets of those sinful jeans. "Miss Bridget, you ready for a good time today?"

As hyper as my daughter had been moments before, she was suddenly shy now. She nodded, her eyes wide, before repeating the same question she'd asked me a few minutes before. "Will they like me?"

"Honeybunch, they already like you. Your grandma and your aunts—they can't wait to meet you for real." He leaned in as though sharing a secret. "In fact, and don't let on I told you, but there just might be presents with your name on them at my house."

That brought out a smile. "Really? How come? It's not Christmas, and my birthday already happened."

"I think we have a little catching up to do on Christmases and birthdays." He glanced at me and winked. "Don't worry, nothing outrageous. And they'll rein it in after this."

"That's fine." I couldn't think of anything else to say. Yeah, I didn't like the idea of Flynn becoming the indulgent dad who could afford to give our daughter everything I couldn't, but I wasn't going to argue with the fact that they had years to make up. As for it becoming too much . . . I'd deal with that if and when.

"Okay, well, you all set?" He stretched out a hand for Bridget. "Grandma's chomping at the bit for you to get there."

Bridge took his hand and jumped down the two steps. "Yep!" She paused and turned back to wrap her arms around my legs. "Bye, Mama."

"Bye, sugar." I knelt down in front of her and hugged her tight. "Be good. Mind your manners. Have a nice time, and I'll see you tonight."

"Okay if I have her back around eight?" Flynn took hold of her hand again.

"Sure. Of course." I managed what I hoped was a good approximation of a genuine smile. "Enjoy yourself."

"We will." He tossed the words back over his shoulder as Bridget dragged him toward the car. "Thanks, Ali. See you later."

I watched as they moved slowly down the driveway and out of my sight. And then I dropped to the top step and buried my face in my hands.

"Hey." Meghan's hand squeezed my shoulder at she sat down next to me. "You okay?"

"Yeah." My voice was muffled by my hands. "It's just . . . harder than I thought."

"Ali, you're not losing Bridget. Just because she'll have more people to love her doesn't mean she'll forget those of us who loved her first." She bumped against me. "Besides, if anyone should be freaking out, it should be me. After all, she's not going to meet a new mom. She's going to meet new aunts. What if she likes them more than me? I mean, I'm not even a blood aunt." She sighed. "I'm not even an aunt by marriage. I'm just . . . her uncle's girlfriend."

I wrapped my arm around Meghan's back. "Don't be silly. Bridge loves you. You'll always be her coolest aunt, no matter what. And the marriage part is just a matter of time."

She raised one eyebrow. "What've you heard?"

I smirked. "Wouldn't you like to know?" When her eyes widened, I just laughed. "No, I don't know anything. But even if I did, I'd never rob you of the joy of a surprise proposal, so don't even try."

"Great. Have I mentioned how much I don't like surprises?"

"Too bad." I stuck out my tongue at her. "Someday you'll thank me."

"Maybe." She hunched over, arms folded across her chest. "So for real, are you all right? Was it hard to see her go?"

I grimaced. "Yeah, but will you think I'm horribly shallow if I tell you the real reason?"

"Too late. I already think it."

"Bitch." I rolled my eyes. Meghan was the first female best friend I'd had in adulthood. It'd taken a little while to get used to some of her humor—affectionate insults, in particular—but I'd embraced it all eventually, to Sam's horror. He liked to complain that his house had been overtaken by estrogen, but I knew that he secretly loved it. "It's just that I'm not really worried about losing Bridget. But I felt so left out when they left. Here my daughter and her dad are going off for a big family reunion and dinner, and I'm Cinderella who gets stuck at home, alone."

"Aw, sweetie. I'm sorry. That sucks." Meghan laid her head on my shoulder.

"You know, when I was dating Flynn, that was one of the

things I loved, being part of his family. Or just about. Maureen and I were best friends, and I was in love with Flynn, and his parents were awesome. They always included me—and Sam, too, if he'd come—in their family stuff. I was starving for parent love, and they helped fill some of that. I couldn't wait until I was really one of them."

"You know I'm more than happy to share my wacky family with you, right? Mom keeps pestering me to bring you and Bridge down to the Cove for a visit. She'd have a blast."

"Someday, we'll do that. Of course, maybe before too long we'll have a good reason to go down . . . like, say, a wedding."

She stared at me, her eyes narrowing. "You're evil. You are really and truly evil." She stuck out her tongue and jumped to her feet. "Just for that, I'm abandoning you to your brother for the rest of the day."

"Aw, really? Are you leaving already?"

She stretched her back. "Well, yeah. Remember I was supposed to leave Thursday night, and then circumstances kept me here." She arched her eyebrows, reminding me that those circumstances involved me coming clean about my child's father. "I need to go back, catch up on some homework and see what I missed in class on Friday. So you and Sam have the rest of the day together."

"Fun." I couldn't remember the last time I'd been alone in our house with my brother. Bridget was always with us, or during the school day, he was in the fields and I was at the stand. Which reminded me . . ."I think maybe I'll go open the stand for a while."

"Really? I thought you didn't open on Sundays until summer time."

"We don't usually, but today's so pretty and warm, we might get traffic." Plus, it'd get me out of the house and keep me from moping all day, which would in turn probably save my life, since my moping would likely drive my brother crazy.

"Okay, chick. I'm going to grab my bags and hit the road. See you Friday night." She leaned down to kiss my cheek. "Behave, and call me if you need to talk this week."

I heaved myself up and walked down the steps and around the house toward the path that led to our stand. Being away from the house when Sam and Meghan said goodbye was never a bad thing.

My hunch about traffic at the stand proved to be correct. We had a steady stream of customers over the course of the afternoon, and I was grateful for how busy they kept me.

About mid-afternoon, as I was helping an out-of-towner select some souvenir jams, I saw a familiar black car pull into the lot. Guilt niggled in my chest; I hadn't talked to Alex since before Brice Evans' funeral. He'd texted that afternoon, but I'd been in the middle of the big reveal to Sam, and after that, I'd been too miserable and nervous to talk to anyone.

I finished up the jam sale, wrapping the glass jars and bagging them carefully. Alex wandered around the produce, trailing a hand over the oranges. I caught his wink just before he spoke.

"Miss, I have to tell you, this is the greatest farm stand I've ever seen. And I'm an expert, because roadside produce stands are my business."

"Thank you, sir." I struggled to keep a straight face. "Just what kind of business is that?"

"I write books about the stands. I travel the world, finding the best and brightest and spotlighting them in my books, *Roadside Gourmand: Eating My Way Across the Country One Stand At A Time.*" He winked at my customer. "Volumes One through Eighteen."

"That's intriguing. I've never heard of those books." The

woman smiled at him. "Are they in bookstores?"

"You should definitely ask at your local bookstore. You'll be mesmerized." He shot her the smolder, and I watched her melt. "But if you wait for Volume Nineteen, you'll be able to see this very business as the highlight feature."

"Well, isn't that wonderful?" She beamed at me. "You've got to be so excited. I can't wait to tell my friends that I was here when you found it!"

Alex sketched a bow, like the goof he was. "Of course."

The woman glanced around. "You know, I was on the fence about buying that big basket of preserves and pickles . . . but I think I'll get them. Do you mind ringing them up? Even though I've already paid?"

Did I mind? That was our single most expensive item in the stand. Hell, yeah, I'd ring her up again.

Once my new favorite customer had paid and left, happy about her purchases, I turned to Alex. "You, my friend, are devious."

"But effective." He stood in front of me, hands on his hips. "Now to business. I just stopped by to say two things. I'm mad at you, and what the fuck?"

I winced. "I'm guessing those two things are related. Okay, I'll grovel. I'm sorry. I know it was shitty of me not to answer you. Or call. I have no excuse except that it was a really, really hard few days."

"Yeah, I know. Because Meghan, who is a good friend—but not my *best* friend—was good enough to answer my texts." He leaned his hip against a table. "So how're you doing?"

I blew out a breath. "Honestly, I'm not sure. On one hand, it went a lot better than I had any right to hope. I mean, yeah, Flynn was furious. He was shocked, and he was hurt." I wrapped my arms around my middle, remembering. "But he actually got beyond it a lot faster than I'd expected."

"So are we talking happily ever after? Should I be getting

out my tuxedo and working on my man of honor speech?"

I barked out a sharp laugh. "Hardly. Flynn's willing to deal with me in order to see Bridget. He wants a relationship with his daughter, so he's going to be as pleasant to me as he can. But nothing more than that's going to happen between us."

Alex reached across to brush his hand over my arm. "I'm sorry, Ali Baba. That sucks."

I managed a smile. "What? Like I was expecting Flynn to come back into town, find out he has a kid with his high school girlfriend and declare his undying love to me? Nah. It's been a long time. Too many years. I'm just happy that he's sticking around to get to know Bridge."

"And how's our girl dealing with the newfound daddy?"

"Amazingly well. It's almost weird. She didn't ask that many questions about where he's been all this time. She just kind of accepted it. I expected . . ." I spread out my hands. "I don't know. I thought she might be upset and want to know why I'd never talked about Flynn before. But she didn't."

Alex nodded. "Well, count your lucky stars, I guess. Who knows, maybe she'll have a delayed reaction and flip out when she's a teenager."

I shuddered. "I don't even want to think about it. Let's change the subject. Are you on your way back to Hotlanta? Did you see the boy toy last week?"

"There might've been a sighting. I'm still not ready to dish, though, so no digging. And yes, I'm heading west. I don't know when I'll be back in town again, but don't worry, I'll be keeping my eye on you. I have my ways."

I fiddled with the hem of my T-shirt. "Did you see Flynn? Did you talk to him?"

Alex shook his head. "Just at the funeral. I was planning to stop by yesterday, but after Meghan let me know what was going down, I figured he needed a little space."

"He's staying in town, you know. Indefinitely. He told me

yesterday that he's going to make Burton his center of operations, whatever that means. But he's giving up his apartment in
New York."

"Wow. That's huge." He quirked one eyebrow at me.
"When I talked to him on Thursday, at the wake, he made it
sound like he couldn't get out of town fast enough."

"It's just Bridget. He wants to be a good father, and what
more can I ask?"

"Sexy times? A little hard-core romping in the sack with
the guy who took your V-card back in the day?"

"Nice, Alex. C'mon. Nothing's going to happen between
us. He can barely tolerate me."

"Uh huh. I'm going to reserve the right to dance the I-told-
you-so all over your face when Flynn 'tolerates' you onto your
back. In a good way."

I rolled my eyes and flipped back my pony tail, channeling
my inner-teenager. "Whatever."

"Hmm? Aren't you even the littlest bit interested? You're
telling me Flynn Evans doesn't still make your heart go pit-
ty-pat?"

I turned my back to Alex and busied myself with the day's
receipts. "Whether he does or doesn't is immaterial. I need to
be an adult and make sure we have a good relationship for the
sake of our daughter."

He whistled. "That did sound very grown-up. And I almost
bought it. If your eyes weren't saying, 'I want Flynn Evans between my legs, pronto' I might've believed you."

I shook my head. "You're insane. My eyes were so not saying that. They were saying, 'I'm a mature, well-adjusted woman who doesn't need a man between her legs to be happy.'"

"Oooh, baby." Alex faked a leer. "The dudes like a lady
who can take of her own needs."

"You're despicable." I couldn't help grinning as I swatted
at his arm. "Don't you have some place to go?"

"Sadly, yes. But I'll be texting you for updates, and if you don't respond, I'll text Flynn. Oh, and I'll be back in town in two weeks." He winked and grinned lasciviously. "Another, ah, business meeting in Savannah. And this one might just close the deal."

"Oooh, baby!" I mimed his words and leer. "And if *you,* my friend, don't decide to tell all, I might just hold out on you when it comes to Flynn and me."

"Aha!" Alex held up one finger. "I knew it. I knew there was something going on."

I sighed, shaking my head. "You're such a pain in the ass. Go home, Alex. Go terrorize the good people of Atlanta."

"Going." He grabbed me and gave me a smacking kiss on the cheek. "But I'm coming back. And when I do, I want the juicy stuff."

Chapter Nine

Flynn

"DADDY!" BRIDGET RAN OUT of the school, her smile wide. Her dark hair was in braids that bounced on her back as she trotted toward me, and her backpack dangled from one shoulder.

"Hey, pretty girl!" I caught her with both arms and swung her up. "How was school today?"

Her grin began to fade. "It was okay."

I set her back on her feet. I'd been told that eight years was too old to hold her for more than just a hug, and I was conscious of not embarrassing my daughter in front of her friends at school. Fatherhood was new, but I remembered being in second grade. "Why was it just okay? Did something happen?"

She shrugged as I led her toward my truck. I'd returned

the Audi to the rental company two weeks before and leased a Chevy pickup from the dealership. I'd never considered myself a truck man, but it felt right, what with my new life in Burton. Opening the passenger door, I boosted Bridget into the cab, and she climbed into the small backseat.

I didn't press her for an answer as we drove to my mom's house. She was quiet, and that worried me. One thing I'd learned about my daughter in the past three weeks was that she was a bubbly, happy kid. Nothing seemed to bother her, not even when Graham, my little demon of a nephew, tortured her dolls. Glancing at her small face in the rearview mirror, I saw only troubled brown eyes. No sparkle, no laughter.

I turned into my mother's driveway, pulling to the side so that Mom could get to the garage after she got home. I knew she wouldn't be long behind me; she'd gone back to work at the library last week, but she always cut out early on Tuesdays, when Bridget stayed with us.

After I shut off the engine, Bridge undid her seatbelt and slid into the front seat. Before she could open the door, I caught her arm. "Hey, kiddo. Why don't you tell me what's going on? What happened today?"

She frowned again and twisted the end of one braid around her finger. "Nothing."

I sighed, rubbing my hand over my jaw. "Do you miss your mom? Do you want me to drive you home? I mean, back to the farm?" It hurt that she might feel that way, but seeing her smile again was more important than how I felt.

Bridget shook her head. "No. I mean . . . I miss Mom, but I know I'm going to see her tomorrow, and I want to be with you, too." Her lip stuck out, trembling just a little.

"Bridget, honey, talk to me. I want to know what's wrong." When she didn't answer, I dug into my pocket and brought out my cell phone. "Want to call your mom and talk to her? Would that help?"

"No, thanks." She clamored onto her knees. "Can we go inside now? Grandma said she was making me brownies for today."

"Okay." I climbed out and went around to the other side to help her down. We went into the house, and as was her habit, Bridget hung her backpack on the newel post and followed me into the kitchen. I cut two brownies, poured us some milk and was just about to join her at the table when my phone buzzed. The readout on the screen blinked twice, signaling an incoming call. *Ali.*

I hit the button and answered. "Hey, Ali. Everything okay?"

Her voice, low and coated with a lifetime of Georgia, filled my head. "Uh, hey, Flynn. Yeah, I think so—but can I talk to you just a minute? Is Bridget right there with you?"

I glanced at my daughter, who was completely involved with her chocolate. I couldn't help smiling at the sight. "Yeah, we just got home. She's elbow-deep in Grandma's brownies."

"Mmmm. Color me jealous." Ali's near-purr went straight down through my center and settled between my legs. I coughed and turned my back.

"So what's up?" I didn't mean to sound gruff, but Ali's voice changed to all business.

"I got a call from the school just now. Bridget's teacher, Mrs. Hazelbeck, said there was some kind of dust-up on the playground."

"Bridge was fighting?" My daughter was a scrapper, but she was usually a pretty chill kid.

"No, she wasn't, but someone was. I guess it was a kid named Charlie and Graham."

"Graham? My nephew?"

"Yeah." Ali exhaled long a long breath. "Mrs. Hazelbeck said no one wanted to talk, but she finally got the whole story out of Charlie. Apparently, Graham was giving Bridget a hard time, and Charlie was defending her."

A lump formed in my stomach. "What do you mean, a hard time? About what?"

"Ah, Flynn, they're kids, you know. Kids say stuff all the time." She hesitated, and I knew she was reluctant to speak the next words. "Graham was telling the other kids that Bridget wasn't really your daughter. He said she was just pretending because her real daddy left her when she was just a baby."

I closed my eyes. *Damn it.* Forcing a smile, I patted Bridget's back. "Honey, I'm going to step outside and talk to your mama for a minute, okay? I'll be right back in."

I opened the screen door and stood on the back stoop. "Ali, what the hell? What was he talking about?"

"I don't really know. I'm just telling you what the teacher said Charlie told her. Is Bridget okay? Mrs. H. said she was a little shaken up. That's why she called."

"She was quiet all the way home, but she wouldn't tell me anything. Shit. What's wrong with Graham? Why would he be such a jerk?"

Ali didn't answer for a minute. "Well, maybe he's not so happy about his new cousin. He's been the only child, the only grandchild for a long time. Could be he doesn't like sharing the spotlight."

I thought of his interaction with Bridget at my mom's house. I'd noticed he didn't seem to be welcoming her with open arms, but he was a boy. Boys didn't do warm and fuzzy. I figured in a few weeks, they'd be playing together in the backyard, the best of friends.

Clearly I'd been wrong.

"So what do I do?" This was beyond my meager parenting skills. I'd only screw it up. "Do you want me to bring her home? Or do you want to come out here to talk to her?"

Ali laughed. "No, Flynn. If you bring her back to the farm, she'll think she's being punished. And if I drive all the way into town, she's going to think it's a bigger deal than it is. Maybe just talk to her. Give her some assurance. Oh, and if I were you, I'd talk to Iona and find out what's going on with her son."

"Yeah, you can bet on it." I cleared my throat. "Listen, Ali. Thanks. You could've made a big deal out of this. But you're trusting me to handle it, and I really appreciate it."

"You're her father." Ali spoke softly. "I know most guys get a little ramp up time to this kind of deal, and I'm sorry you're getting tossed into the deep end, but you can handle it."

"I hope so." I turned as I heard my mom's car. "Listen, I'll call you tonight and let you know how it goes, all right?"

"Uh . . ." She sounded a little flustered. "You don't have to report back to me, Flynn. We can just talk tomorrow."

"No, I'll call tonight." Ali trusted me, and I wanted to repay that with full disclosure. "I'll talk to you then, okay? After Bridge goes to sleep."

"Okay." She spoke on a whisper. "Talk to you then."

I ended the call and was about to go back inside when I changed my mind. Mom was in the kitchen now, pulling Bridget onto her lap and laughing about something shared between grandmothers and granddaughters. I scrolled through my contacts and hit my oldest sister's number.

"Hey. I was just about to call you." Iona sounded weary. "Listen, Flynn. I'm sorry. I'm so sorry. I had no idea Graham was even in the house, but he must've overheard us talking—"

"Heard who talking about what?" I was pissed, but I knew my sister would never do anything to hurt my daughter. Both Iona and Reenie had been great with Bridget. Which, of course, probably had only made Graham unhappier.

"Right after everything came out about Bridget, I was telling Mark the whole story. I mean, he knew it, mostly, but you know he's a guy, and he'd forgotten you'd even dated Ali. Crazy, right? So I was trying to explain it to him, how Ali married Craig, and we all thought Bridget was his, and then about Craig leaving. Graham must've come inside without me hearing him.

I never knew he'd been eavesdropping until the principal called today to say he'd been fighting. When I heard the whole story, I wanted to die. I'm so sorry. You know I love Bridget."

"Yeah, I know." I was silent for a few beats, trying to rein in my mad. "Did Graham say why he did it?"

She sighed, long and deep. "He's a spoiled brat, Flynn. It's not a nice thing to say about your own kid, but it's the truth. And we're trying to make it better, but eight years of only kid can't be undone in a month." She paused. "We were worried about this anyway, with the baby coming."

"Baby? Iona, are you knocked up again?" Gladness filled me.

"Yeah, surprise, surprise. We never planned to space our kids out this far, but you know Mark's been trying to build up his practice, and what with one thing and another." She sniffled. "I wish I'd known to tell Daddy. Wouldn't he've been thrilled?"

"You know it." I thought about how much I hated that my dad had never known Bridget was his granddaughter. I didn't want to do regret, but I could still be sad. "Iona, I'm not upset with you or Mark, but you got to make sure Graham understands that he can't go around telling people I'm not Bridget's father. He needs to know I'm her dad."

"I just talked to him hard for twenty minutes, but I'll talk some more when Mark gets home. And Graham's grounded for two weeks, if that makes you feel any better."

I laughed. "It doesn't, but thanks. Talk to you later." I ended the call and went back inside, where Mom and Bridget were still giggling over brownies. The sound of my daughter's laughter had the miraculous power to release all the knots in my chest, and I slid into a chair to join them.

I'd only known about this kid's existence for about a month, but I was ready to lay down every dream I'd ever had to make her happy. I'd do whatever it took.

For the rest of the evening, I didn't bring up Graham or what he'd said. Bridget was having too good a time with my mom and then with Reenie when she got home. We all made dinner together, and my sister taught my daughter how to do the Twist when it came on the radio. I sat at the kitchen counter with a beer, breathing in the smell of my mother's fried chicken and biscuits and watching Reenie and Bridge giggle and dance. For just a fraction of a breath, I felt my dad near me, his hand on my shoulder as he watched them with me. Then it was gone, and so was he. At the stove, my mother lifted her head to meet my eyes. She smiled a little and nodded.

Once Bridget was tucked into bed—Mom had given her Iona's old room—I dropped down on my own bed and called Ali.

When she answered, her voice was soft and sleepy. "Hey, Flynn."

Memories of a hundred different late night telephone calls with her pulled me back into the past. How many times had we whispered until long after midnight, talking about nothing but nonsense, neither of us willing to say goodnight even though we'd see each other next day? More than I could count. I wondered if Ali were remembering, too.

"Hey." I whispered, too, even though my mom's room was way down the hall, and I didn't think she was going to come in and yell at me for being on the phone anymore.

"Did everything go okay tonight?"

"Yeah, it was fine. I talked to Iona. Apparently she and Mark were discussing what happened with . . . with Craig, and Graham overheard it. She was really sorry, and Graham's being punished." I stared up at my ceiling, looking at the same cracks in the plaster that I used to see when I was eighteen. "I didn't talk to Bridge, though. She was having such a blast with Mom and Reenie, I just couldn't ruin it." I held my breath, half-expecting her to be pissed that I'd ducked the issue.

"That's probably smart." To my surprise, Ali didn't sound upset. "Sometimes with kids, it's knowing when to say something and when to leave it alone. Half the time, it all blows over without us making a fuss." She yawned, and I heard a rustling.

"Are you in bed?" I asked the question before I thought better of it.

She laughed softly. "Yeah, I am. Sorry, this time of year, the days are long. I worked the stand from eight this morning until five, and then I weeded the vegetable garden at the house, and then I went out into the fields with Sam to plant tomatoes."

"Whew." I laced my fingers behind my head, cradling the phone on my shoulder. "I'm exhausted just hearing about it. Did I wake you up?"

"No. Not really. I was maybe dozing just a little."

"Were you dreaming?" I couldn't stop myself.

Ali didn't answer right away. "No. I don't dream anymore."

I knew she was talking about more than just what happened when she slept.

"Really? I do." I let my eyes drift shut. "I thought I didn't, but since I've been back in Burton . . . it's weird. Like my brain's catching up on all those years."

"I don't think it works that way. We dream every night, even if we don't remember. I read that somewhere."

"Hmmm." I lay there for a minute, just enjoying the peace. The quiet I was sharing with Ali. I could hear her soft breathing, and I wished with sudden gut-strong need that she were here with me. It rolled over my body like a truck, shocking the hell out of me.

"Hey, Ali. Do you still sleep in the same room you did in high school?"

"Um . . . yeah. Bridge slept in with me when she was a

baby, and now she's right next door, where Sam used to sleep. He took Mom and Dad's room."

"Ah."

"Why did you ask?" Her tone was curious, but a little apprehensive, too.

"I wanted to picture where you are." And when I did, I got hard, thinking about her room. Her bed. Ali and me together there, on nights when Sam had late meetings with the Guild. "Hey, Ali."

"Yeah, Flynn?" There was something else in her voice now. Something cautious but yearning. I plunged ahead.

"Do you ever think about what would've happened if I'd stayed? Or if you'd come with me?"

I nearly felt her sigh. "At first, I didn't think about anything else. It was all that I could imagine. I wished a million times or more that I could change what we did. What we said." Silence stretched between us until she spoke again. "But it hurt too much. After I knew Bridget was coming, I had to make a decision. I could keep wishing and crying and hurting, or I could put on my big girl pants and grow up. I had to do that for my baby." She drew in a shuddering breath, and it killed me to think she might be crying again. "So I stopped thinking about what might have been. I stopped wishing, and I stopped dreaming."

If I could've crawled through my phone and somehow ridden the cell waves or however it worked, I would've gathered her into my arm, pressed her head into my chest the same way I had in the days after her parents' death. I couldn't do that tonight.

"Ali, I want—"

"It's late, Flynn." She sounded sad but definite. "Go to sleep. I'll see you this weekend." There was soft click, and I was alone again in my room.

I tossed my phone to the other side of the bed and stretched my arms above my head. *Damn.* I was restless now. Horny, if I were honest with myself. It'd been a long time since I'd been with a woman, but this was more. It wasn't just the need for any woman. I wanted the girl who'd just hung up on me.

"Dude, you are so fucked up." I muttered the words, rubbing one hand over my eyes. I'd thought I could handle being back in Burton, and maybe I would've been okay, if I hadn't ever laid eyes on Ali. But the minute I'd seen her, standing on my mom's front porch with her sad and worried eyes, I was sinking back into the quicksand that was Ali Reynolds.

She'd always been my biggest weakness. I rolled to my side, staring through the blinds into the black velvet of night, but in my mind, I was sixteen again, parked in my old Chevette at the lake on the Nelsons' farm, with Ali laying halfway over my lap as I kissed her senseless.

From the very beginning, we'd moved slowly when it came to our physical relationship. Not that I didn't want her— God, did I. And in my dreams nearly every night, I did things to Ali that made it harder—no pun intended—to stop myself from pushing our boundaries.

We'd talked about it, because one thing Ali and I had going for us was complete openness. After I'd kissed her the first time on New Year's Eve, she'd told me that she'd been afraid I'd never get around to it.

"I thought maybe . . . maybe you didn't want to kiss me." She'd glanced up at me through her eyelashes, her brown eyes unsure.

"I wanted to kiss you from that first day, when we covered the stupid sign dedication." I traced one finger over the curve of her cheek, my heart skipping a beat when Ali closed her eyes and leaned her face into my palm. That small gesture of absolute trust made me fall in love with her a little more. I hadn't thought it was possible.

"Then why did you wait?" She smiled, soft and dreamy.

"I wanted it to be special. And I wanted to make sure you knew that I like you for *you,* not just because I wanted . . ." My face went red. "You know."

"That's the most amazing thing anyone's ever said to me." Ali slid her hand into mine. "It makes me feel . . . treasured." She shook her head. "Does that sound hokey?"

"Nope. It sounds perfect." I'd kissed her again, heady with the realization that I could do it any time I wanted. Well, within reason. We were careful around Ali's parents and her brother, who always looked at me with narrowed eyes of suspicion. And we didn't have a whole lot of alone time, other than moments stolen on her front porch when I dropped her off after dates. That was more than a little awkward, since we had to be driven by my sisters or my parents. We'd gotten adept at finding the shadowed spots on the porch, where we couldn't be seen from the car.

But now, finally, I'd gotten my license, and even better, I'd inherited the ancient Chevette that had been Iona and Maureen's first car. It wasn't fancy or remotely cool, but it ran, and it meant freedom to drive out to the Reynolds' farm whenever I wanted. And even better, freedom to drive out here on the old dirt road that connected Alex's family farm with Ali's, through the woods until we got to the edge of the small lake.

I pulled the keys out of the ignition and ratcheted my seat back as far as it would go, stretching my legs. Ali unclicked her seat belt and turned toward me, a smile of promise on her face.

She leaned over the gear shift and rested her forearms on my chest. "Hi." The single whispered word shot straight to my crotch, making my jeans a lot tighter than they'd been a minute before. I felt the soft promise of her boobs teasing against my chest, and I swallowed hard.

Ali lowered her mouth to mine. I circled my arms around her waist, running my hands up and down her back as her lips angled, needing to get closer. I teased her with my tongue until she opened to me, giving me free access to sweep over her teeth, stroke the inside of her lips and tangle with her tongue. She slid her arms up, around my neck, so that the upper part of her body was pressed against me. I was pretty sure she had to be feeling my heart thudding.

"Ouch!" Ali jerked back, rubbing her hand over her hip. "Sorry. The parking brake poked me in the side." She pushed back to sit in her own seat. "Don't get me wrong, Flynn, I love that you have a car now, but I wouldn't have minded something with a bench seat in the front."

I laughed, shifting to hide the bulge between my legs. "They don't make cars with bench seats anymore." I turned to look behind us. "There's always the backseat, I guess, but it feels a little cliché. And it's not much bigger." I picked up her hand from where it rested on her knee and kissed the inside of her wrist. I was still riled up and getting more desperate by the minute to touch her again. "I have a blanket in the trunk. I guess we could go sit out by the lake."

Ali cocked her head. "You don't sound like you want to do that."

I laced my fingers into hers and squeezed, pressing our palms together. "Ali, don't ever think I don't want to touch you. God, right now, all I want is . . ." I took a deep breath. "I can't even say it, because if I do, I'll end up making it happen."

"Why don't you?" She smiled and raised our joined hands to her lips.

"I think . . ." This wasn't going to be easy. Not when part of me—the part that was a distance south of my cerebral cortex—was screaming that I was an idiot. "I want you, Ali. I want to kiss you all the time. I want to touch you all over. I want to peel off all your clothes, and let you take off mine, and lay out there on the blanket, skin to skin, nothing between us but the night air." *God, I was a fool.* "But I like you a lot. You're more than just my girlfriend, you're my best friend." I reached across and tucked a strand of her silky hair behind her ear. "I want to make love to you." Saying the words made it so real, the throbbing under my zipper became almost unbearable. "But I want us to be ready. Both of us. I want us to make the decision together, so we have no regrets. When we're together, really together, I want it to be the best moment of our lives. Something we never forget. Something we think about for the rest of our lives."

When I dared to look into Ali's eyes, I was half-afraid I'd see incredulity and maybe even scorn. What I was saying wasn't exactly popular philosophy among high school students. But instead, I saw the sheen of tears and the unmistakable glow of love.

I recognized that expression. I'd seen it in my mother's eyes when she looked at my father, and in Iona's when she talked about Mark. I'd known for a while it was how I looked at Ali. Love was more than just the girlfriend/boyfriend stuff that went on all around us at school. It was a big deal, life-changing and forever. It was Ali and me, together against the world for the rest of our lives.

That was exactly what I wanted. And why I was willing to wait for sex. Getting it right was more important than getting it right away.

"How did I ever get lucky enough to deserve you?" Ali laid her head on the back of the seat. "What do you see in me? I'm not special."

"You're the most special. Ali, you're beautiful, and not just on the outside. You're nice to people, you're funny, and . . ." I shrugged. "I don't know. I can't describe it. I just know it."

"I love you, Flynn." She said it as though she couldn't help it, as though the words surprised her as much as they did me. "I—I know that sounds weird, or maybe you're not ready—"

"I love you, Ali." I spoke before she could backtrack anymore. "I've loved you for a long time. It's not weird. It just *is*."

"When did you know?"

I hesitated. I wasn't sure she'd want to hear this, to know the truth. But I'd promised to be honest and open with her always. "It was after your parents. After the accident."

There was a brief flare of pain on her face, but she didn't look away, so I went on. "You were hurting so much, and you were so sad. Crushed. I knew then that I never wanted to leave you. I wanted to do anything to make sure you never had to feel that way again, for the rest of your life. I never want to be away from you." I sucked in a breath and for the first time, I spoke the words that would both define us and doom us. "I want you to come with me, Ali, when I leave Burton. This town, it's just . . . too small. I'm getting out of here as soon as we graduate. I'm going to see the world. I'm going to travel as far as I can, for as long as I can. And I want you to come with me."

For a moment, Ali didn't move. She watched me, and I could tell she was digesting what I'd just said.

Finally, she pushed herself up, and crawling over the parking brake and gearshift with great care, she slung one leg over mine and settled her body on my lap. Instinctively I brought my hands to her hips, keeping her steady.

"Flynn, I'll go with you anywhere. To the ends of the earth and back again. As long as we're together, I won't ever need anything but you."

She kissed me with abandon, and I held her against me, knowing I'd never need anything or anyone but this girl in my arms.

A car backfired on the street outside my mom's house, jerking me back to the present. Had I dozed off? I wasn't sure. What had happened a decade ago sometimes felt more like a dream than reality.

I sat up and pinched the bridge of my nose between my finger and thumb. It was late, and I knew I had to be up early to take Bridget to school. But talking to Ali had given me a hell of a hard-on, and remembering us together in the past hadn't helped that condition. I stood up and grabbed my towel from the hook behind my door.

"Cold showers. And I thought I was beyond this shit." I slung the towel over my shoulder and headed down the hall to the bathroom, muttering to myself the whole time.

Chapter Ten

Ali

"MOMMY, DID YOU TALK to Daddy about Maisie's party yet?" Bridge dropped her drawing pad and pencil bag on the kitchen table with a clatter and climbed into a chair. "I have to tell her if I'm coming. I can go, right? All the other girls are going, and it's going to be so much fun, and I don't want to be the only one who misses out."

Crud. I'd meant to mention the party to Flynn last week, but it had slipped my mind. Actually, most things slipped my mind when I was near him anymore, which annoyed the living crap out of me. I was trying to be a grown up, for criminey's sake. But one look at those blue eyes and I was as gaga as I'd been at age fourteen.

"Pitiful," I muttered under my breath as I drained the kitchen sink and wiped off my hands.

"What'd you say?" Bridge cocked her head at me.

"Sorry." I cleared my throat. "I'll ask him today when he comes to pick you up."

"But you're going to be at the stand. Remember? I'm staying so Aunt Meghan can give me my art lesson and Daddy's getting me here."

I turned around and leaned against the counter. "I'll text him and ask if he can stop to see me on his way here." I tugged my phone out of the pocket of my jeans and skimmed my fingers over the screen.

I need to talk to you about something before you get Bridge. Can you stop at the stand on your way to the farm?

His answer came back quickly. *Sure. Everything okay?*

I paused. *Yeah, just parenting stuff.*

Okay. See you in an hour or so.

I stared down at the screen for a few minutes more. I could've just called Flynn and asked him about the party, but, I reasoned, it would be easier to do it in person. Plus we could catch up on Bridget's still-rocky relationship with her cousin Graham, who apparently had not taken well the news of his expected sibling. He continued to harass Bridge, though he'd toned down his behavior at school.

Meghan sailed into the kitchen, glowing from every portal in her body. She ruffled Bridget's curls and grinned at me. "Miss B and I are heading to the peach orchard for her lesson. Are you off to the stand?"

"Yeah, I was just about to head there." I tucked my phone back into my pocket. "I'll walk with y'all."

Bridge gathered her supplies, and Meghan stopped at her car to retrieve her portable stool, easel and paints. We trudged down the path that led through the orchard to the stand as Bridget skipped ahead.

"Something up?" Meghan nudged my arm as we walked.

"Hmmm? With me? Nah."

"You're quiet. And you have that look on your face."

I rolled my eyes. "Okay, Mom, what look is that, specifically?"

Meghan smirked. "I call it the Flynn Evans is back in town expression."

"Bite me."

"No, thanks. I've had a better offer. Is there any reason you might be wearing the Flynn look today?"

I shrugged. "He's stopping by the stand on the way to get Bridge. Which, by the way, thanks for doing her lesson this morning so she can still go with her father. I appreciate it."

"Not a problem. Don't change the subject. Flynn's stopping to see you at the stand? Hmmmm."

"No 'hmmmmm' about it." I stuck out my tongue at her. "I asked him so we could talk about Maisie's birthday party. Bridge keeps pestering me to say yes, and I didn't want to make a decision like that without checking with Flynn." I slanted a glance in Meghan's direction. "I call that growth. Remembering to co-parent."

"That's the party in Savannah?"

I sighed. "Yeah. I think it's a little over the top, having an eight-year old's birthday in a different city. It's like a destination party. I'm not happy about letting her go, but she's so hyped up about the whole thing."

"Are you hoping Flynn'll say no and take the bad-cop role for you?"

"God, yes!" I laughed. "I've been freaking bad-cop for eight years. About time someone else took a turn."

Meghan grinned. "I can only imagine." We picked our way along the dirt in silence for a few minutes. "What if Sam and I went with her?"

"What?" I'd lost track of the conversation for a minute.

Okay, full disclosure, I'd started think about Flynn again.

"The party. If it's in Savannah, Sam and I could drive her over there. We could stay in my apartment, but we'd be close by in case anything happened."

"You'd do that?"

"Of course. I'd do anything for you and Bridge. Plus . . ." She lowered her voice. "I get to drag your very sexy brother off for a night in the city. Alone. No one else sleeping down the hall, no having to get up early to head out into the fields . . ."

"Ugh! My ears." I clapped my hands over the sides of my head. "Please. I still choose to believe that you two are playing charades every night after we all go to bed."

"Why are you allowed to have a sex life and your brother isn't?" Meghan was teasing, but it still cut.

"Who says I'm allowed to have one? I haven't had the pleasure—and I do mean pleasure—in so long, I forget how to do it."

"It's like riding a bike. It'll all come back to you."

We'd arrived at the orchard, and Bridget was busy examining the blossoms and branches of the trees. Meghan stopped and turned to me. "You know, if Sam, Bridget and I are all in Savannah, you'd have the house all to yourself. In case you needed it."

I turned to walk backwards for a minute. "And why would I need it?"

She grinned. "If you have to ask, you're farther gone than I'd thought. I'm just saying."

Shaking my head, I called to my daughter. "Hey, Bridge! Come give me a hug. I'll see you tomorrow night."

She barreled into me for a hug and then turned up her face for a kiss. "Okay, and you'll tell Daddy about the party?"

"I'll ask him," I corrected. "Be good. And have fun with Aunt Meghan."

"Ali? Hey, didn't you hear me?" Cassie Deymeyer, the high school student who helped us out at the stand on weekends, stood in front of me, waving her hand in front of my face. "I've been talking to you for five minutes."

I flushed. *Busted.* "Sorry, Cass. I'm a little preoccupied." I picked up the sheaf of papers that lay on the cash register stand. "All the orders for next month have to be filled out." It was a good excuse, anyway, for why I'd been standing there, staring off into space.

"Uh huh. So that moony look on your face doesn't have anything to do with the pickup that just pulled in?"

My eyes flew to the parking lot, where Flynn was slamming the door of his truck. This time, I swore the blush went all the way down my body. *Pull it together, woman.*

"Cassie, don't be ridiculous. Flynn's just here to discuss some stuff about Bridget."

"Hmmm. Well, that's a waste of good man candy on your part."

I shook my head. "Cass, you're seventeen years old."

She giggled. "I have eyes." She leaned closer to me. "You know, my cousin Lu had a massive crush on Flynn Evans. She used to swoon over him, and I never saw why. Being I was only, like eight or nine. But now . . ." She nodded. "I get it. Totally."

"He's too old for you." I didn't mean to sound so mom-like, but the words came out harsh.

"Who's too old?" Flynn's voice held a familiar note of humor.

I raised one eyebrow at Cass. "No one. Cass, would you please start re-stocking the asparagus? It's going fast."

"Sure." She headed toward the back, where we kept the extra stock. As soon as she was behind Flynn, out of his line of vision, she turned back to me, and with eyes wide, fanned her face. I stared hard at her, one eyebrow raised, until she finally got the hint.

"Thanks for coming over. I appreciate it." I hooked my thumbs in the front pockets of my jeans.

"I didn't mind." He smiled, and for the first time since he'd come back to Burton, it was all for me. His eyes were warm, and he let them skim down my body in a way that almost left me in a puddle.

Keep it business. I had to be firm with myself. Firm, like the abs that rippled under his black T-shirt. Firm, like the muscles in his arms . . .

No. I swallowed hard and tried to remember why he was here. Bridget. And the party. Yup, that was it. "So I needed your input on something. Bridget was invited to one of her friend's birthday party. It's in two weeks, and it's in Savannah."

Flynn's eyebrows drew together. "Savannah? Why? Does the girl live there?"

I sighed and shook my head. "Nope. It's a pirate-themed party, and they're the taking the kids to the Pirate House restaurant and then spending the night at a hotel. I think the idea is to let them have fun at the hotel pool and stay up late."

"Okay. Not sure I love the idea of Bridget going all the way to the city with people I don't know." He paused. "Do you know the parents very well?"

"I know them a little. I probably would've said no right off the bat, but all Bridge's friends are going, and she's desperate not to be left out." I bit the corner of my lip, mulling over whether or not to share Meghan's offer with him. In the end, loyalty to my daughter won out. "Meghan and Sam offered to drive her up and stay in the city the whole time. Meg's got an apartment there, so they'd be close if anything happened."

"That's really nice of them." Flynn shifted his weight, and I thought distractedly that it ought to be illegal for jeans to look that good on any guy.

"Yeah, well, it's not that altruistic." I smirked. "They don't get much alone time, living in a house with a sister and a niece. Sam doesn't get up to stay with Meghan very often, since he has to be at the farm, so I think this would be as much for them as for us." My face heated. *Damn.* "For Bridget, I mean. To make sure we felt okay about Bridget going."

"Still cool that they'd do that. If they really don't mind, then I'm all right with Bridget going." He hastened to add, "If you are, of course. You know more about Bridget's friends and their parents, so I'll defer to your wishes."

"Thanks." We stood there, not knowing what to say next, and in a moment of weakness, I let myself look at him, really look. For the first time in almost nine years, I saw Flynn without the haze of pain, guilt and regret. Under the new sharper planes of his face, I could still make out the boy who'd loved me. And within the outlines of his broader, more muscled physique, I saw the arms that had once held me as our bodies trembled with passion.

And speaking of trembling . . . my eyelids fluttered as Flynn reached out a hand to brush my hair away from my face.

"You let your hair grow longer." His fingertips traced my cheekbone. "I like it."

"I don't have a lot of time for haircuts these days." I whispered the words, almost afraid to move too much. Everything around us was still, quiet; no cars passing by, no customers milling around. Vaguely, I registered the noise of Cassie in the back, unloading asparagus.

"Ali." Flynn slid his palm against my cheek. "I'd forgotten how smooth your skin is." His chest rose as he breathed deep. "And how good you smell. Like lilacs."

"What are you doing, Flynn?" I wanted to make myself step backward, but I was afraid if I moved at all, it would be closer, into his arms.

"I'm remembering." His breath tickled me, and I shivered. Flynn let his hand wander down my arm. "Goosebumps. Do you remember the night—"

"No." I forced myself back. "Flynn, I can't do this. I can't let myself remember that night, or any of our nights together. It hurts too much. It's easy for you to talk about memories and then walk away. But I can't walk down that road. It took me too long to get over you last time."

He frowned. "Ali, I didn't mean—"

I held up one hand. "It's fine, Flynn. We have to learn to be together, for Bridget's sake, without it being awkward." I paused, staring over his shoulder. "Given our history, it's natural that there'll always be a pull between us. But we can't let that go anywhere."

"What if it's more than just history?" Flynn's voice was rough.

"It's too risky to test that theory." I wrapped my arms around myself. "What if we did, and we broke our hearts, again? Bridget was the collateral damage last time. I can't let that happen again. We have to focus on being parents together."

"And that's it? We were friends once. Couldn't we try that again?"

I considered. "Sure. Friends is good. I can do that."

Flynn nodded. "Okay, friends. And parents." He put his hands on his hips. To the casual observer, he seemed loose, relaxed, but I could see the tension in his jaw.

I searched for a change of topic. "So, do you and Bridge have any plans for tonight?"

He lifted one shoulder. "Actually, I'm being kicked out of the house. Mom and the girls are doing a spa night. They told me no boys allowed."

"What're you going to do?" I wondered if Flynn had been in touch with any of his old buddies from high school. Not that he'd had that many, now that I thought of it; he'd been friendly with guys from the football team, but they never hung out beyond practice. I'd been his best friend, and he'd been mine. Other than Alex, who was equally loyal to us both. As though I'd summoned him, Flynn spoke his name.

"Alex is in town, and he asked if I wanted to go check out Mason Wallace's new place. Guess I'll do that." He studied me, his expression blank. "How about you? What do you do with yourself when Bridget's with me?"

"Go to bed early." I managed a smile. "I've actually taken a few long baths, which is something I haven't had the time to do until lately. Oh, and I read an actual book. One for grown-ups."

Behind me, I heard a car pull in. Flynn's eyes flickered over my head and then back down to me. "Well, looks like you have customers. And I'd better go fetch our daughter."

"Thanks. Have fun tonight." I took another step away and gave him a quick wave.

"Will do. You, too. Enjoy your, ah, bath." He made it sound so much dirtier that it was. "See you tomorrow afternoon around five?"

"Sure. I'll see you then." I moved back behind the register and pretended not to watch him go. Once he was out of sight, I took out my phone and began to text.

Hey, best friend. Are you in town?

Alex didn't respond for a few minutes, and I wondered what going was on with him. Finally, the phone beeped.

I'm on my way. Almost there. News travels fast. Or someone's been talking to lover boy.

I rolled my eyes. *Yeah, right. Were you going to tell me?*

Of course, doofus. I was going to come by this afternoon. Okay?

Alex never called me before he came to town. Why should this weekend be any different? Why was I making this such a big deal?

Okay, sure. See you in about ten.

Cassie came back out, carrying a wooden crate. "Is it safe to come out yet?"

"What're you talking about? Of course it's safe." I glanced at the gray-haired woman who was poking at tomatoes. "Why wouldn't it be?"

"I didn't want to interrupt anything hot and heavy. And the way Flynn was looking at you . . ." Her eyes widened. "Definitely hot."

"You're a delusional child." I shook my head and took the crate out of her hands. "Give me that. I'll stack while you—" I jerked my chin in the direction of our customer. "Handle the floor."

I pulled the top off the box and began unloading the vegetables with hands that weren't quite steady yet. I hated that Flynn still had that kind of power over me. Not that I thought he knew it . . . I didn't think he wanted to hurt me. Not on purpose. But I had a hunch that what for him might be a casual stroll down memory lane would be for me a treacherous dash off the edge of a very steep cliff.

I finished with the asparagus and carried the crate to the back. As I turned around to head back into the stand, I heard a familiar voice that made me grin.

"Cassandra Deymeyer, you young vixen. Why were you born too late?"

Cassie giggled, and I rolled my eyes. "Alex, stop dangling sugar in front of the jail bait. And Cass, I think the customer's ready to check out. Can you handle that, please?"

She sighed. "You hog all the uber-babes who come here, you know that? Fine. I'll go."

I shook my head as she slipped past me, and Alex cocked his head. "All the uber-babes? Were there other uber-babes here today? Should I feel threatened?"

I swatted his arm. "She was drooling over Flynn when he

stopped by. I'm getting a little worried . . . Cassie used to be the most level-headed teenager I knew. Now she's a big ball of hormones."

"We've all been there, done that. She'll survive. So will you. Now would you like to tell me why Flynn was here earlier?"

"We had to discuss some Bridget stuff." I couldn't quite meet Alex's eye, and of course he noticed.

"Was that all? The pretty pink creeping up your neck says different."

"I don't know, Alex." I leaned against the side of the sliding wall. "When Flynn came back to town, all I could think about was him finding out about Bridget. After I told him, it was all about how angry he was, how hurt. Now things have kind of . . . leveled out. And sometimes he says things. I'm not sure what it means. Today he looked at me . . . almost like he used to."

"Remind me why that's so bad and scary, Ali Baba." Alex's voice was gentle.

"It's bad because I don't think he really means any of it. He's back in town, dealing with his dad's death and his new daughter, and he's got all this nostalgia going about what used to be. It's making him say and do things he never would, otherwise. And it's scary because . . ." I pressed my lips together. "I might start to believe in him again."

"Oh, angel." Alex pulled me into his arms. "When did you stop believing that good things can work out for you?"

I sniffled against his chest. "Probably around the time I found out I was pregnant, and the guy I was crazy in love with was gone for good. You remember those days, don't you?"

"Yeah, I do. I know what it was like for you then. But you're not the same person you were nine years ago, sweetie pie. Did you ever stop and think maybe Flynn isn't, either? You might give him a chance and find out."

"I'm not sure I can. What if I can't handle it when he leaves again?"

"Let's take it one bungee jump at a time, okay? Who says he's leaving? And even if he did, who says you don't have more options now than you did back then?"

I pushed away from Alex and wiped at my face. "I don't see any new ones. Feels pretty much the same." I sucked in a deep breath. "So I hear you're going out with Flynn tonight. Did you get tired of boring old me?"

"Not at all." He flicked my nose. "Flynn's been texting with me the last few weeks. I got the feeling he was a little lonely, feeling a little at loose ends. So when I found out I was going to be passing through, I suggested a boys' night out. It just happened to work." He slanted a look at me. "Want to join us? The three musketeers ride again?"

"Thanks, but no. I'm not looking to be a third wheel."

Alex frowned. "You wouldn't be. We never—"

"Excuse me."

I turned, surprised by the soft voice behind me. The girl who stood twisting her hands together had almost white-blonde hair and huge blue eyes. She was petite; her head barely reached my shoulder, and I wasn't tall by anyone's standard. She bit her lip as she glanced from Alex to me.

"Can I help you?" I softened the words with a smile.

"I'm sorry to interrupt. The girl over there told me to talk to you." She licked her lips. "I'm Rilla Grant. I live a couple miles down the road from here."

"Grant?" Alex nodded. "Is your dad Emmett Grant? I think I've met him." He stuck out his hand. "I'm Alex Nelson. My mom and dad farm next door."

"Nice to meet you." Rilla seemed flustered by Alex's hand. Her face turned red, and I noticed that her fingers shook a little as she clasped it.

"I'm Ali Reynolds. Stand owner and person in charge.

Are you looking for something specific?" I was curious; at first glance, I wouldn't have thought she was even as old as Cassie, but once I saw her eyes, I realized she was probably closer to Meghan's age.

She took a deep breath. "I'm starting up a business. I just got my degree in advertising and public relations, and I'd like to begin raising the visibility of the commerce in this area. Mostly what I'd do is online, social media type of promotion, at first at least, but I hope to eventually expand to print and broadcast." She finished what was obviously a well-rehearsed speech and met my gaze with what appeared to be a great deal of effort.

"And you think you could do something for us? The stand, I mean?" Sam and I'd never really done any kind of advertising other than word of mouth. There were a few old wooden signs in either direction of the highway, but beyond that, we'd relied on the power of the passing motorist.

"I'd like to try." Rilla smiled, and I was struck by how pretty she was. It was odd; I couldn't remember ever seeing her before. If she lived nearby, I was pretty sure I'd have known her at least by sight. Burton wasn't so large a town that I couldn't identify the entire population, even if I couldn't name them all.

"Do you have a card? Or some information? My brother and I own the farm and the stand together. I couldn't make any decision without running it by him."

Alex pushed away from the table he'd been leaning against. "Not that this high-level business talk isn't fascinating, but I'm going to head home, check in with the parentals and get ready for big fun tonight." He glanced at me, one brow raised. "You sure you don't want to come with?"

Oh, hell yeah, I did. But I shook my head. "Another time, Alex. But thanks."

He grimaced. "Whatever. I'm not going to beg you. But if you change your mind, you know where to find me. Nice to meet you, Rilla." He kissed my cheek, waved to Cassie and headed to his car.

Rilla handed me a folder. "This has my contact information and some statistics for what I think I could do to help you. I'd appreciate it if you'd take a look, and if you like what you see, or if you have questions, give me a call."

"I'll definitely do that." I smiled at her. "Are you working for anyone else in the area?"

She glanced away. "Um, actually, you're the first person I've approached. I was hoping if I could start with a few clients, or even just one, I could start to get some referrals."

"That's smart. Especially in a small community like this." I tapped the folder against my leg. "Let me talk to Sam, and I'll get back to you next week. Does that work?"

Rilla smiled again, but this time it was genuine and brilliant. "Yes, that would be terrific. Fine, I mean. Thank you so, so much." She turned to leave and then stopped, coming back and extending her hand. "Sorry. I almost forgot. Thank you for talking with me, and I hope we can work together in the future."

More canned speech, but I couldn't help liking this girl, as full of nerves and jitters as she was. I hoped her information was decent; Sam and I didn't really have an advertising budget, but maybe it was time to rethink that.

Cassie came to stand next to me as I watched Rilla climb into an older model sedan and pull slowly onto the highway.

"Do you know her?"

I shrugged. "No, not until today. I was thinking it was sort of weird I've never met her, if she lives this close. I know where the Grant farm is. Why, do you know her?"

"Yeah. Well, I know who she is. My brother dated a girl from her church, and I went with him to one of their youth group meetings. She was there, too."

"She's older than you. Said she graduated from college. You didn't know her in school?"

"She didn't go to Burton. I think she went to the private

elementary school at their church, and then she was homes-chooled for high school. I only remember her from the youth group deal because she was assisting the youth pastor. Some-one told me they were like, together, but they don't really date. No hand holding, no kissing, no nothing, until they get married. I remember thinking that was just crazy."

I raised one eyebrow in her direction. "I don't know, Cass. Might not be such a bad idea. Hmm, wonder if I could get Brid-get to buy into that before she's old enough to date."

Cassie hooted with laughter. "Good luck with that."

The rest of the afternoon was steadily busy. We didn't have more than a few minutes between customers, keeping both Cas-sie and me occupied with answering questions, ringing up sales and restocking the tables and shelves. The entire time, my mind kept darting back to Flynn and Alex. I mentally debated texting Alex, changing my mind on his invitation for tonight, but then I worried Flynn would think I was tagging along like a lovesick idiot. I couldn't do that. I wasn't ready to take any risks when it came to him, no matter what Alex had said.

On the other hand, the idea of sitting home tonight, with a front-row seat to the Sam and Meghan show didn't sound like much fun either. They hardly ever went out, preferring to spend their time together having quiet dinners and evenings on the porch. A DVD night every once in a while. Come to think of it, those two could use some shaking up, too. A little excitement wouldn't hurt anyone.

I got home just as Meghan was putting a roast chicken on the table. Sam was already sitting down, and they both had that smiley glow that told me they hadn't spent the afternoon play-ing pinochle. Excellent. I needed them to be in a good mood.

"Come in early from the fields today, brother dear?" I gave him a wide smile over my shoulder as I washed my hands.

"Might have. I worked hard all week to get a little ahead. I could afford to take a little time off."

"Wonderful. And how about you, Meghan? Did you have a nice, quiet afternoon of painting after Bridge left?"

She put a bowl of potatoes on the table and shimmied around a chair with a little shriek as Sam reached out to pat her ass. "Behave yourself, you! Yes, I did, actually. I had four hours of peaceful sketching and painting before your wicked brother came home."

"Good, good. I, on the other hand, spent all day at the very busy stand, selling and stocking and schmoozing. And keeping Cassie from making a fool of herself over any man over fifteen and under fifty who came in. And more selling. And more stocking. All. Day. Long."

"Oh, I'm sorry, Ali." Guilt covered Meghan's face. Awesome. I could work with guilt. "I could've run over to help you."

Sam, having more experience with my ways as well as a good healthy dose of suspicion when it came my motives, was not as easily moved. "You had Cassie there. She's a hard worker. Besides, you love when the stand's busy."

Hmmm, he had me there. "True, but I'm just saying. You two've had a relaxing day, while I worked my ass off. Don't you want to do something nice for me?"

"Meghan made you this beautiful dinner, which is getting cold while you whine." Giving me a hard look, he closed his eyes, bowed his head and said the blessing before I could get another word in.

But I wasn't that easily put off. I served myself some green beans and continued as though I'd not been interrupted. "So I was thinking, wouldn't it be fun for the three of us to go out tonight? Do something fun?"

Sam sighed, but Meghan's face brightened before she could stop it. "What were you thinking, Ali? Like a movie or something? Over to the diner for ice cream?"

"I kind of thought maybe The Road Block. Music, dancing, some lovely adult beverages . . ." I smiled at her and kept my eyes pointedly off my brother. "We haven't gone dancing in ages."

"The last time you two went out together, it didn't end well." Sam pointed his fork at me.

"Clearly we don't have the same memory. As *I* remember it, Meghan and I had a blast, and after we got home, you finally gave in to your baser instincts and made out with Meghan on the porch."

Sam flushed, and Meghan's eyes grew wide as they flicked from my brother to me. Maybe that was information that had been meant to stay between us girls. Oh, well, all was fair in love and dancing.

"Anyway, that doesn't matter. You come with us tonight and make sure we behave. It'd do you good to get out a little with people who don't only talk soil and motor whatchamacallits and crops."

He groaned. "Ali, I hate all the noise and the crowds. Bunch of drunk cowboys just looking for a skirt to nail."

"Please . . ." I gave him my best little-sister eye bat. "I really need it, Sam. And Meghan wants to go, too. Don't you?"

Meghan looked a little a deer in headlights. "I, um, oh Ali, don't put me in this position." She laid down her fork. "Yes, Sam, I'd enjoy the dancing." She leaned a little closer. "I'd particularly enjoy the dancing with *you*. But if you really don't want to go."

Sam shook his head and scooped a bite of potatoes into his mouth. "Fine. We'll go. But we're not staying late, and you, baby sister, owe me big time. And don't think I'll forget it."

I jumped out of my chair and hugged him hard from the back. "Thank you! I promise, the next time you two need alone time, I'll clear out, no questions ask." I clapped my hands. "I'm going to do the dishes and get changed. Put on your best boots, brother mine. We're going dancing!"

Flynn

"**M**OM, YOU'RE SURE YOU don't want me to hang out here tonight? I can just stay in my room. I won't interfere in spa night. Though I have been told I do a mean facial."

My mother shook her head. "Ew, and I don't even want to know who would've told you that. No, you're out of here. Go have fun with Alex. See some of the guys. Bridget's fine with us. Right, darlin'?"

"Right." My daughter turned from the kitchen table, where she was helping my mom mix up some kind of hair conditioner goop. "No boys allowed tonight. It's girls' night."

"Fine, fine. I can see where I'm not wanted." I stood up, pushed in my chair and tugged on one of Bridget's braids. "I'll get changed. Alex is picking me up in twenty minutes."

I passed Reenie coming down the steps as I was going up. She carried a stack of towels and shot me a wide smile. "Getting your cowboy on tonight, Flynnigan?"

I stopped, my hand gripping the bannister. "What did you call me?"

Maureen turned to look back at me. "Flynnigan. Why?"

"No one ever called me that but Dad." I almost whispered the words.

"Oh." She nodded. "I'm sorry. I didn't mean to . . . step on anything there. I didn't even think of it."

"It's okay." I shrugged it off. "Just took me by surprise."

"I miss him, too." She hugged the towels to her chest. "So much has been happening the last few months, but every now and again, I swear I hear him singing, or smell his aftershave."

"Yeah." I rubbed my jaw. "Think he's hanging around to make sure we're behaving?"

"Knowing Dad, probably the opposite. Hoping we won't behave." She grinned. "So I stand by my original sentiment: go get your cowboy on tonight, Flynnigan."

I changed into a faded white and blue cotton dress shirt and rolled the sleeves to just below my elbows. Opening my closet door, I looked at my beat up old boots, the ones Ali had given me for Christmas in our junior year of high school. I'd left them behind when I fled Burton, not wanting any reminders of Georgia or the girl I'd loved.

But tonight, I was feeling the need to go old-school. I reached for the boots and sat down to pull them on, feeling them mold to my feet again, just as comfortable and perfect as they'd been a decade before.

Back downstairs, I kissed Bridget good-bye and teased all the girls about sneaking back to take pictures of them in their clay face masks. I heard the purr of Alex's Porsche as he turned into the driveway.

"Behave yourself!" My mother had to get in last word. "But have fun."

I stood in the open doorway and winked at her. "No promises." Closing the door behind me, I slid into the passenger seat of my friend's fine machine.

"Check you out." I slammed the car door and tugged my seatbelt across my lap. "Business must be good."

"No complaints." Alex turned in the driver's seat to back out, and the scent of his very expensive cologne drifted my way.

"Hey, do guys really dig that smelly stuff?" I stretched out my legs.

Alex glanced at me. "Why do you ask? You looking to change teams?"

I rolled my eyes. "No. Just curious."

"Well, then, in my experience, yes, they do. At least some. But it's just like with girls. There's no one size fits all."

I grunted. "If it's just like with women, I don't see the point. I mean, I hang out with dudes because chicks are confusing."

"Yeah, well, it's the same the world around, buddy. Sorry to burst your bubble." He sped up as we left the town limits, turning onto the county highway. "Is there any one chick who's particularly confusing to you?"

"I live in a household of women. They're all that way."

"I thought maybe you were thinking of one who doesn't live with you."

Alex was about as subtle as a freight train. "Why don't you just come out and ask me how things are going with Ali?"

"I would, but I saw her this afternoon and got the scoop. She thinks you're messing with her."

I frowned, my forehead drawing together. "Messing with her? What the hell's that supposed to mean?"

"She thinks you're just interested in her because she's here, she's part of your past, and you're being nostalgic. Or some shit like that." He slowed as we approached a huge building with bright neon letters on the side. "I know the truth, though. She's scared. She doesn't remember how to trust, and she's afraid you'll hurt her again."

"*I'll* hurt *her?*" A pinprick of guilt pierced my chest. "The fuck? Who's the one who changed the plan at the last fucking minute? Who's the one who decided I wasn't important enough to leave her precious farm?"

"Whoa there, dude. Don't kill the therapist. I'm just telling you what I think. Maybe if you understand where she's coming from, you two can figure out where to go from here."

"We don't go anywhere from here. Except we're both Bridget's parents. She's the only thing we've done well together, and even then, we almost screwed up. Ali told me today that we need to stick to being parents only, for Bridget's sake. Maybe she's right."

Alex found a parking spot in the back. I checked out the small groups of girls who clumped together around the lot, dressed in short skirts, tight tops and boots. Then there were the guys who were checking out the girls, tipping back longnecks and slapping each other on the shoulder.

Oh, yeah, I was back in Georgia.

Alex and I made our way inside, waving to a few people who shouted out greetings to us as we passed. I noticed more than one girl flash an invitation to me with her eyes, and one who was either braver or drunker flashed more than an invitation.

"Now that's class." There was laughter in Alex's voice. "Nice to see you haven't lost your touch."

"Thanks. But no thanks. I'm just here to let off some steam and hang out with you. And maybe get a little wasted."

The atmosphere inside was surprisingly upscale for Burton, Georgia. The circular bar dominated the huge room and was already surrounded by people ordering or waiting to order.

To the left of the bar, tables circled by chairs filled the space, and to the right was the dance floor. A band was setting up on the stage that ran along the back wall.

Alex and I pushed through to the bar. A tall guy with black hair and a shorter, bald man were waiting on patrons, moving with between the people and the liquor with relaxed grins that belied their speed. I was impressed by how laid-back they both seemed to be, considering how many people were calling out, demanding attention and booze.

"Hey, Mason!" Alex cupped his hands around his mouth and hollered. "How's it hanging, dude?"

The black-haired man turned, and catching sight of Alex, grinned. "You son of a bitch, you back in town again? You sure you really live in Atlanta? I'm thinking of calling bullshit on that."

Alex spread out his hands. "What can I say? The charms of Burton keep luring me home." He hooked a thumb in my direction. "Mason, do you remember Flynn Evans? He's back in town, too."

"Evans." Mason extended an arm over the bar, and I shook his hand. "Long time, no see. Heard you got out of Dodge, too. What brought you back?"

I laughed. "Too much to get into with this many people around. Let's just say, a death brought me back and a birth kept me in town. For now." I waved my hand in a circle between us. "Great place you have here. Seems like you're packing them in."

"Every weekend, bro." Mason nodded. "We bring in some hot new music acts, serve good liquor at decent prices, give 'em a place to dance." He leaned closer to be heard when he lowered his voice. "Dance floor is for the ladies, of course. All of them told me they had no place to dance until we opened. They come and they bring their boyfriends, or they come here to hook up, so plenty of guys want to be here, too. It's a win-win."

"Works for those of us not looking for ladies, too. Some of us come to dance and pick up hot dudes." Alex wiggled his eyebrows, and I was happy to see Mason throw back his head and laugh. Most people in Burton accepted Alex as he was, but there were always a few rednecks ready to give him shit. Nice to see Mason wasn't one of them.

"Touché, dude. Absolutely, we don't discriminate on the basis of sex, race, coolness or who finds who attractive." He glanced over his shoulder at the other bartender. "So what do you guys want to drink? First round's on the house."

"Hey, you don't have to do that. But thanks." Alex cast his eyes upward, thinking. "I'll have boilermaker."

"Make it two. Thanks."

Mason pulled our beers, poured the shots and slid them all across the bar to us. "Bottoms up, guys. Have a good time tonight." He started to turn away and then stopped, staring over my shoulder with big eyes and whistling low. "Holy shit. Check out the legs that just walked in."

I followed the direction of his gaze, grinning when I spotted what he saw. Yeah, he wasn't wrong. The platform just inside the door was raised above the rest of the floor, so her face was hidden by all the people between us, but those legs . . . fuck. Her feet and ankles were covered by heavily overstitched black cowboy boots, but the expanse of skin between the top of the leather and the hem of her very short flowered dress was smokin.' Lightly tanned, ultra-toned and . . . bare. I poked Alex in the ribs, but the look on his face stopped me from saying anything.

"God almighty. Shit just got interesting." A broad smile spread over his mouth, but he was still looking at the legs. No, he was looking at the body that went with the legs. The crowd had parted just enough for us to see the rest of her, and my heart thudded deep into my stomach when I saw the face.

"What the hell's she doing here?"

Alex shrugged. "Looks to me like she's getting her party on." He wagged his head, grin still in place. "Damn, I forgot how good our girl cleans up."

He wasn't wrong. Her light brown hair was down, falling in fat curls over her shoulders. That was about all that covered her shoulders; the little dress she wore had the tiniest straps, making me wonder how it was staying up, because her tits were definitely on display.

I'd always been a boob guy, and Ali's were my favorite. The first boobs a guy gets to touch always stay in his mind. Since being back in town, I hadn't had the chance to really appreciate her rack, but now there it was, for all the world to see. I shifted on my bar stool, because suddenly my jeans were tight in the crotch.

The dress dipped low to give a tantalizing view of her cleavage, clung to her figure and then ended just about an inch below her ass. The fabric fluttered, giving the illusion that it might offer a better view yet, should just the right breeze come along.

Ali flipped her hair back, her smile huge as she spoke to someone behind her. *Sam.* Okay, so she was here with her brother. That was okay, right? And then I spied a redhead and realized Meghan, Sam's girlfriend, was here, too. As I watched, another guy, in jeans, a black T-shirt and a cowboy hat approached her and laid his hand on her bare shoulder.

I was on my feet before I knew it, and if it hadn't been for Alex's hand on my arm, I might've bolted through the crowd and slugged the guy. But he held me back.

"Don't do it." His words were low, but I could hear them well enough. "At least, don't do it if you're not ready to follow through."

"Follow through? What's that supposed to mean?" I growled, still on my feet.

"I mean, if you're going to punch that guy for touching

your woman, you better make damn sure she *is* your woman, and that you're willing to throw her over your shoulder and haul her out of here. Not just for tonight, not just for this month . . . for good."

I swallowed hard. Alex was right. The fury that pounded in my veins and in my head was still pushing me to rip that douchebag's hand of Ali and knock him flat to the floor, but what would I do after that? Bow to Ali and walk away? Grab her and kiss her crazy? I didn't know. And if I didn't know, I needed to back down.

I swung back to the bar, dumped the shot of whisky into the beer and slammed it down. Mason had moved to the other side of the bar to attend to other customers, but I caught the attention of the shorter man.

"Tequila shots. Double and keep them coming, okay?"

The bartender flicked a glance at me, over my shoulder and then back to my face. Whatever was there must've told him I was serious, because he pulled out the bottle and set me up.

Alex met my eyes. "So we're doing this?"

"Fuck, yeah." I poured the first shot down my throat and without pausing, followed it with a second. "We're doing it."

Across the room, the band began to tune up, and the crowd roared in anticipation. Baldy, the bartender, set up me up again while I leaned against the wooden bar, scanning the crowd, seeking out one light brown head. I spied her in the middle of a group of men. One of them handed her a shot—I was pretty sure it was whiskey—and like any good Georgia woman, she tossed it back without hesitation and with nary a grimace. Another guy supplied her with a second.

The DJ who was playing the music before the band kicked off started another song—I was pretty sure it was Luke Bryan. Ali grabbed the hand of the nearest man and hauled him onto the dance floor. She danced with the same abandon I remembered from our high school dances, tossing her head, gyrating her hips and running her hands over the back of her neck, lifting her hair. She used to do that when we were making love, too—a sudden, vivid memory flashed across my mind of her straddling my body, grinding herself against me, fingers dug into her hair to get it away from her sweaty neck. Her eyes were closed and her lips just slightly parted as pleasure washed over both of us . . .

Fuck. I wasn't near drunk enough yet if I could still remember that. I reached for the shot glasses again and began to remedy that situation.

"Hey. Aren't you Flynn Evans?"

I glanced to my left. A pretty blonde with wide brown eyes and a tight tank top over a denim skirt that barely hid her bikini line was smiling at me.

"Yeah, so I hear. Do I know you?"

She giggled, and it went up my spine, until I had to grit my teeth to stop from wincing. "You were three years ahead of me in school. I'm Shayna Parkins."

The name didn't ring a bell, but I smiled and nodded. "Sure. Good to see you again."

Whether or not Shayna bought my line didn't seem to matter. She clutched at my arm, rubbing her tits into the side of my body. *Shit.* She wasn't wearing a bra. I waited for the same reaction from my body that the memory of Ali had evoked, but there was nothing. Absolutely frickin' nothing.

She was holding a beer in her free hand. Draining it, she set the empty glass on the bar and leaned into me. "Want to dance?"

I didn't. I wanted to stay on this bar stool and brood about Ali, but since the girl in question was currently on the middle of the dance floor, grinding against the guy who stood behind her with his hands way too close to her breasts, I nodded and stood up. "Sure."

Alex shook his head. "Are you sure you know what you're

doing?" He shouted it into my ear.

"Maybe you should be asking your other best friend that question." I jerked my head toward Ali.

"I'm not here with Ali. I'm here with you." His fingers curled around an empty shot glass. "Sam and Meghan are in charge of Ali tonight. I just want to make sure you don't do anything you regret."

"Way too late for that one, buddy." I clapped a hand on his shoulder. "I'm going to dance. Keep my spot warm, okay?"

There were so many bodies undulating on the wooden floor that at first I wasn't sure there'd be room for Shayna and me. But I'd underestimated her determination. She dragged me through a couple of groups and between a few couples until we found a space big enough for the both of us . . . providing we stood very close together.

I dropped my hands to her hips as she linked her hands behind my neck. The front of her body pressed into mine, swaying side to side. Gazing over her head, I tried to look for Ali without being obvious about it. Her back was to me, as she faced her partner, who I realized with dawning horror was Trent Wagner.

"What the fuck is she thinking?" I spoke out loud without realizing it.

"What'd you say?" Shayna stood on her toes and shouted over the classic Garth Brooks song playing.

"Nothing. Sorry." I wracked my brain for any kind of conversation I could possibly have with the girl in my arms. "So, uh, you still live in Burton?"

"Oh, yeah." She nodded. "I work at the Piggly Wiggly. You left town for a while, didn't you?"

For a while. Like, nine years. "Yeah, I did. I'm a photojournalist." I didn't play the status card often, if ever, but what the hell. I wasn't sure this chick even knew what a photojournalist was.

"A photowhat?" Her pretty brow wrinkled in confusion.

Nailed it. "Photojournalist. Ah, I take pictures of news stories for different magazines and newspapers. A few TV news shows, too, now and then."

"Oh, awesome! So do you, like, cover the People's Choice? Do you get to take pictures of all the celebrities?"

I lowered my hands to her ass, just to remind myself that conversation wasn't all she had to offer. "Uh, no. I don't cover any of the award shows. Mostly I do political news."

"Oh." Clearly I was a disappointment. "Are you living back here now?"

"For a while. Hey, do you know that guy over there?" The crowd had parted enough that we had a perfect view of Ali and company. Shayna followed my gaze.

"Oh, yeah. Trent. He was in your class, wasn't he?"

"Mmmhmm. Haven't seen him since I've been back in town. What's he up to?"

She wrinkled her nose. "Not much. He's here every weekend, picking up a different girl. Works out on the Benningers' farm during the week."

"Huh. Doesn't sound like you think much of him."

"Well, he's hot, no question, but he's dumb as a box of rocks."

I bit in the inside of my lips to keep from laughing. *Takes one to know one.* And then I felt guilty, because I didn't know this girl. She might've been perfectly nice. A perfectly nice girl who picked up guys in bars.

"I was so excited to see you here tonight." She gazed up at me through her lashes. "I probably shouldn't tell you this, but I had the biggest crush on you when we were in high school."

"You did?" Now I felt even worse that I couldn't remember her at all.

"Yup. Not that I ever did anything about it, because you didn't see any other girl but . . . what was her name? Amy? Addy? It was like the rest of us were invisible."

"Ali." I said her name softly, but almost as though she could hear me over the ear-splitting volume of the music, her eyes met mine across the dance floor. They flickered to Shayna's face, down to my hands on the other girl's ass and then back to me. Although she was still smiling at Trent, it didn't reach her eyes, which were solemn and almost sad.

"That's right. She got married right after graduation, didn't she? To some other guy in your class. I remember we were all shocked. Like, we all totally thought you guys were going to end up together, and then you're gone and she's married to someone else. Funny how life turns out, isn't it?"

Truer words. "Yeah, it is. Hey, you want another drink? All this dancing's making me thirsty."

Shayna beamed up at me. "I'd love that." She clung to my arm as we pushed back toward the bar. "This is just a dream come true. It's like in a book, you know? When the girl finally gets to hook up with the guy she's crushed on for years?"

Shit. I plunged ahead, my focus on the bar. Once we reached it, I ordered Shayna another beer. "And another double of tequila for me." I searched for any sign of Alex, guilty that I'd abandoned him. Finally I spied him at a table with Meghan and Sam. Well, at least he wasn't alone. They seemed to be absorbed in their conversation, though I noticed Sam never looked away from his sister, who was still dancing with Trent.

Shayna maneuvered herself to stand between my knees, and halfway through her beer, she tilted her face to mine, clearly waiting for me to kiss her. I closed my eyes and sighed.

"Shayna, look. You're a nice person, and really pretty, but I'm just not in a place where I can, uh, pursue anything with you. I'm sorry. But I had a good time dancing." It was the classic rejection sandwich my dad had taught me: let girls down easy by hiding it between two sets of compliments.

Apparently, though, it was too complicated for this girl. She frowned as though trying to figure out what I meant.

"You don't have to pursue me. I'm right here." She moved in a second time for a kiss.

I gently pushed her back. "No, what I meant was—well, I have a daughter, and right now, she's got to be my priority. I came out tonight just to hang with my friend." Alex, bless his perceptive heart, was wending his way back toward me. "And here he comes, so I'd better say good night and let you go have fun with someone who can really appreciate you."

"You're turning me down?" Disbelief colored her face. "Guys don't turn me down."

"Sorry." I realized that nothing I said was going to change anything for her at this point.

"You're an asshole." Shayna slammed her still half-full beer onto the bar so that it sloshed over the sides and stormed away.

"Nice to see you're still making friends and spreading sunshine." Alex reached the bar, smirking at me. "So what's it gonna be? Are we going to be grown-ups and head home now, at a sensible hour, when we still have at least some of our hearing? Or are we diving back into the tequila and getting stupid?"

I raised my shot. "Alex, my friend, we may be older and wiser, but we ain't dead yet. We're staying. Night is young, and . . ." I looked over his shoulder in Ali's direction. She'd stopped dancing and was leaning over the table, talking to Meghan. While I watched, she skimmed one hand down her side, smoothing her dress, and then lifted that same hand to rake through her hair. I was pretty certain all the men in a twenty-foot radius were now drooling.

Ali picked up a drink from the table and drained it before she went back to the dance floor. Meghan stopped her with a hand on her arm, and I saw Ali shake it off. The room went dark, except for a spotlight on the stage as Mason introduced tonight's act. The music started, and everyone in the bar went crazy.

"And what?" Alex poked my arm. "You were in the middle of saying something about the night being young."

"Yeah, you know what? Doesn't matter. We're going to shut them down tonight. We're going to shoot tequila until I don't remember my name. Until I don't remember her name."

Alex stared at me. "Masochist much?" When I didn't respond, he lifted his shoulders. "Fine. Your funeral, buddy. I'll hang around for the ride. I just hope you're prepared for the crash landing."

Chapter
Twelve

Ali

THE SUNSHINE POURING INTO my room was going to burn me alive from the inside out. I was sure of it. Groaning, I rolled over and tried to yank the blanket up higher, to cover my head.

"Morning, glory." Meghan sang off-key as she opened my door. "Are you ready for breakfast?"

"Oh, God, no. Never. I don't want to think about food for the rest of my life. And maybe even longer."

"You'll probably feel better with a little something in your stomach. And you need to eat before you can take the ibu, which I have a feeling you're going to need sooner rather than later."

"Just put me out of my misery. Smother me. Hell, shoot me for all I care. Just do it fast."

"Sorry, sweetie, you don't get out of it like that. You danced, now it's time to pay the fiddler. Trust me, I know what I'm talking about." The bed dipped a little as she sat on the edge. "Hangover queen right here. Or used to be. I'm reformed now, but I remember what it felt like."

"What was I thinking?" I moaned. "I'm too old for this shit. I'm a mom, for criminey's sake. How can I tell Bridget not to get drunk if I can't even do it?"

"Ali, she's eight years old. I think you've got some time."

"Yeah, but still. I'm not a teenager anymore. I need to re-member that."

"You're not exactly ancient either. It's okay to get a little crazy now and then, if you're smart and responsible about it, which you were. So stop beating yourself up."

"Is Sam pissed at me?" I might've been almost twenty-seven, but I still hated disappointing my big brother.

"Not at all. He's already out in the fields, but he said to tell you to rest this morning and feel better."

I buried my face in the pillow. "Have I told you how glad I am that you're dating my brother? He's much nicer now that you're around."

"Happy to be of service. Now I'm going to leave this tray right here, and you eat some of it, okay?"

"Yes, Mother."

"Don't be a smartass, or I'll put you in timeout."

"Hey, Meghan?" I lifted my head from the pillow just enough to call to her. "Did I dream it or . . . was Flynn singing on the bar last night?"

Meghan paused in the doorway of my room. "Not a dream. Sadly. Bet he's waking up in the same shape you're in this morning. Only Sam and I kept you from making a fool out of yourself."

"Huh. Did he sing . . ."

"Elvis, Tim McGraw and Hank Williams." She ticked them

off on her fingers. "You know, I was going to let you rest a little before I asked you about this, but you brought it up. Why do you think Flynn got so wasted last night?"

I shook my head and regretted it immediately, wincing. "I don't know. Because he could? Because Alex is in town and he wanted to hang with his friend?"

"Because *you* were there, looking damn hot and dirty dancing with other guys. Alex said they'd planned just to grab a couple of drinks and have some fun, but that all went out the door—when you came in the door."

"He doesn't care about me, Meghan. It was just coincidental."

She sighed. "Fine. Then what about you? Why were you so eager to go to The Road Block last night, when you knew Alex and Flynn were going to be there?"

"Isn't it against the Geneva Convention to interrogate a prisoner who's on the verge of death?" I burrowed into the pillow again.

"Um, first, no, I don't think it is. Second, you're not on the verge of death. Third, I'm not interrogating you. I'm just asking questions that might reveal some truths."

"Well, I'm not ready for it yet. Maybe tomorrow."

"Tomorrow I'll be back in Savannah."

"Bingo."

Meghan didn't respond, but I heard the exasperation in her sigh as she stomped out of the room and down the steps. Or maybe it just sounded like she was stomping, since each step reverberated in my pounding brain.

I dozed off and on for the next hour, and by the time I opened my eyes again, the drill team in my head had taken a break and my stomach was more receptive to the idea of food. I sat up, moving slowly and experimentally. When it didn't kill me, I ventured one hand out to snag a piece of toast. It was cold, but I managed to nibble at it until I got half a slice down.

At that point, I felt safe enough to swig some water along with the headache meds.

By noon, I'd crawled out of bed and into the shower. I couldn't manage anything more ambitious than a pair of sweat pants and an old oversized T-shirt, but at least I was upright. I braided my wet hair into a single plait down my back and descended the steps, into the kitchen.

"She lives!" Meghan still sounded far too chipper as she wiped the counter. "And just in time. I'm getting ready to leave."

"Isn't it a little early?" She usually stayed at the farm through Sunday night and drove back to Savannah Monday morning, since she didn't have an early class.

"Yeah, but my mom and Logan are coming up to visit me tomorrow, and I want to make sure my apartment's in decent shape."

"That's nice." I eased myself into a kitchen chair. "Are you excited to see them?" Meghan's mother and her husband, who'd been a lifelong friend of Meghan's late father, were usually so busy with their restaurant that they didn't make it up to Savannah often.

"Yeah. Though I'm pretty sure it's a fact-finding mission disguised as a family visit."

"What kind of facts?"

"The what-is-Meghan-planning-to-do-after-graduation-this-year facts. They act like they're laid back and fine with whatever I decide—and they probably are—but they want some definite plans."

"Well, you've got a job already. That's more than most college grads have."

"And they're thrilled with that. I think maybe they just want some assurance that Sam's intentions toward me are honorable and long-term." Meghan shook her head. "Like he could ever be anything else."

"In other words, they want a ring on your finger before you move in with us for real?" I leaned my chin on my hand.

"Maybe. Which is so weird, because my mom's never been like that. She raised me to be strong and independent, not to need a man to make me complete."

The kitchen door creaked open, and my brother came in. "You don't need me to make you complete?" He snagged Meghan's hand and pulled her in to him.

"How did you hear that? Were you standing outside the door eavesdropping?" She sounded offended, but her hands snaked up to clasp together behind his neck as she fit her body to his.

A pang of wistful envy hit me in the chest. I loved my brother and Meghan, and their happiness made me happy. But it also had the unpleasant side effect of making me painfully aware of my own lacking. The memory of Flynn, standing on the bar last night and playing the air guitar as he belted out one of my favorite Elvis songs, flashed across my mind with odd clarity.

"I wasn't trying to listen. The window's open." Sam kissed the top of her head and winked at me. "Didn't expect to see you up and around yet. Quite a night you had."

I laid my head down on my folded arms. "Don't remind me. It happened, it's over, let us never speak of it again. The next time I beg you to take me dancing, lock me in my room."

"I'd like to get that in writing." Sam rubbed his hand up and down Meghan's back. "Are you heading out, babe?"

"I am. If you're sure you've got everything covered here."

"Yeah, we're good." But he didn't make a move to let her go. Instead he looked at me again. "I stopped at the stand on my way back from the fields. Cassie says she's got everything under control, and she'll call us if things get too busy. And she said she hopes you feel better."

I frowned. "What'd you tell her?"

Sam quirked his eyebrow at me. "What, you didn't want me to tell her you got ripping drunk last night and now you're hung over?" He smirked. "Don't worry. I told her you had a little stomach bug."

"Thanks. Not that she won't hear what happened from someone else, since no one in Burton knows how to keep their mouth shut."

"Which isn't a problem if you know how to behave." Sam shot me the big-brother glare, but it didn't carry much heat. I stuck out my tongue at him.

"On that note, I'm out of here." Meghan wriggled away from my brother and came over to give me a hug. "Feel better, sweetie. Call me tonight and let me know how it goes with Flynn."

"What? How what goes with Flynn?" Panic sliced through me. *What had I forgotten from last night?*

"He's coming over to drop off Bridget later this afternoon, right?"

Crud, he was. I'd blocked that out. "Yeah, so?"

"So I thought he might say something about last night. Maybe you two could start to do something radical, like be honest with each other about how you feel." She patted my shoulder. "Just something to think about." She offered her hand to Sam. "Walk me out?"

I put my head back down and concentrating on wishing this day were over. I might've fallen asleep again for a minute, but I jumped awake when the door slammed.

"God, Sam, you scared the life out of me."

"Sorry." He didn't sound very contrite as he pulled out a chair to sit across from me. "Do you want to talk about last night?" The way he spoke, I knew he'd rather plow the south forty naked than have this discussion. I toyed with the idea of dragging him through a chick-talk about my feelings and what seeing Flynn dance with that bleach-blonde bimbette had done to me, but in the end, I decided he deserved a break.

"Nah, I'm good. I talked to Meghan. And it really doesn't matter anyway. I just want to forget it all." My eyes fell on the counter, where sat the bright blue folder Rilla Grant had given me the day before. That seemed like a good way to change the subject. "Hey, Sam, do you know the Grants?"

He frowned, rubbing the back of his neck. "The ones who have the farm out on 72? Yeah. Well, I know Emmett a little. He was part of the Guild for a while, until they got too liberal for him."

I raised my eyebrow. "Since when is the Guild liberal?" They were a group of farmers and town businessmen who met to support each other and the community. After our parents had been killed, the Guild had taken Sam under their collective wing and helped us keep the farm. My brother never forgot how much we owed these men.

"Since they decided to meet on a Sunday afternoon once a few years back. Mitch Jones' daughter had her wedding on the Saturday when we usually got together, and so we voted to postpone to the next day. Emmett left the Guild right then."

"Sheesh. That seems a little extreme."

Sam shrugged. "Well, to each his own, and I respect his wishes. I think he was heading toward leaving before that anyway. The whole family is kind of stand-offish. I guess Emmett's wife ran off when their daughter was a baby, and he closed ranks after that."

"Hmmm. That fits with what Cassie told me, too. Rilla Grant came by the stand yesterday. She's starting up an advertising business, and she wanted to know if we might be interested in being one of her first clients. She gave me that info." I nodded to the folder.

"Advertising? For what, the stand?" Sam snorted. "Since when do we need to advertise?"

I rolled my eyes. "I don't know, Sam. But moving with the

times wouldn't kill us. We don't do anything to promote our business. I'm not saying we go full-throttle or spend a ton of money, but I looked over what Rilla gave me. She's got some good ideas. Wouldn't hurt to talk to her, at least."

"I'll take a look." Sam reached for the papers, but before he opened the folder, he gazed at me. "You're right, Ali. Sometimes things need to change. I spend a lot of time and energy working to keep everything going just like it was before. The same old, same old is comfortable. But sometimes we need to shake things up."

"Okay." I was a little unclear about where he was going with this. "You're not firing me, are you?" I laughed. Sam and I were co-owners of everything: this house, the farm and the stand. Since I'd moved home with Bridget, after Craig left, we'd made every decision together.

He didn't join in my laughter. "I'm just saying, even though things have worked well for us like they are, it doesn't mean change is a terrible thing. I never want you to feel like you're stuck here."

Now it was getting clearer. "You talked to Meghan, too, didn't you?"

He scowled, looking uncomfortable. "A little. I asked her the other day if she knew what'd happened between you and Flynn, back after graduation, I mean. We talked about the choices you made then. At the time, I never asked you. I didn't know until you told me about it last summer. Back then, I was afraid to say anything, because you were so upset. And after it just seemed like it didn't matter. It was over." He heaved a sigh. "I'm sorry, Ali. Sorry I didn't ask, and that I wasn't a better big brother back then."

I reached across to lay my hand on his arm. "Don't, Sam. There wasn't anything you could've said that would've changed anything. No matter how much you pushed. Okay? Stop feeling guilty."

"You were going to leave with Flynn, and you didn't because of me. Because of the farm. You gave up what you wanted to do to stay here for me."

I took a deep breath. "That was part of it, or at least it was the reason I used. Yes, I'd told Flynn I'd go away with him. He was just chafing here, you know that. As much as he loved his family, Burton was too small to hold him, I think. But that morning before graduation, you were so excited. You laid out all the plans you'd been making, how if we worked together, I could go to college right here and work the stand, and we could keep the farm going. You'd figured out all the timelines and the budget, and how it was going to happen." I smiled, remembering. "I was so impressed, and it felt like Mom and Dad would've been proud. It felt like what they'd have wanted us to do."

"And that's why you told Flynn you weren't leaving." Sam leaned back in his chair, dropping his head against the top of it.

I nodded. "Yeah. And I didn't handle it well. I was so confused. Just torn over what to do. I loved him, Sam. Loved him like—" Tears gathered and threatened to choke me. "I think he was probably it for me. But after all you'd given up for me, I couldn't just run off and leave you holding the bag."

"Why didn't you tell me?"

"I thought Flynn and I could work it out. I figured he might be a little upset, but I was counting on him understanding. We'd never really had a fight before, you know? But that night, when I told him I couldn't leave, not then at least, he exploded. He told me he wasn't getting stuck in this town, and if I didn't love him enough to leave with him—" The horrible things we'd both said that night echoed in my head. "Well, it was bad. He stormed out, and I cried, but at the back of my mind, I never thought we wouldn't make it up. I expected him to come back the next day, and we'd figure it all out. But he didn't call, and he didn't answer when I called. Finally, Reenie came over and told me he'd gone."

Sam drew in a ragged breath. "I wish I'd known, Ali. I wish you'd told me."

I managed a smile. "You know what, Sam? All these years, I've wished I'd told you, too. I kept thinking what I would've done different. But lately, I look at the farm, and what you and I've done together, and I'm not sorry. These were good years. I know they were hard, and I know we both worked ourselves to the damn bone, like Dad used to say. But I wouldn't trade them."

He nodded, and I thought maybe he was afraid to speak. I gave him a few minutes before I went on.

"Are you going to propose to Meghan?"

He jerked his head up, surprise etched on his face. "What? Where did that come from?"

I smiled. "We're talking about change and about holding onto what's important, right? Come on, brother mine. It's no secret you're hung up on her, and she's so crazy in love with you, it's almost sickening. She's moving in here come June, right? I figure it's just a matter of time before you make it official. You and I need to talk about what happens after you do that."

He had the grace to look sheepish as he scratched the back of his head. "I was planning to ask her right after she graduates. I already talked to Jude and Logan, and I was going to discuss it with you, too. Just didn't seem to be a good time to bring it up." He gazed at me from under drooped eyelids. "I was scared, if you want to know the truth."

"Scared of me? Well, hell, of course you were." I teased him a little and then sobered. "Change is scary. It's one thing to have your girlfriend here on weekends, hanging out and having fun. It's another thing altogether to bring your wife into the house where your sister's been running the show for almost ten years. We need to be realistic. I think it's time for Bridge and me to find our own place."

Sam flinched. "No. That's exactly what I didn't want to happen. I don't want you to feel like you can't live in your own house. We own all of this together. Nothing's going to change that."

I rubbed his arm. "You're right, nothing's going to change that. Not even us living in different houses, like most brothers and sisters do." I paused, searching for the right words. "Sam, if I'd told you on my graduation day that I wanted to leave with Flynn, that we planned to move away and go to college together, would you've told me to stay? Would you have let me make that sacrifice for you?"

He shook his head. "Of course not."

"Then don't you see this is the same thing? I'm not going to stand in the way of you and Meghan being happy. I want you to have the best chance you can to make a family, together. I'm not abandoning you, Sam. Bridget and I'll find a place close by, and I'll still work the stand. We'll be here to help you with planting and the harvest, and we'll come for dinner every Sunday night, like in the old days when the whole family gathered at the farm. This is how it's supposed to be." I stood up, swaying just a little.

"You okay?" Sam reached for me, but I brushed him off.

"Fine. Just a little light-headed. I think I'll grab a nap before Bridget gets home." I started for the steps, and then hesitated. "Hey, Sam? You planning to give Meghan Mom's engagement ring?"

His voice was gravelly as he answered me. "Yeah. I was thinking of it. I think Mom would like that. Is it okay with you?"

"More than okay. Exactly as it should be."

Chapter
Thirteen

Flynn

"WHAT'S WRONG, DADDY? DO you still feel sick?" Bridget's small forehead wrinkled in concern as she looked up at me from the back seat of the truck.

"I'm good, honeybunch. Just the bumps are making my stomach feel a little rough." I clamped my teeth together as the Chevy bobbed up and down on the Reynolds' driveway. We rounded the bend, and I pulled to the rear of the house. Somehow in the last weeks, I'd fallen back into the old habit of parking here and going into the kitchen.

As soon as we came to a halt and I turned off the ignition, Bridget unbuckled and opened her door, flying out of the car and up the back steps. "Mommy! I'm home." I followed her at a much more sedate pace.

"Hey there, sunshine." Sam met us at the door. "I'm about to walk over to the stand to help Cassie close up. Want to tag along?"

"Yeah, but where's Mommy?" Bridget peered past her uncle's legs.

"She's on the porch, resting. She was feeling a little sick this morning, so she stayed home."

"That's funny. Daddy was sick this morning, too. He had a really bad headache."

Sam smirked at me. "I can only imagine. Well, c'mon, pipsqueak. Let's get moving." He held the door open behind him, fastening his eyes on me as Bridget scampered down the steps. "You can go on through the house. You probably want to talk to my sister."

Shit, no. Talking to Ali today was not on my list of top ten of things I wanted to do. But Sam's face wasn't asking, it was telling, so I just nodded and walked through the door.

I went into the silent kitchen and past the living room, opening the front screen door. Ali sat on the swing, her feet curled up under her as she stared out into the yard. She was wearing sweats and big T-shirt, and with her hair down her back in a braid, she looked about fifteen again.

God, I wanted her.

The realization took me by surprise, which was stupid, given how many times the sight, thought or memory of her had given me a painfully hard erection over the last weeks. Yeah, I knew my body still reacted to her. But this was different. I *wanted* her. I wanted to gather her into my arms, feel her head on my shoulder and her breath against my neck. I wanted to lay her out, with care and tenderness, and kiss her lips until they were swollen and every one of her heartbeats belonged to me. I wanted to laugh with her about all the funny things our perfect daughter said. I wasn't sure about anything else in my life right now, but this I knew with perfect clarity.

Ali turned her head a little to see me. "Hey." Her voice was soft and husky, as it used to be after we made love. I cleared my throat and adjusted my pants as subtly as I could.

"Hey. Okay if I come out?"

She held out her hand in a be-my-guest gesture. "Sure. Have a seat."

I sank into the deep wicker chair and stretched out my legs. "So how're you feeling today?"

She laughed, though there was little humor in it. "Better now. I was thinking the swing wasn't such a great idea when I first came out here, but it feels okay. This morning was rough. I asked Meghan to shoot me."

I grinned. "I offered to pay Alex to hold a pillow over my face. He wasn't game. Said he made enough money without resorting to murder for hire."

"Did you go home with him?" There was hint of vulnerability in her voice that made me want to sweep her onto my lap.

"Yeah. Wasn't the plan, but he said it was really late by the time we left The Road Block, and I was practically passing out, so he was afraid to take me back to my mom's. He texted her first thing this morning and drove me back after breakfast." I grimaced. "Breakfast made by his mom and accompanied with a side of loud scolding about being old enough to know better."

Her lips curved up into a smile. "I lucked out. No one here gave me a hard time. Just a little teasing."

"Well, as far as I remember, you left before I did. And I hear things got kind of wild even before that."

Ali pulled her braid forward and twisted it around her finger. I saw a teasing gleam in her eye. "I was there for the concert. I mean, I wasn't completely sure it really happened when I woke up this morning, but Meghan assured me you rocked the house."

"Oh, God." I dropped my head back, screwing my eyes

closed. "Yeah, I hear I was quite the hit. I already called Mason this afternoon and apologized. He's a decent guy. Just laughed and said if his bar couldn't stand up to a pair of boots, it wasn't worth its weight."

"Maybe you missed your calling. Ever think about giving up your camera for a cowboy hat and honkytonks?"

"Nah, I think I'll stick with the quiet life." I lifted my head and regarded her. She'd dropped one foot to the porch floor and was slowly pushing the swing back and forth. "So. Trent Wagner?"

"Oh, my God." Ali covered her face. "Don't remind me."

"So there's nothing between you two?" I had to ask it, even though I was pretty sure I knew the answer.

"Trent and me? Stab me, shoot me, flay me. No. He was just . . . convenient last night."

"Good." I spoke the single word with enough meaning that her eyes flew to my face. I held her gaze without looking away until she did. The pink tinge on her cheeks gave me an unexplainable happy.

"You seemed kind of cozy with the blonde. Not that I was paying attention or anything. Trent said he'd, ah . . . known her." I couldn't miss the arch tone.

"Yeah, I guess she was a freshman when you and I were seniors. Said she'd always had a crush on me." I rubbed my hand over my knee. "She also said everyone knew I only had eyes for one girl back then."

This time, I couldn't miss the blush. "That was a long time ago."

"Some things don't change." I bounced my leg up and down, needing an outlet for the nervous energy that had suddenly filled my body. "Ali, can I ask you something? Not because I'm trying to dig up painful crap or anything. I just have to know."

Her mouth tightened, but she nodded. "Okay."

"Why Craig?"

She swallowed hard and turned her face away from me. "Flynn, I don't . . ." She worried the corner of her lip between her teeth, silent for a moment. "All right. That's an explanation I owe you. I told you, after you left town, I was a mess. I didn't want to do anything. Alex would come over and sit with me, and let me cry on his shoulder, but he was worried about me. He talked me into leaving the house, finally. A bunch of kids from our class were hanging out at the river, just drinking and talking . . . you know the deal. I sat on the hood of Alex's car, not talking to anyone. It still hurt too much."

She closed her eyes as a single tear leaked out, running down her cheek. I wanted to wipe it away, but I wasn't sure she'd want my touch just now.

"Then Craig came over and sat next to me. He didn't make me talk. He didn't try to get me to join in. He just sat there. And then the next night, he came over to the house, and we sat . . . here. On the porch. And he still didn't make me talk. I mean, he talked to me, and I listened, but he didn't get upset when I was quiet. He was just an ear. A shoulder, I guess. I was so lonely."

I thought about Craig. We'd been friends all during high school; not as close as Alex and me, but we'd hung out regularly, played together on the football team and gone to the same parties. In the back of my mind, I guess I'd always known Craig had a thing for Ali, but I also knew he'd never act on it. Until I gave him a huge open door to walk through.

"I knew people were talking about us. A couple of girls made some snide comments when I was in town, about how fast I jumped from one guy to another. I didn't care, because I knew the truth. There wasn't anything romantic between Craig and me. He was just . . . there.

"Then I found out I was pregnant. I freaked out. Alex was the only one who knew, and I made him swear not to tell anyone else. I wouldn't see Craig when he came over, I'd just hide in my room, but one day, he came while Sam was out in the fields. He came to my room and told me he'd figured out I was pregnant. Alex didn't tell him, but he'd seen me getting sick, and when I started pushing him away, I guess he put the pieces together. He asked me if I was planning to tell you, and when I said I couldn't, he offered to marry me."

I nodded. I could see it, could almost feel her pain. Craig would've loved her from a distance forever if I'd been the man I promised her I'd be. When I fucked up, he stepped in to save her.

"I didn't want to, but he kept pushing, and I was so tired. I was sick, I was sad, and it felt like my life was over. I knew Craig thought he loved me. One day I just gave up. I said yes. I told Sam what we were doing—he didn't know I was pregnant, but he knew I'd been seeing Craig—and he tried everything he could to talk me out of it. Offered to fly me to wherever you were. But by then I'd made up my mind." She shifted a little, and the swing creaked. Her tongue darted out to touch her lips, and I sensed she was struggling with what she was going to say next.

"The day we went to get married . . . we drove to Savannah to do it, so I didn't have to deal with anyone in Burton. That morning, though, I knew I was making a mistake. I had a huge panic attack, and I couldn't breathe. I did the one thing I'd sworn I wouldn't. I called you."

"What?" I gripped the arms of the chair. "No, you didn't. If you had—Ali, you've got to know I would've come back here if you'd called."

"It was early in the morning. About an hour before Craig was supposed to pick me up. Alex was there with me—he drove into the city with us that day—and he told me I should talk to you before I did anything, if I wasn't sure about marrying Craig. So I called, and someone answered. But it wasn't you."

"God, no." I had a sudden ache in the pit of my stomach

as I remembered. "Ali, she wasn't anything to me. Reenie had called me the night before to tell me you were marrying Craig. She told me I needed to get back to town and stop you. I was furious, I was hurt . . . I got smashed and went home with one of the girls who was interning with the same photographer. But I didn't do anything. I just slept on her couch."

"She answered your phone, this girl with a sleepy voice, and I just shattered. I didn't ask for you, I didn't even speak to her. I just hung up. I felt like . . . I'd gotten my answer."

"I'm sorry. When I think . . . if I'd just called you. Or come home." *So much wasted time.* "So you went ahead and married Craig."

Ali turned to look at me. "I never slept with him, Flynn. Not until after we were married. And even then . . ." She bowed her head, and this time the tears fell faster, hitting her folded arms. "On our wedding night, he tried to hold me, and I . . . just cried. Every time he touched me, I felt like I was cheating on you."

"God, Ali." I fisted my hands. "I'm sorry. I'm so sorry."

"Why are *you* sorry, Flynn? I'm the one who broke all our promises."

I shook my head. "No. I left you, and I put you in a position where you had to . . . do whatever you could to survive. I'm sorry." I gave us both a few minutes of quiet. "Why did Craig leave, Ali?"

Her shoulders shook. "He tried his best. He stuck with me the whole pregnancy, while everyone was . . . judging us. People talked, you know. They said Craig and I'd been together before you left, and you found out, which was why you took off. Once I started showing, a few people actually asked Craig if he was sure the baby was his. He swore up and down that she was. He was by my side the day she was born, and until she was three months old. And then one day, he came into the living room—we were living in a little apartment over the flower shop downtown—and he had his suitcases. He told me he was leaving. He'd gotten accepted to a small college in Arkansas, and he was leaving. He'd applied there as a surprise for me, thinking we could all three start over fresh, where no one knew us. But then he realized that it was never going to work. I was never going to love him, not the way I'd loved you."

My throat was so tight, I couldn't speak. I raked my hand through my hair.

"He was right, of course. I'd have been better off marrying Alex, because him I loved as a friend. Craig was just the guy who came along when I was lonely. I remember he said to me, right before he walked out the door, 'I thought I could make you love me. But I want more for myself than to be a safety net for a girl who can't love me.'"

She inhaled deep and blew out a breath. "So he left, and that day I packed up Bridget's stuff and mine and called Sam to come pick us up. I told him that Craig and I hadn't worked out, and that was that. We moved back in at the farm, and life went on. And eventually, one day I realized I was happy again. Not in the same way I'd been with you. But happy as I could be. And for a while, it was enough."

She brought her knee back up to hug to her body again, and a strand of her hair fell out of the braid, onto her face. I got up and knelt next to the swing. Reaching with one finger, I tucked the hair back behind her ear.

"Ali, you are the strongest, bravest woman I've ever known. I am . . . so awed that you are my daughter's mother. If she grows up to be even half the woman you are, I'll be the proudest father ever. I'll never forgive myself for leaving you. For putting you in the place where you had to make those kind of choices. I can only say . . . I'm sorry."

I laid my head against her legs, letting the wet from my eyes seep into her sweat pants as my shoulders shook. I wrapped my arms around her feet, and after a moment, I felt her hand slowly, tentatively, stroking over my hair.

Everything changed that week.

By the time Sam and Bridget returned from closing the stand, Ali and I were both calmer, still sitting on the porch as I entertained her with stories from my some of my shoots.

"Have you taken any photos since you've been back in town?" She trailed one hand lazily over the chain of the swing. "You know, seems to me it's about time for them to replace the town sign again. You might be able to get in on that gig."

I laughed. "Yeah, maybe. I've done a little shooting. I got some great pictures of Bridget the other day. Remind me, I'll send them to you."

"I looked beautiful in the pictures Daddy took, Mommy." Bridget nodded in agreement, and we all laughed. Not an ounce of false modesty in this kid.

"Of course you do. You take after your uncle." Sam poked her in the ribs, and she giggled. "Are y'all hungry? Since my personal chef took the day off, we're just having leftovers. But Flynn, you're welcome to stay, if you want."

I glanced at Ali, and she gave me a small smile and nodded.

"If you're sure you have enough, I'd love to eat with you. Thanks."

When I left after dinner, Bridget hugged me with her usual exuberance, Sam shook my hand, and Ali walked me to the door. As I turned on the top step to say goodbye, she leaned forward and kissed my cheek.

It was a start.

That night as I lay in bed, I thought about everything that Ali had told me that afternoon. I remembered about all the years I'd spent blaming her and running. Refusing to return to my hometown, because I was afraid of what would happen if I saw her again. All the years of wasted time.

I picked up my phone from the nightstand and hit Ali's name. It rang a few times before I heard her voice, soft and relaxed.

"Everything okay?"

"Yeah, fine. I just . . ." I rubbed my forehead. "Would I sound like a wuss if I said I just wanted to hear your voice before I went to sleep?"

She laughed. "Do you care?"

I thought about it for a moment. "No, I don't. Actually, I just wanted to say thank you, for telling me everything you did today. I know it was hard. But I do appreciate it."

"You're welcome. It felt good to get it out."

"I've missed talking to you before you bed."

She sighed. "Flynn, you haven't talked to me before bed for a long time."

"I know. I've missed it for a long time."

"What are we doing?"

I paused, considering. "I'm not sure, but I think we might be . . . finding our way back."

"Back?" I heard a rustling, as though she were shifting in the bed. "Do we want to go back?"

"You might have a point. What if we're finding our way forward?"

"It's still scary as hell."

"That's why we're finding our way. No big leaps, no rushing. Just . . . taking our time." I sensed I'd pushed enough for one night, so I added, "How's our daughter tonight?"

"She crashed early, right after you left. She always had a lot of trouble falling asleep, did I tell you that? But lately, she's been doing well. Anyway, she told me she had a wonderful time at girls' night. She said Grandma put cream on her hands that smelled like roses, and Aunt Iona gave her a special hair treatment, and Aunt Maureen painted her toenails. She was in seventh heaven."

"Mom was, too. She said they laughed and played until late. Everyone loves Bridget. Oh, I forgot to tell you, she and Graham actually got along today when he was over. I caught them playing like real, live cousins out in the backyard. Bridge told me she was teaching him how to play Robinson Crusoe."

"That sounds like her." She yawned. "Quite the imagination."

"I should let you go to sleep."

"Morning comes early. Thanks for calling, Flynn. Good night."

"Good night, Ali. Sleep well."

Ali

FLYNN CALLED ME AT bedtime every night that week. We didn't talk about anything deep; sometimes, I only told him about what Bridget had been up to and maybe a few stories from the stand that day.

"You still like working at the stand?"

I thought about it for a moment. "I do. I know it's kind of mindless, but I like meeting new people and talking to our regulars. I think Sam and I are going to start doing some advertising—Rilla Grant's going to handle it for us."

"That's exciting. You know, Ali, what you and Sam have done with the farm is pretty incredible. When I think of the two of you, having that thrust on you as young as you were, it just blows my mind. You should be proud of it."

"I think we are. Sometimes I worry that we let it take too much priority. Last year, Sam almost lost Meghan over the farm."

Flynn made a noise of surprise. "Really? How'd that happen?"

"Oh, you know Sam. He has an overdeveloped sense of responsibility. And he thought Meghan wouldn't want to live here. She thought he didn't love her. They were a mess. I was ready to slap them both silly."

He was quiet for a heartbeat. "Sometimes people have trouble seeing what's right in front of them."

I wrapped a strand of hair around my finger. "Are we still talking about Sam and Meghan?"

"Maybe. Who else would we be talking about?"

"I have no idea."

When Saturday came around again, Flynn picked up Bridget at the farm while I worked the stand. I half-hoped that he might stop and see me again, as he'd done the week before, but when he didn't, I scolded myself for being disappointed. Expectations were not my friend. They'd only lead me down dangerous paths.

Cassie had a date that night, so I let her leave early. I'd just begun closing up, locking the register and boxing the perishables, when I heard a truck pull in the lot. Moments later, my daughter came running into the stand.

"Surprise, Mommy!"

Flynn stood at the edge of the shed, leaning against the end of the sliding door, smiling as he watched Bridget and me.

"What's this? What're you two doing here?"

"We came to take you on a picnic." Bridget tugged at my hand. "Come on, Mommy. Daddy and I made fried chicken and potato salad, and Grandma made chocolate chip cookies. We have a basket, and a blanket, and I made sweet tea all by myself."

I looked across at Flynn. His eyes were steady on me, waiting for my response. Bridget jumped up and down, still chattering.

"Well, if I'm getting kidnapped for a picnic, I'm going to need help closing up the stand. Bridget, can you cover the tables? And Flynn, can you help me move these boxes to the cooler?"

While Bridge got to work, Flynn lifted up a stack of boxes. When I tried to take one, he refused. "Nope, I got this. You just lead the way and open the cooler for me."

I held the swinging door open for him and then slid open the huge cooler. He set the boxes inside it, moving each one so that everything fit perfectly.

"So whose idea was the picnic?" I leaned back against the side of the stand, appreciating the view of Flynn's arms flexing as he lifted and his very fine ass when he bent.

He glanced at me over his shoulder. "It was mine. Is it okay? I never stopped to think you might have plans tonight." He shot me a wicked grin that just about curled my toes. "You know, like another Saturday night at The Road Block?"

I shuddered. "Not hardly. No, my Saturday nights are usually an exciting blend of eating dinner and going to bed early. Sometimes I sneak in a chapter or two whatever book I'm reading." I reached for my phone. "That reminds me, though. I need to tell Meghan I won't be there for dinner. They're probably waiting for me."

"No, they're not. Bridge and I took care of that." Flynn closed the cooler and fastened the lock for me. "Your only job is to relax and have fun. Let us take care of you for once."

With everyone working together, we were climbing into the truck a few minutes later. Bridge scrambled over the front into the tiny back seat, and Flynn handed me up into the passenger seat. I wasn't sure if he held my hand a little longer than necessary to help or if it was just my imagination.

They'd chosen a spot by the river, on the far side of the Nelson farm. We'd never paid attention to any kinds of property boundaries growing up; Alex and I ran back and forth from their family farm to mine without thinking about it. I'd always liked this particular bend in the river, which formed a protected bank. The trees shaded us from too much sun in the summer but allowed enough filtered light to keep it from being too dark in the spring or fall.

Flynn stopped the truck and helped us get out. He and Bridget spread the blanket and began to unpack the food.

"I can't believe how delicious this all looks. Did you really make it?" I picked up a wing and broke off a piece of the succulent skin.

"Yep. I'm a pretty good cook, you know. You want more than a wing, don't you?"

"Hmmm." I peered into the container. "Maybe a thigh."

"I'm a breast man myself." Flynn winked at me as he bit into the meat, and I felt my face turn pink.

We all ate until we thought we'd burst, and then Bridget asked if she could play in the water. It was a warm evening, and once I'd gotten her promise that she'd be careful, stay in the ankle-deep shallows and within view of her father and me, I gave my permission.

Flynn lay back on the blanket with groan. "I don't think I can move again for at least a week. You'll have to stand guard over me until I can get up."

I laughed. "You're on your own, buddy. I happen to know the mosquitos've started coming out, and down here they bite like a son-of-a-bitch."

He feigned shock. "Why, Miss Reynolds, such language. And in front of your child." He shook his head, tsk-tsking the whole time.

"She can't hear anything from down at the water, and she's not paying any attention to us at all. She's playing water sprite."

"Well, in that case . . ." Flynn reached for my hand and threaded his fingers through mine. "I've been waiting all evening to hold your hand."

I couldn't help my smile. "Oh, really? Well, you've shown great restraint, then."

"I'd say so." He tugged a little, throwing me off balance so that I landed on his chest, my boobs pressed against him and my hand pinned between us. "Now, this is even better."

"What're you doing, Flynn?" I swallowed, wondering if he could feel my heart pounding against him.

"I'm holding you. I'm enjoying feeling you against me. You might even say I'm canoodling with you. Isn't that what people do on picnics, after they eat? They canoodle?"

I shifted, bringing my head back just far enough that I could see him better. "I don't know. Is that what's traditional?"

He rubbed his hand in slow circles, up and down my back. "I remember being on a picnic with you, at another spot on this very river. Just the two of us. And after we ate, I undressed you. And kissed you. And touched you here." He slid his hand to cover one of my breasts. "And touched you here." The same hand shimmied lower, to cup me between my legs. "And I made you come for the first time. Do you remember that?"

My breath was coming in shallow gasps. "Of course I do."

Flynn lifted his head to whisper in my ear. "If we were alone right now, I'd do it again. I'd make you come, over and over, until all you could remember was my name and all you could feel were my fingers and my lips."

"Mommy? What're you doing?"

I jerked away from Flynn, trying to sit up, but he had a grip on my arm. "Mommy's fine, honeybunch. She's just canoodling with me." He grinned, and I was pretty sure my whole body was about to burst into flames.

"What's canoodling?" Bridget crossed her arms over her chest, one eyebrow raised in skepticism.

"It's what two people—two grown-up people—do when they like each other very much. And I like your mother very much."

My daughter shifted her stare to me. "Do you like Daddy very much, too?"

I licked my lips, and Flynn rubbed his hand on my hip. Like I needed another distraction. "I—yes, Bridget. I like your daddy very much."

She nodded. "Okay, I guess that's all right. Is it time for cookies yet?"

Flynn pushed himself to sit up, holding onto my hand all the while. "I think we can make that happen." As he reached for the basket, he lowered his voice so that only I could hear him. "Funny, I was just wishing for the taste of something . . . sweet."

I swatted his arm. "Flynn Evans, you're incorrigible."

Laughing, he brought my hand to his lips and kissed my knuckles. "Oh, I try, sweetheart. I do try."

The week after our picnic, the nightly telephone calls between Flynn and me took on a decidedly sensual tone. His game of do-you-remember tended toward very private moments we'd shared.

"Do you remember the first time you let me touch your boobs? I thought I'd died and gone to heaven. And the first time I got your bra off? I could hardly walk for a week after."

I giggled, which was something I was doing a lot lately on these calls. "Why couldn't you walk?"

"Because every time I saw you in school, if you were passing me in the hall or worse, if we were in class together, all I could see was you lying next to me, with no shirt or bra on. Instant hard-on."

I stuffed my pillow over my mouth to muffle my laughter. The last thing I needed was to explain to Sam or Bridget what was making me laugh. "Oh, God, Flynn, really?"

"Yeah, really." He sighed, long. "You have no idea how tough life is for teenaged boys."

Another night, another phone call: "Do you remember the first time *you* touched *me?* And the first time you went down on me? Oh, my God."

I smiled. "What I loved was that you and I were so open about everything. Remember? When we wanted to try something new, we talked about it. We discussed it before we did it."

"Yeah. I used to hear other guys talking about how things were with their girlfriends. No one was like us. I never said anything about you or our sex life, because I knew they'd be so jealous, they'd try to win you away from me."

"It wouldn't have worked." I brushed the hair out of my eyes. "I never wanted anyone but you, Flynn. From our first day of freshman year until . . . until graduation. There was no one else who existed for me but you."

"It was the same for me." The silence that followed was comfortable, filled with promise instead of regret. "Ali, this weekend, when Bridget's in Savannah with Sam and Meghan . . . would you have dinner with me?"

I had been hoping he would ask but telling myself not to expect it. I hugged my arms around my middle. "I would. But why don't you come here, and let me cook for you?"

He didn't answer right away, and I wondered if I'd pushed too far. After all of our conversations this week, I was so turned on that I could only think about getting him alone, recreating out some of the memories we'd been discussing. But maybe I was moving too fast. I opened my mouth to take back my offer, but Flynn spoke first.

"I don't want to push you, Ali. But I have to tell you, if I'm alone with you in a house where no one's going to be there all night . . . I can't promise I won't . . . push a little. I'm back to having trouble walking around. And my mother thinks I've developed a weird clean fetish, I've been taking so many damn cold showers. So before you ask me to dinner at your empty-all-night-house, are you sure this is what you want?"

I was about to tease, to play bashful, but I remembered what we'd both said. Being open was who we were. "Flynn, I was hoping you'd get the hint if I invited you over to my emp-ty-all-night-house. I want you. Although I'm pretty sure at this point, all you'll have to do is look at me to push me over the edge."

Flynn groaned. "Can I make it two more nights? God, Ali. I could be there in fifteen minutes. Climb up the house to your window . . ."

I laughed softly. "Sometimes anticipation is good for us. Saturday night, Flynn. I'll have to figure out what to cook for dinner. What's your pleasure?"

His answer was fast and succinct. "You."

Flynn

"HEY, MA, I'M HEADING out. See you later." I stood at the front door, calling into the kitchen.

She came into the foyer, drying her hands on a dishtowel. "Okay. Have you heard anything from Bridget? Is she having a nice time in Savannah?"

"Yeah, they got there fine—Meghan texted me—and then Maisie's mom sent Ali a picture of all the girls at the Pirate House. Looks like they're having a blast."

"Good." My mother opened her mouth as though she were about to say something and then shut it. "Well, enjoy your dinner tonight."

"I will. Oh, and uh, Mom, don't wait up. I'm pretty sure I'll just spend the night out at the farm."

Mom's lips pressed together, but she nodded. "Oh, yes, of course."

I paused, my hand on the doorknob. "Mom, do you have something you want to say to me? You look like you're about to burst."

"No, I just . . ." She sighed. "Flynn, I know you're old enough to make your own decisions. You're a father now, you've lived on your own for a long time. But I'm going to be a nibby-nose mama anyway. Are you sure you know what you're doing with Ali?"

I leaned back against the door. "Yeah, I am. I'm probably surer about this than anything else in my life." I looked up the steps, into the shadows. "Ma, I never stopped loving Ali. Never. We were young and stupid, and we made mistakes, but we've been given a second chance. I'm not going to screw it up again."

She regarded me steadily. "And it's not just because of Bridget? Because you won't be doing Ali any favors if it is. It's admirable to want to be there for the mother of your child, but be sure, Flynn."

"I thought you liked Ali. When we were dating . . . you treated her like a daughter."

"I adore Ali. I always have. And if you truly love her, Flynn, no one will be happier for you than me. Your father . . ." She paused, shut her eyes for a minute and crossed herself. "God rest his soul. He always told me you and Ali were going to end up back together. He loved that girl, and it hurt him that we were estranged. We never stopped liking her, sweetie, but we didn't want to interfere with her life after you left."

"I never want to lose her again, Mom. I'm going to do everything in my power to make sure I won't."

My mother nodded. "What're you going to do about work, Flynn? I know you've been turning down jobs. But pretty soon, you'll need to do something."

I rubbed my hand over my chin. "I know. I've been hoping for a shoot to come along close by, where I could go do it and be back in a day. Even DC would be doable. But everything I've been offered has been overseas. I don't know what to do."

She patted my shoulder. "You could always teach photography at the high school. Think what you could offer those kids."

The idea of teaching in Burton unleashed a torrent of dread in my chest. As long as I focused on Ali and Bridget, staying in Burton was fine. But when I began contemplating taking a job, becoming part of the community . . . it felt like I had a heavy weight around my heart.

"It's something to think about. I gotta run, Mom. Ali's cooking, and I don't want to ruin her dinner."

"Of course, sweetie. Run along. Oh, and why don't you plan to bring both Bridget and Ali to Sunday dinner tomorrow?"

I leaned to kiss my mother's cheek. "You're pretty awesome, you know that, Cory Evans?"

She smacked my backside. "Get out of here, you. Behave yourself."

"Never." I waved at her and closed the door behind me, climbed into my truck and aimed it for the highway. I couldn't get to Ali fast enough.

The ride out to the farm seemed to take three times as long as it normally did. I was unreasonably nervous, my leg bouncing up and down as I cruised down the road. I hadn't even been this keyed up the first time we'd had sex. Of course, then I'd had no time to be nervous.

Ali and I had stuck to our promise to talk about everything when it came to our physical relationship. Although we hadn't taken the final step to actual intercourse yet, by the early spring of our junior year, we'd done pretty much everything else. I'd given Ali her first orgasm, and then she'd given me my first hand job—by someone who was not me, of course. We'd ventured into oral sex, although I'd never expected Ali to take to it so enthusiastically. She was open to trying almost anything, and I was diligent about finding new things for us to try. It wasn't exactly a hardship.

We had more freedom than many of our friends, because Sam was so consumed with the farm and the stand that he couldn't be around to keep his eye on us all the time, or even very often. We spent lazy afternoons next to the lake or down at the river, and when we could, we took advantage of her empty house and her bed.

On the first truly warm evening of that spring, we'd gone to our favorite spot by the lake. We'd long since abandoned the car for a blanket on the grass, and after a particularly chilly winter had confined us to her porch and a few heated sessions in the front seat of my car, I was more than anxious to be out on that blanket with Ali.

We made short work of our clothes, and I was raised over her body, kissing the slope of her breast. She clutched the back of my head when I moved to take one taut pink nipple between my teeth. At the same time, I slipped two of my fingers between her legs, groaning when I felt how wet she was.

"God, babe, you feel so good."

Her hips pistoned against my hand, and her small fingers captured my cock, which was the best feeling in the world ever. I caught my breath and growled.

"Flynn." Her whisper floated down to tickle against my ear.

"Yeah, babe." I was focused on not coming too soon, trying to hold back.

"Don't stop."

"I won't. Wait, don't stop what? You mean here . . ." I

swirled my tongue around her nipple. "Or here?" I rubbed my thumb over her clit, expecting her to tell me both.

"I mean, don't stop. Let's not stop tonight. I want you . . . inside me. I don't want to wait anymore."

My heart stuttered, and I pushed up to look at her face. "What? You want . . . tonight? Now?"

"Yes." She curled her hand around my dick and moved them up and down. "Now. Tonight. Please." She hesitated, opening her eyes to meet mine. "Oh, damn, do you have . . . you know? A condom."

"Yeah." I rolled to the side and brushed my hand over her flat stomach. "I've kept a package in the glove box of my car since we started talking about it." I stood, still nude, and leaned in through the open car window to fumble with the box. I managed to get one in my hands and went back to lie down again.

Ali tilted her head back and touched her lips to mine. "Are you okay with this? I mean, we don't have to if you don't think . . ."

"Oh, my God, babe. No. I mean, yes. Yes. I'm ready and I'm okay with it. As long as you are."

"I love you, Flynn. I want to be with you, all the way."

I brushed her hair out of her face. "I love you, Ali. All the way." I slid my hand back down her side and between her legs.

"What are you doing?" She sucked in a breath as I circled my thumb over her clit. "Aren't you going to—aren't we—"

"It'll be better for you if you come this way first. I want to make it as good for you as possible. If you come before I enter you . . . it might not hurt as much. Or so I read." I slipped two fingers inside her, stroking the spot on her inner walls that made her go wild. She arched her back, her breath coming in short gasps, and then I pressed my thumb over the small bundle of nerves and brought my mouth to her nipple. Ali tensed, her hips raised as her fingers dug into my back.

"Flynn . . . oh, my God, Flynn. Oh, God." She fell back

onto the blanket as I stroked her down from the orgasm. "That was incredible."

"You're incredible." I kissed down her neck. "You're the sexiest, most beautiful woman in the world, Ali. Do you know that?"

"Flynn." She reached back between my legs. "Please. Make love to me."

I knelt up and ripped open the condom package. With hands that weren't quite steady, I rolled the rubber over me for the first time in a situation of real need. I'd practiced putting one on before in the privacy of my own room, but this was a whole different deal. Ali leaned up on her elbows, watching me, which somehow made it even hotter.

"Are you sure?" I needed to ask again, to make sure she knew she could change her mind any time.

"Flynn, I'm so sure, I'm about to roll you onto your back and take you myself."

I choked on a laugh. "Okay, I get it." I held her face and lowered my lips to hers. "I just want you to know, Ali, that I love you, and I'll never leave you. As long as I live."

She wrapped her arms around my back. "As long as I live."

I positioned myself between her thighs. I'd listened to enough guys in locker rooms and read enough stuff on line to realize that taking a girl's virginity was a dicey business. It might hurt her. She might cry. She might bleed. I was going to do my best to make it good for her. But she was taking my V-card too, so we were all newbies here.

I balanced on one arm and with the other hand, I rubbed the head of my cock over her slick folds. Ali hummed, kneading her hands into my back. When I felt like I was going to explode if I didn't do something, I entered her, just a little.

"Are you okay?" I gritted my teeth, trying to keep from going too fast.

"Yes, I'm good. It just burns a little—but it's good. Don't

hold back." She tilted her hips up, and on instinct I could no longer deny, I plunged into her.

For a moment, I couldn't think of anything except *Oh. My. God.* The sensation was the most incredible thing I'd ever felt in my life. Tight, slippery heat surrounded me, and I never wanted it to end.

Then Ali hooked her legs around my hips, trying to bring me even closer. "Flynn, more. It feels so good."

"I'm afraid I'll hurt you." I clenched my jaw.

"You're not going to hurt me. Please. Faster."

I didn't need to be told twice. I stroked into her, moving with more force and intent. Ali's breath began to quicken, and I could feel how close I was to the edge. "Ali, babe, I'm going to come. I'm sorry, I can't hold back anymore. God, I'm going to come." I pushed into her one last time and then my entire body was quivering as I came, harder than I ever had.

I knew Ali hadn't come again, and once I could breathe, I slipped my hand between us and found her clit. Pulsing in and out of her in shallow thrusts, I pressed my fingers to her in tight circles until she cried out my name as her body convulsed around me. It was the most amazing thing I'd ever felt.

I fell onto the blanket next to her, pulling her to the side with me. "God, Ali, I love you." I stroked her hair back. "Are you okay?"

"I am so far beyond okay that it should probably be illegal." She grinned at me with sleepy eyes. "Thank you, Flynn."

"*You're* thanking *me?*" I snorted. "Ali, you blow my mind. I can't believe we did this. It was . . . amazing."

"Do you think it's always this way? I mean, you and I don't have any comparisons."

"Does it matter? I don't want any comparisons. I only want you."

Ali framed my face with her hands. "Now and forever." She pulled my lips down to cover hers, and I was lost again.

We'd had a little over a year together after the first night, and we'd made love countless times. But that night never left my mind, and wherever I was in the world, if the air had a certain softness and the scent of lilacs, I was transported back to a river bank in Georgia.

"Oh, my God, Ali, that was fabulous." I leaned back in my chair, stretching. "When did you become such a great cook?"

She laughed. "It happens when you're the one doing it all. I'm glad you enjoyed the chicken, though. It was one of my mother's recipes. One of her favorites."

I watched as she moved across the kitchen, carrying plates to the sink. I'd asked her to wear the same dress that she'd worn to The Road Block two weeks ago, and now I was cursing myself, because seeing her ass moving under the flowered cotton was about to kill me.

She returned to the table and leaned her hands down, pressing her arms against her sides and throwing her tits into prominence. When she bent at the waist to look me in the eye, I could see down the low-cut neckline to the tops of her luscious boobs. I couldn't look away.

"Flynn?" Ali was speaking to me, a smile playing around her lips and one eyebrow quirked at me. "I said, do you want dessert now, or later?"

I raised my eyes to hers with no small effort. "If you're dessert, I want it now."

She cocked her head. "I made chocolate cake."

I reached for her hand and laced our fingers together. "You now, chocolate cake later."

"That sounds like a good plan." Ali moved around the table to stand next to me. She bit the corner of her lip, and I felt some of my earlier nerves coming back.

"Hey." I traced her mouth with my finger. "It's just me. Are you freaking out?"

She closed her eyes and blew out a breath. "I am. I know it's crazy, but I'm nervous. All week, I couldn't wait for tonight. I've been so . . . so damned keyed up, wanting you, but now that you're here in person, I'm second-guessing everything."

"Come here." I pulled her down onto my lap. "Ali, it's me. It's us. We lost our virginity together. Or rather, we gave it to each other."

"I know." She toyed with the collar of my shirt, and the slightest brush of her fingers against my skin was setting me on fire. "But since then . . . a lot has happened. A lot has changed."

"The important things haven't changed." I hadn't planned to say this yet. I didn't want to ruin anything by jumping the gun. But maybe it was essential to say it first. "Ali, I love you. I've loved you since we were fourteen, and I'm pretty sure I'm going to love you until I'm a hundred and fourteen. Probably longer. So no matter what's happened or changed in the last nine years, that hasn't. And it won't."

"Flynn." Ali pressed her forehead against mine. "I want to tell you I feel the same way. I do. But I'm still so afraid."

"Don't be afraid. I was an idiot to leave you before, and I'm not going to do it again."

She nodded. "I believe you. I want to. But it's more than that. I'm worried about . . . not being good enough."

I would've laughed if I couldn't have seen how serious she was. "Why the hell would you think that?"

Her throat worked. "First, because I haven't been with any man for a very, very long time. I told you Craig and I had . . . trouble. I couldn't stand to have him touch me. We only were together twice. Once before Bridget was born, when I was pregnant, and then after. I think he thought—hoped—it was just the pregnancy that made it so awkward the first time. So when the doctor gave me the green light after I had Bridge, Craig really tried. He set up this romantic night, plied me with lots of wine and was so patient. It was okay during, for him at least, but after, I couldn't stop crying." She sighed. "I'm pretty sure that's when he decided to leave."

My heart ached for her. "And no one else, Ali? In all that time?"

She flushed. "Men weren't exactly knocking down the door, and I didn't have any time to go find them. No, no one else." She linked her hands behind my neck. "I didn't want anyone. Not until you came back to town."

I smiled. "That's not something to be nervous about, babe. I know it makes me sound like a huge chauvinist pig, but I'm glad you weren't with other guys. You've been mine for a long time. I like that."

"And that's the second thing that worries me. You've been with other women." She said it definitively. "They've probably been . . . experienced. I'm not. What if you realize I'm a letdown?"

"Ali, no way." I exhaled. "I'm not going to lie to you. Yeah, I've slept with other women. But you need to know . . . I didn't have sex with anyone else until after you married Craig. One night, a few weeks after, I got ripping drunk, and I slept with a girl I'd met at the office where I worked. It didn't mean anything. She knew it and so did I." I lifted my shoulders. "Other than that, yeah, there've been women here or there. Not as many as you probably think. No relationships. Just nights when I couldn't stand to be alone anymore."

Ali nodded, but her eyes were fastened on my chest. "I didn't think you were a monk. It still makes me feel like I might be inadequate." She tightened her hands behind my neck. "And I'm scared . . . because I don't have the same body I did ten years ago. I had a baby, Flynn. And I'm not seventeen anymore. What if my body disgusts you?"

I couldn't help it. I dropped my head back and laughed.

"You're insane, you know that, right? Your body? Didn't you hear what I told you the other night, on the phone? Seeing you makes me hard. You're fucking perfect, babe. I promise." I paused, thinking for a minute. "I have an idea. You game to try something?"

Interest sparked in her eyes. "Like what?"

"You said you were getting turned on when we were talking on the phone. Go up to your room. Take your phone. I'll call you from down here, and we'll . . . talk. And then when you're ready for me to come upstairs, I'll be there faster than you can say the words."

She giggled, but I could see the prospective intrigued her. "Really? Isn't that kind of silly?"

"Hey." I tilted her chin with one finger. "Nothing's silly when it comes to you and me. Remember, we talk about everything. And we work through it together. So get your phone and go up. Oh, but first . . ." I slid my arms around her waist and drew her closer to me. "First, I'm going to kiss you. If nothing else happens tonight, I've been waiting and wanting to kiss you for weeks. That's happening."

Before she could respond, I pulled her to me and angled my mouth over her lips. I started soft, with just a touch, but the moment we connected, desire surged. I coaxed her mouth open and trailed my tongue over hers and around her inner lips. Ali moaned a little, just a low sound, but it drove me freaking crazy. I wanted her now, spread open and begging for me.

But I could feel that she was still nervous. Still tentative. So reluctantly I leaned back and pushed her off my lap, my hands gentle on her hips. "If you don't go upstairs now, I'm going to forget why I'm sending you there." I gave her a light swat on the ass. "Hurry up before you miss my call."

Ali grabbed her phone from the counter and sprinted up the steps. I gave her a few seconds to get settled on her bed before I called her.

"Hi, Flynn." Her voice was low, like it was every night when I called her. I settled back in my chair.

"Hey, Ali. Everything okay there?" It was how I started out every conversation with her.

"Yes, everything's fine." She paused, and I figured she was waiting for me to bring up a do-you-remember, as I usually did. But before I could think of what I wanted to say, she spoke again. "Do you remember the last time we made love?"

I closed my eyes. *Hell, yeah, I remembered it.* "I do. We were down at the lake again. It was the night before graduation. And we went skinny-dipping that night, because it was so hot."

"You chased me into the water, and I thought we were just going to cool off and then get out. But you caught me after I surfaced from going under, and you pulled me close, and I could feel how . . . aroused you were. And you looked at me, and without either of us saying a word, I wrapped my legs around your hips, and you entered me. We didn't say anything. There wasn't any sound but the slosh of the water around us, and when I started to come, you did, too. I had one of the most intense orgasms I'd ever had."

My cock pulsed between my legs, and I was having trouble breathing. "Yeah. And then I carried you out of the water, still inside you, and we laid down on the blanket, and just . . . touched each other until I was hard again. I rolled us over so you were on top, and you rode me. Your tits were gorgeous, right in my face, and I leaned up to suck your nipple. You told me to do it hard. You ground down on me and started to come. And I—"

"Flynn." Her voice sounded strangled. "Flynn, come up here. Come up here and make love to me. I want you."

I dropped my phone and took the steps two at a time. Ali's door was open, and she lay on her bed, her dress hiked up just enough that I could see she wasn't wearing any underwear.

"Ali. Holy shit." I dropped to my knees next to her bed and

wrapped my arms around her, kissing her open-mouthed and hard. "God, I want you. I want to take you so hard, babe."

"Yes." She buried her fingers in my hair. "I need you right now. I'm on fire for you, Flynn. I want you inside me. Now."

"In a minute. First . . ." I grabbed her leg, moving her so that she lay crossways on the bed. I ducked between her thighs and then tugged down so that my mouth was at her core. "First, I'm going to blow you away."

I covered her with my mouth, teasing with my tongue. Ali cried out, arching toward me. She was already so wet, and I knew she was on the verge of coming. I sucked lightly on her clit and then speared my tongue into her.

"Come for me, babe. Come right now."

"God, Flynn! Oh God oh God oh God . . ." And then she was coming apart around me, her fingers clutching me to her as her sex spasmed.

I pulled back and stood up, shedding my shirt and pants as fast as I could. My cock was aching with the need to be inside her.

"Do I need a condom?" I ground out the words as I hovered over her.

Ali shook her head. "I've been on the pill since I had Bridget. I'm fine. If you are."

"Oh, thank God. I'm clean, I promise. I've been checked out. I brought some, but I left them in the car. Don't think I could wait that long." I looked down at her, disheveled and flushed, her lips swollen and red. She was the sexiest woman I'd ever seen, and I loved her more than I loved my own life.

"Ali, take off your dress." I'd been crazy to get inside her, and I still was, but more than that, I wanted to savor this moment. I helped her lean up and pulled the cotton material over her head. As I tossed it to the side, she reached behind her and unhooked her bra, releasing her tits. Oh, my God, Ali's tits. I palmed them, letting my thumbs rub over her nipples before I lowered my mouth to take one between my lips. I sucked, hard, the way I remembered she liked, and I was rewarded with a moan.

Her hands wandered down, seeking, until she had her fingers around my cock. For a moment, she explored me, circling one finger around the head and then gripped the base. She stroked me, driving me back into a frenzy.

"I can't wait." I growled into her ear. "Next time, slow. This time, now. Fast. Hard."

"Yes." She guided me to her entrance and arched her hips as I drove into her. "Faster. Harder."

"God, babe, you're so tight. So fucking perfect." I plunged harder, feeling the build of an orgasm that I'd been working up to for weeks.

Ali cried out my name, her nails digging into my arms as she came. Her channel clenched around me, pushing me over the edge into my own insanity. I ground out her name as I came deep within her.

It took a few minutes before I could manage regular breathing again. I rolled onto my back, and Ali curled her body against me. She reached to the foot of the bed and pulled a light blanket over us.

I stroked her hair, lost in the quiet of a moment I thought I'd never experience again. My heart was still thumping against my rib cage.

"Flynn." Ali spoke into the silence. "I love you. I'm still scared. But I love you. I never stopped. And I never will."

"Don't be scared. Or if you have to be scared, we'll be scared together. Okay?"

She smiled. "That works."

I closed my eyes, listening to the sound of Ali's breathing. I let my hands wander over her skin, reveling in the softness.

Ali traced one finger over my chest, touching one side. "What's this?" She sounded curious, and I grinned.

"Are you checking out my ink, babe?" I covered her hand with mine, squeezing before I let her go.

"Have you had it long?" She rested her chin on my chest, and her hair tickled my stomach.

"About five years, I guess. I spent three months in Jerusalem on assignment, and it really affected me. There's so much beauty, and so much history, but so much hate, too. Violence."

"What does it mean? The last word is peace, I know, but what are the other two?"

I turned my head to suck her earlobe into my mouth. "They all say peace. The top is in Hebrew, the middle is Arabic, and then as you said, the bottom is English. It's a trilingual word-mark."

"Very cool." She shivered when I darted out my tongue to tickle her ear again. "You've been all over the world. Just like you always wanted."

"How do you know?"

The ghost of a smile flitted over her lips. "I followed you via the internet. It was like rubbing salt in a wound sometimes, but I got to see where you were."

"I've been very lucky. But you want to know a secret?" I threaded my fingers through her hair and twisted the heavy length around my hand.

"Of course. I want to know all your secrets." She smirked.

"And so you shall." I put on a deep, accented voice. "But this one first. I did travel the world. But you did, too."

Her brow wrinkled. "What do you mean?"

"I mean that everywhere I went, I saw you there. I pictured you on the green hills of Ireland. On the snowy plains of the Ukraine. In the slopes of the Alps. In the gondolas of Venice. In front of the Kremlin. On the Temple Mound. I'd take a picture, and then I'd turn and catch you out of the corner of my eye. Just beyond my sight. I never went anywhere that I didn't see you, Ali. You were with me all the time."

Her brown eyes filled with tears that overflowed and landed on my chest. "Flynn, that's the most beautiful thing I've ever heard. And you have no idea how much that means to me."

I trailed one hand down her spine to her perfect ass. "Does it mean enough for you to go downstairs and bring us some chocolate cake?"

She rolled her eyes. "Why don't we just go downstairs and eat it at the table, like civilized folk?"

"Because." I rolled her under me again and sucked lightly on her neck. "If you bring it up here, I can eat it off your boobs. And your stomach. And your—"

"Okay, okay." She wriggled out from under my body. "You convinced me." She pulled the blanket off me and wrapped it around her, tucking it beneath her arms. "But only if I get to eat the vanilla ice cream off you."

"Oh, baby. It's a deal."

Ali

I WOKE UP SUNDAY morning with Flynn's hand on my breast, his cock at my back and the lingering scent of chocolate in the air. I smiled. I couldn't think of a better way to begin a day.

Turning in his arms, I wriggled downward until I was eye-to-eye with his morning wood. Since I was going for the element of surprise, I didn't touch him until I took him into my mouth.

Flynn groaned, and his hands groped for my head. "Ali?" His voice was groggy with sleep.

"I should hope so." I licked around the head, holding him in one hand. "If you're going to wake up with your dick in someone's mouth, it better be mine."

"My sentiments exactly. Fuck, Ali. Aw, fuck. You're killing me."

"Not yet." I bobbed my head up and down, sucking lightly. When his breath had turned to strangled gasps, I sat up, positioned myself over him and sank down, taking him completely inside me.

"Oh, my God, Ali. Yeah. Ride me. Ride me hard."

I lifted up until he was nearly out of me, and then plunged down again. He was close, and so was I. I undulated my hips, taking him as deep as I could.

"Ali—babe—touch yourself. Let me see you make yourself come."

"Like this?" I brought my fingers to my boobs, pinching my nipples. The sensation shot straight to my center.

"Yeah. Like that. Now your pussy. Touch your pussy."

I kept my eyes on Flynn's as I slid my fingers between my legs. I was already so close, and feeling my own wetness at the spot where our bodies joined pushed me over the edge.

I gasped out his name as I came. Flynn grasped my hips and arched into me, his body tensing as he found his own release. I collapsed onto his chest, still panting.

"That's about the nicest way to wake up ever." Flynn's breath caressed my ear. "Can I sign up for that every day?"

I smiled. "It might be a little bit of a hardship for me to get over to your house every morning. And your mom might object, too."

He stroked my spine. "What if you didn't have to go that far? What if . . . we were all in the same house, you and Bridge and me?"

I stilled. I wanted what he was saying. I wanted it to be reality. At the same time, it still terrified me.

"Hmmm." I kissed the edge of the tattoo over his heart. "That's something to think about."

"That doesn't sound very enthusiastic." He was teasing,

but I was afraid I heard hurt in his voice.

"I want that, Flynn. But we need to move slowly. We need to ease into this, into the new idea of us."

"Because of Bridget?"

"Partly. And because of me, too. I just need a little time."

He studied me, his eyes unreadable. "We've been together twelve years, Ali."

"No, we were together four years, nine years ago. The past is our foundation, but we need to build something on it."

He sighed. "You're probably right. I just—I'm ready for us to be a family. I want to wake up next to you every morning. I want Bridget to come jump in bed with us. I want to snuggle with you on the sofa after she goes to bed at night." He skimmed his lips up my neck. "I want to make love to you every night. And I want to make more babies with you. I want to see you pregnant, and be there for all the morning sickness and late-night cravings. I want to be in the room when you give birth."

I was crying again. What the hell was the matter with me? Flynn was offering me everything I'd ever wanted. All I had to do was reach out and grab it. Why was I dragging my feet?

"I want all that, too." I sniffled against his chest. "Just give me a little bit of time to catch up with you, okay?"

"As long as you need, babe." He wiped the tears from my face. "Now let me get some clothes on. I'm going to make you breakfast."

"Speaking of babies." Flynn set down his fork and took a sip of coffee.

"Were we? Speaking of babies?" I nibbled on a strip of bacon. "I don't remember."

"Yes, we were talking about the six babies we're going to

have, bringing our grand total to seven kids."

"Holy shit. Just who do you think is going to pop all these kids out?"

"You're the only person who's ever going to have my babies, sweetheart. I'm willing to negotiate on the number, by the way. But I'd like to have one son, if we can. I want to name him after my dad."

"Oh, Flynn." I reached across the table to squeeze his hand. "Of course. I mean, I can't promise the son part. That's your job. But I'd love to name our hypothetical potential son after your father. I loved him. I wish he'd known Bridget."

"Me, too." He studied our joined hands for a minute. "That's not really what I was going to say, though, when I brought up babies. I keep meaning to ask you why you named our daughter Bridget."

I leaned back and sighed. "I didn't plan to do it. I was going to name her Elizabeth, after my mom. And then the day she was born . . ." I swallowed hard. "It was an awful day. My labor wasn't that bad, but it was all just so wrong. Craig was there with me, but I only wanted you." I looked up at him. "After she was born, I just cried. I couldn't stop. They laid this perfect little angel in my arms, and I could only think how terrible it was that you weren't with us. So when they asked what we were naming her, I remembered you talking once about wanting to name your daughter after your grandmother. The next thing I knew, I had a baby named Bridget Elizabeth, and Craig was so mad. He stormed out of the hospital and went out drinking. If Alex hadn't been there with me, I don't know what I would've done."

"I'm sorry, babe." He rubbed his thumb over my knuckles. "I promise, the next time you have a baby, I'll be right by your side. We'll get through it together." He smiled. "But thank you for naming her after my grandmother. I hate that I missed so much with Bridget. At least I feel like I was part of her naming."

"There was never a time I didn't think about you and wish you were there. You know what you said about me being around the world with you? I guess in a way I kept you here with me. I could never quite convince my heart to give you up."

"I hope you never do." He kissed my fingers. "Now, tell me something. How do you feel about shower sex?"

For the next few weeks, I was happier than I'd ever been in my life.

Flynn and I fell into a routine of sorts. On Saturdays, he and Bridget picked me up at the stand after closing, and the three of us went out on a family date. We went bowling or to the diner for ice cream. I loved those evenings when it was just the three of us, learning to be a family.

The only bad part of the evening was when Flynn dropped me at the farm and took Bridget back into town to spend the night at his mom's. He'd suggested that I come for a sleepover, too, but I wasn't quite comfortable enough to sleep with him at his mother's house. So I had to kiss them both good night and go inside to my own lonely bed.

I drove in for Sunday dinners at the Evans' house each Sunday afternoon, after which Bridget came home with me. She still spent Tuesday nights with Flynn, too; he picked her up after school and dropped her off in the morning.

"Ali, this is crazy." Flynn was exasperated. "We're adults who have a child. We're in love. And we never see each other."

"That's not exactly true," I countered. "I saw a lot of you on Thursday." Flynn had come over to the house while Sam was out in the field, and I'd done the unthinkable by closing the stand for two hours in the middle of the day. Two hours in bed with Flynn was worth the risk of Sam finding out and yelling at me for potential lost business.

"I want to see you first thing in the morning and last thing at night, Ali. Not just for stolen sex hours."

"Okay, Flynn. I get it. Me, too. But there're a lot of complicated things to work out. I need to figure out how to balance my commitment to the farm and Sam with my commitment to you. And you still need to figure out what you're going to do with the rest of your life."

He sighed. "I know. I'm just . . . ready for the rest of my life to begin."

"Still no local shoots coming up?"

"Nope. I got a call this morning about one in Madagascar."

"Madagascar." I tried to sound enthusiastic. "That's . . . far."

"Yeah, I know." He was quiet for a minute. "Ali, stop freaking out. I can feel you doing it all the way from here."

"I am not."

"Yes, you are. Every time I tell you about a possible shoot, you quietly melt down. Until I tell you I'm not taking it. Don't you trust me yet?"

"Of course I do. I'm just still . . . figuring it all out. Now tell me what you and Bridge did today."

"What is it exactly that you're figuring out?" Meghan asked me the question as she and I sat on the porch on Friday night after Bridget had gone to bed. I'd just related to her my latest conversation with Flynn.

I shrugged. "Life. Life with Flynn. Where we should live, what he should do . . . he loves his job, Meghan. It's killing him each time he turns down a shoot. He says no, but I see it."

"And he can't get anything that would let him live here?"

I snorted. "You might have noticed, Burton's not exactly the cosmopolitan center of the world. He's talked about trying to find a magazine or paper that would let him shoot just in the south, but even so, he'd be traveling most of the time. I'm selfish, Meghan. I want it all. If I'm going to live with Flynn, I want to be with him, not just be a stop for when he's between jobs."

"Why doesn't he move in with us at the farm for the time being? Sam wouldn't care, and then Bridget doesn't have to adjust to a new place."

"Well, it's a thought. But we're going to need our own place, and I'd rather start in a place that belongs to *us,* you know?"

"Yeah, I get it." Meghan patted my arm. "Well, hang in there, sweetie. It'll work out."

My phone buzzed with a text, and I smiled when I saw Flynn's name. Meghan poked my arm. "Is that lover boy now?"

"It just might be." I touched the button to read the text as Meghan returned to her book.

Can I come over?

I frowned. We hadn't made any plans for tonight, and Flynn rarely just popped in.

Sure. Everything okay?

His reply was swift. *Yeah. Be there in 20.*

"Everything all right?" Meghan looked up from her book.

"I think so. Flynn's coming over."

She wiggled her eyebrows. "Oooh la la!"

I rolled my eyes. "I don't think so. I just . . . I hope nothing's wrong."

"What would be wrong?"

"I don't know. Just a feeling."

For the next twenty minutes, I fidgeted, pushing the swing back and forth with the toe of my shoe until Meghan shot me an exasperated look. When Flynn's truck finally came bouncing down the driveway, I jumped up and ran to meet him in the back.

"Hey." He slammed his truck door and held open his arms. "How's my best girl?"

I wrapped my arms around his waist and lifted my face for

a kiss. "Happy to see you." I slid my hand down to take his and tugged him toward the house.

"I was thinking we could take a walk. Maybe go sit by the lake."

I quirked an eyebrow. "Oh, is this *that* kind of visit? You should've given me some warning. I would've shaved my legs."

He smiled. "Not that unshaved legs would ever slow me down, but no. I just want to talk."

"Okay." We walked around the barn to the path that led into the woods. It was dark, but I knew the way without light. I'd been walking it as long as I could remember. Flynn swung our hands between as we meandered.

"I got a call today about a job." He spoke hesitantly, and my heart plunged into my stomach. *This was it.* This was what I'd been afraid of since Flynn had come back to town. He was leaving me again.

I tried to quell my fears. Flynn wouldn't just run off again. This was different. We were different. "Where is it?" Somehow I kept the tremor out of my voice.

"It's more than just a shoot. The job's with World Wide News, a monthly magazine out of New York. They're looking for someone to take the permanent position of photo editor for the US."

I nodded. "What does that mean, exactly?"

"It'd mean a job, not just free-lancing. Most of it would be assigning shoots to the staff and then working out what we use, what makes it to the magazine's website and what makes it to the hard copy. That's all office work, so I'd have pretty regular hours when I was in New York. But I'd have my choice of one assignment of my own a month, which would give us the chance to travel—but just one week every month." He looked down at me, and for the first time, I saw the excitement in his eyes. "This is a big deal, Ali. I've never looked for a job with just one publication, because I liked the variety of taking whatever assignment came up when I wanted it. It fit me. But now I want something steadier."

"Uh huh." I didn't trust myself to form actual words yet.

"I was thinking, what if we homeschooled Bridget? We could all travel together to wherever I had to go. Wouldn't that be amazing?" He stopped walking and pulled me to him. "Think of all those places we could see together. We wouldn't have to be apart at all."

"But what about . . . home? We'd be so far away."

Flynn smoothed back my hair. "Yeah, we'd have to be in New York, since I'd be working out of their offices. I know it's a long way, but there're flights directly from there to Savannah. We could come back and visit as much as we wanted. And the opportunity . . . Ali. You could do whatever you wanted. You could write, like you talked about when we were in high school. Or you could go to school. You'd have all the museums in the city, and the chance to travel wherever we wanted."

My mind was reeling. Everything I'd been afraid of was happening right now, and I was having a horrible feeling of having been in this place before. If I said no, would he leave me again?

"Flynn, what about the farm? And the stand? I can't just up and leave Sam without any help, and he can't afford to hire someone yet."

Flynn raked his hand through his hair. "Ali, don't do this. Don't start looking for reasons why this won't work. Give it a chance. Let's talk about it, like reasonable adults."

That stung. "Maybe I *am* being the reasonable adult in this case, Flynn. I'm the one who has to figure out how all your big ideas would actually work out. Homeschool Bridget? Guess who'd be doing that? And who'd be dealing with her when we pull her away from the grandma she just got, plus the place she's lived her whole life and the people she loves?"

"I'm not asking you to leave town tomorrow, Ali. I'm asking you to at least consider the possibility."

"I don't want to consider it. So if this is what you're planning to do, just do it. Just go and leave us, like I always knew you would." The inevitable tears were coming.

"Ali, no." He grabbed me by the upper arms. "I'm not leaving. Not without you and Bridge. Understand that. I don't care if my dream job's dropped in my lap—if you're not on board, neither am I. You come first. You are my priority. I told you I wouldn't leave you again, and I won't. Trust that. Trust me."

I buried my face in his chest. "Trust hurts. I can't do that again, Flynn. I can't live through losing you again. Please don't leave me."

"Shhh, baby. I'm not. I promise."

We stood clinging to each other in the dark of the woods until my sobs subsided. Flynn stroked my back and kissed my temple, but my stomach still clenched. I believed him when he said he wasn't going to leave me. But knowing I was the reason he was going to lose this opportunity worried me. This was why I hadn't told him about being pregnant with Bridget. I loved him too much to stand in his way. I wasn't sure I could be brave enough to do that a second time.

I walked Flynn to his truck, and he framed my face with his hands. "We'll talk more tomorrow. But no worries, okay? We'll figure it out. Sleep well, babe. I love you."

I watched his truck until the tail lights disappeared around the bend. I knew I should've felt comforted that Flynn had chosen me this time. But instead, I felt as though I'd destroyed his dream. Again.

When I went inside, Sam was sitting at the kitchen table with a mug. He looked up and smiled as I came in. "Hey. Didn't expect you back so soon. I thought you and Flynn were heading down to the river."

I sat down across from him and shook my head. "No. He just wanted to talk about something. He just left. What are you doing up?"

He shrugged. "Couldn't sleep. Meghan conked out, but my mind wouldn't shut off." Sam cocked his head. "Everything okay with you?"

I folded my arms on the table and laid down my head. "I don't know. Probably not." I took a deep breath. "Flynn was offered a job in New York with a news magazine. It would mean some travel, but Bridge and I could go with him. But we'd have to live in New York."

"Hmmm." Sam nodded.

"What do you mean, hmmm? You know I can't do that. I can't move to New York."

"Why not?"

I stared at my brother, my mouth open. "Why not? Well, let's see. There's the farm. The stand. You and Meghan. Bridget's home and stability. I think that's a good start."

"Okay. And if you take all those things and weigh them against being with Flynn and thinking about his happiness, what do you see?"

"It doesn't work that way, Sam. I love Flynn. I'm in love with him. I want to marry him and raise kids together. I don't think I can live without him. But how do I choose that over the people who count on me? On the commitments I've made?"

He took my hand. "Last year, after Meghan left the farm and went back down to Florida and I thought I'd never see her again, I did a lot of heavy thinking. You know this farm is important to me. And you and Bridge—well, you're my family. I love you. But I had to decide what—or who—I couldn't live without. And that was Meghan. When I went down to Florida, I told her we could live wherever she wanted, as long we could do it together. I'm so glad she chose the farm, and that she loves it like we do. But if she hadn't, Ali, I would've given it up for her. It doesn't mean I love you less. But Meghan's my life."

"I know," I whispered. "But what would you do if Bridge

and I moved to New York? How would you manage the farm? I don't want to crush your dream anymore than I want to destroy Flynn's, and I know yours is this farm."

"Ali." Sam tilted my chin up so I had to look him in the eye. "You remember Mom and Dad, right?"

"Of course I do."

"They were crazy in love. If someone had told them they had to give up one another in exchange for the keeping the farm, what would they've done?"

I closed my eyes. "They'd have given up the farm."

"Yep. Nine years ago, you sacrificed your own happiness for me. For this farm and the vision I have for it. Never think I don't appreciate that, Ali. I'd have told you not to do it, but from the perspective of it being a done deal, I'm grateful. But now, I'm telling you, it's your time. It's your turn to grab your own chance at happiness. It doesn't come around very often. You're so lucky that you're getting a second chance." He squeezed my hand. "Don't fuck it up."

I blinked back more tears. "I'm scared, Sam. What if I take a chance and it's not the right thing to do?"

"Trust your heart, Ali. And trust that boy. I think he's a keeper. Take a chance." He stood up, stretching. "Now I'm going to bed before Meghan wakes up and thinks I've fallen asleep down here. Good night."

"Good night, Sam. I love you."

"Love you, too, little sister."

Flynn

"**H**EY, YOU COMING DOWNSTAIRS for pancakes?" My sister stuck her head in the door of my bedroom. "Mom made your favorites. Ricotta with lemon peel."

"Yeah, I'll be right down." I waited for Reenie's footsteps to echo down the stairs before I got up, pulled on shorts and followed her down.

"Good morning, sunshine." Mom set a mug of coffee at my place. "Was I imagining things, or did you go out late last night? I could've sworn I heard the truck."

"You weren't imagining anything. I went out to the farm to see Ali."

I didn't miss the look my mother and my sister exchanged.

"Everything all right?"

"Yeah. No. I don't know." I leaned on my hand. "I got a job offer yesterday. For World Wide News, in New York. It's a full-time, permanent position, and we'd have to move up there."

There was silence at the table. "Well, Flynn, congratulations." My mother's smile was forced. "What did Ali say about it?"

"Ali . . . freaked out. I had a few ideas about how we could make it work, but she wasn't willing to listen to them."

Mom nodded. "It would be hard for her leave Burton permanently. What did you decide?"

"I told her I wouldn't take it. I said she and Bridge are more important than any job."

"Okay. And is that how you really feel?" My mother had a knack for getting to the root of the matter.

"Of course it is. Was I a little disappointed she wouldn't even consider it? Well, yeah, sure. But I'll get over it. We'll figure it out. It was just a great opportunity for me. For us."

Mom leaned back in her chair. "Flynn, do you remember what your father used to say about the cornerstone of a good marriage?"

Maureen and I grinned at each other. "Compromise!" We shouted the word together.

"Exactly. And do you know why he knew that so well? Because he lived it. Did you know that your father wanted to be a writer when I met him?"

"Dad?" Maureen frowned. "I didn't know that. I thought he always wanted to teach."

"Yes. Writing was his passion. But then we met in college, and we fell in love, and I couldn't live with the uncertainty of that kind of life. I wanted stability, someone who would support me so I could raise our kids. And so your father changed his major, and he became a teacher instead." A sheen of tears covered her eyes. "Twice your dad gave up his dream. Once in Ireland, when his father forced him into masonry, and then again when I forced him into teaching."

"How come we never knew that?" My dad had been the happiest man I knew. I never would've guessed that he wasn't doing exactly what he wanted.

"Because he chose to be happy. He could've been bitter or resented us. But he never was. Not once did your father ever accuse me of ruining his dream. He always told me he'd chosen the better part: his family. He compromised, Flynn." She smiled at me. "You need to decide how your life can work with Ali's. You're both strong people. You're passionate about what you do, and that's wonderful, son. But try to remember that Ali's sense of responsibility is one of the things you love about her. She wouldn't be who she is if she didn't care."

"But isn't it my turn to be her first choice? Her priority?" I hadn't been aware how much that stung. "Last time she chose Sam. And the farm. When's it going to be my turn?"

"God, Flynn, you sound like a spoiled brat." Maureen rolled her eyes. "Do you know how lucky you are that you found someone you love? Who loves you? It doesn't happen for everyone. Look at me. I'm almost thirty, and I've never had a real relationship. I'd give anything to have what you and Ali have. You love her. You want to build a life with her. Figure out how to make that happen, and stop whining about priorities." She winked at me. "*Compromise.*"

The Colonel's Last Stand was crowded. I eased the truck around to the side and pulled up out of the way of the real customers. Adrenaline buzzed in my system as I climbed out and headed for the front.

People were milling around the tables of vegetables and fruit, chatting with each other and loading up baskets. I spotted

Cassie Deymeyer ringing sales at the register. She saw me before anyone else did and gave me a grin and a wave.

Ali was standing by a table of lettuce, earnestly explaining something to a pair of white-haired women. I waited out of her sight until she began to turn away to handle someone else. And then I called her name.

"Alison Reynolds." She jerked her head toward me, and the smile that was mine alone stretched her mouth. She began to walk toward me, but as I kept talking, she slowed, curiosity covering her face.

"Alison Reynolds, nine years ago, I gave you an ultimatum. Leave town with me, as we'd planned, or we were through. It was a terrible thing to do. Probably the worst mistake of my life. You made the impossible choice I forced you to make: you stayed here to keep the promises you'd made to your brother. To your family. I hated that, because I thought it meant you loved me less."

Some of the women in the crowd had stopped what they were doing and were watching us. I recognized some of them from town. Cassie leaned both of her arms against the top of register and smiled broadly at me.

Ali was frozen, her face tense as she stared at me. Her hands were clenched tightly at her sides.

"I didn't realize that you being a woman who kept her promises was one of the things I loved most about you. I was a stupid, immature fool."

There was a buzz of voices among the crowd. Ali's face relaxed a fraction, but she was still wary about what was coming next.

"When I came back to Burton, back to you, I realized everything that I'd given up by leaving you all those years. I gave up my family. I gave up my greatest chance at happiness. And I gave up the only woman I will ever be able to love."

Whispers and awws came from the around the stand. I ignored them, focusing on the only woman whose heart would ever matter to me.

"Ali, I want a life with you. I want a life where we both get to live out what we're passionate about. If you feel like we need to live in Burton, I'll stay here with you. I'll build you a house, I'll get a job that lets me come home to you every night, and we'll make that family. I promise you, I'll do anything to make you happy.

"But if you might consider a compromise . . ." I smiled, letting the word roll off my tongue and feeling my dad at my shoulder. "I think there's a way for us to work it out. The most important thing, though, is that you know who and what is the most essential to me. And that's you, Ali. There's no future for me without you, because you *are* my future."

I walked toward her slowly, my eyes never leaving her face. "So Alison Reynolds . . . marry me. Marry me, and make me complete. Marry me, and we'll make the family we've always wanted." I reached her and held out my hand, whispering the last words. "Marry me, because I'll never leave you. I've loved you my whole life, Ali, and I'm never going to stop loving you." I dropped to my knee and opened my other hand, where my mother's engagement ring, the beautiful antique Celtic knot, lay on my palm. "Please."

She was shaking now. I could feel it in her hand. Or maybe that was me, because I also tasted the tears that were rolling down my face as I stared into her eyes, willing her to say the only word that I ever wanted to hear.

The most beautiful smile I'd seen in my entire life curved her lips. She reached out her free fingertips to trace the side of my face.

"Yes."

A smattering of applause filled the stand, but I hardly noticed. I stood up and pulled Ali into me, wrapping my arms around her as I buried my face in her neck. She threaded her fingers into my hair, and I knew without a doubt that I was where I belonged.

I was home.

Ali

THE SUN WAS BLAZING down on me as I walked from the house to the tent set up in front yard. It was hot for early May, and I was glad I'd gone with the strapless dress and sandals.

"Hey, Ali." A pretty woman who bore more than a passing resemblance to Meghan greeted me with a hug. "This is absolutely perfect. Thanks so much for throwing Meghan's graduation party. I can't believe the turnout."

I looked around at the crowds of people filling the tables and chairs we'd borrowed from friends and neighbors, at the line of folks enjoying the buffet table and the few who'd take up residence on the porch.

"This town loves Meghan, Jude. She's one of us now." I

squeezed her arm. "Thanks for sharing her."

"You all make her happy. That's what matters." She beamed at me. "And speaking of happy, I hear you've got some good news."

I held up my left hand. The beautiful ring I'd always admired on Cory Evans felt right on my finger. I'd been a little worried at first about taking it away from her, but she'd pushed that away.

"Brice would want you to wear it. And so do I. It has centuries of love and happy marriages built into it, and I know you're only going to bring it more."

"Yes, I do." I answered Jude with a grin. "It was a long time coming, but it's worth every tear I ever cried."

"Hey, are you talking about me?" Flynn slid his arms around my waist and drew me back against him. "I just got Bridget to sit down and eat something."

I laughed. "Jude, have you met my fiancé, Flynn Evans? Babe, this is Jude, Meghan's mom."

"Congratulations to both of you." Jude cocked her head. "So you're moving to New York?"

"Yes. Sort of." I turned my head to smile at Flynn. "Flynn's got a job at a news magazine in New York, and we're going to live up there part of the year, from late fall to early spring. But from May through September, we'll live here in Burton, so I can do my part with the farm. Flynn will telecommute while we're down here. The magazine wanted him enough to make that happen." I covered Flynn's hands where they rested on my middle. "And we'll be traveling, too, about a week out of every month. I'm going to homeschool Bridget, so we have the freedom to go with Flynn, wherever he's working."

"Sounds like a perfect compromise." Jude's lips twitched, and I knew she'd heard the whole story from her daughter.

"I think it works for us." Flynn nuzzled my neck.

"Two weddings in one year. Who would've ever thought?"

Meghan joined us, slipping her hand around her mother's back. She held out her own left hand, where my mother's ring sparkled. It looked absolutely perfect.

"I want to hear the whole story of how Sam proposed." Jude hugged her daughter. "You promised when you called me."

Meghan smiled. "We were on the porch last night, and I was nervous about graduation and the party today. Sam made me sit on the swing, and he told me to sketch something, because he knows it calms me down to draw. So I started doing a picture of our two hands together, and when I had it finished, I showed it to him, and he said it was missing something. I took it back to check, because I actually thought it was a pretty damn good sketch, and when I looked back at Sam, he was on his knee, holding out my ring and asking me to marry him." She smirked a little. "He might've said some other things, too. You know, about love, how I'm his life, and he never wants to live without me again."

"Yeah, you women have a way of turning us inside out and making it so we can't live without you." Logan, Jude's husband, came over and slid his hand through his wife's. He smiled down at her. "Not that I'd have it any other way."

"Hey, is this a family gathering? Did you forget me?" Sam slung his arm over Meghan's shoulders.

"We were just hearing how romantic you are, big brother." I bumped my arm against Sam's.

"We need to talk wedding plans." Jude raised her eyebrows. "I'm so excited about it. Everyone back at the Cove is going to be happy to hear you're getting married on the beach."

"What about you two?" Logan glanced at me. "You know you're welcome to use the Rip Tide if you want to have your wedding on the beach, too."

"Thanks." Flynn kissed my cheek. "But our family and friends would raise a fuss if we didn't finally give them a wedding right here in Burton. We're not doing anything too big, but it'll be in town, at the end of the summer."

Jude nodded. "Well, you're always welcome when you want to come visit." She glanced inside the tent where her toddler grandson was running the length of the buffet line. "I think I'd better go lasso DJ. Lindsay's not feeling well. The heat takes it out of her these days."

"When's she due?" I shaded my eyes from the sun.

"End of the summer, poor thing. Between the Tide, DJ and this new baby, she's going to have her hands full." Jude took Logan's hand. "We'd better go give her a break. Talk to you later, Ali."

Meghan watched her mother hurry over to scoop up her grandson and then glanced back at me. "Sam told me you'd come up with someone to help him with the stand after you move."

"Yeah, for the months when we're living in New York. Rilla Grant's doing the PR for the stand now, and when I mentioned we were looking for someone to help out, she jumped at the chance. I guess she's trying to make a little money to get her own place and jumpstart her business."

"I don't think I know her." Meghan frowned. "Sam said she lives nearby?"

"She does. I don't know her whole story yet, but I think she'll be a good fit. She seems to be a hard worker, and I'll train her this summer before we leave."

"I'm so glad everything's working out for you." Meghan squeezed my arm. "I'll miss you when you're living in New York, but I know you and Bridget are going to love it. You're all three going to be so happy."

Flynn's smile was brilliant. "That's the plan."

Alex was passing us, carrying a plate laden with food to a table where his parents waited. When he heard Flynn's words, he grinned and winked at me.

"Man of honor! Remember, I'm it. I'm serious."

I blew him a kiss. "Who else?" I laughed as I watched him navigate through the people who stood between his table and him.

Sam tugged at Meghan's hand. "You need to eat before this crowd devours everything. Come on."

As they wandered away, Flynn took my hand and kissed it. "You good, babe?"

I looked around at all the people I loved, gathered on the land that had nourished generations of my family, and then at the man who was my every dream, my every wish and my future.

"I couldn't be any better."

"Really? What if I did this?" He used the hand he was holding to pull me tight against his chest. The other hand skimmed over my cheek until he caught my chin between his finger and thumb, using it to coax my mouth open as he lowered his lips to mine in a sweet kiss that held every hope we shared.

I lost myself in Flynn and his touch until breathing became an issue. He leaned his forehead down against the top of my head and whispered so that I shivered.

"See? I told you it could be even better."

"Hmmm." I pretended to consider. "I guess if it only gets better each time you kiss me, you'll have to do it all the time, every day, for the rest of our lives. Think you're up to it?"

His blue eyes sparkled with wicked intent, and his lips curved into a smile of promise.

"Challenge accepted."

The End

If you loved Ali and Flynn, don't miss the third and final book in The One Trilogy.

THE ONLY ONE

The best way to show how much you love a book is by leaving a review on your favorite venue. Please leave some love for THE FIRST ONE. Thank you!

Want to make sure you don't miss any new releases, special content and giveaways? Sign up for Tawdra Kandle's newsletter here (http://eepurl.com/isWKs).

Acknowledgements

The human brain is the coolest thing. The portion where stories are born is an amazing place that makes connections that sometimes blow me away.

A long time ago, I remember being with my oldest daughter in the car as we listened to Tim McGraw's song, *Everywhere.* I told her there was a beautiful story in those lyrics, and it began to unfold in my mind. While I didn't write it then, it always lingered there, just in the back of my mind.

Flash forward to last year when I was writing *The Last One.* Sam's sister Ali had a story, and I knew the vague outline of it. Then one evening, it all came together, and I realized that Ali's story was the one I'd begun to spin years before. Love when that happens.

So thank you to Tim McGraw for that song and many others that have made me laugh and cry over the years.

Thanks also to my wonderful team of book midwives: Kelly Baker for proofreading magic, Stacey Blake of Champagne Formats for making it all pretty, Amanda Long and Olivia Hardin for their help and support, and Mandie Stevens and Jen Rattie for their promo help. Massive love to all of you! L.P. Hidalgo of BookFabulous Designs made this beautiful cover—I appreciate her hard work and patience.

I am endlessly grateful for the support, encouragement and cheering of my readers. Y'all make me smile and keep me going. Big hugs and hearts all around.

And always, always, always . . . thank you to my wonderful family. I love you all.

About the Author

Photo: Heather Batchelder

Tawdra Kandle writes romance, in just about all its forms. She loves unlikely pairings, strong women, sexy guys, hot love scenes and just enough conflict to make it interesting. Her books run from YA paranormal romance (THE KING SERIES), through NA paranormal and contemporary romance (THE SERENDIPITY DUET, PERFECT DISH DUO, THE ONE TRILOGY) to adult contemporary and paramystery romance (CRYSTAL COVE BOOKS and RECIPE FOR DEATH SERIES). She lives in central Florida with a husband, kids, sweet pup and too many cats. And yeah, she rocks purple hair.

Follow Tawdra on Facebook, Twitter, Tsu, Instagram, Pinterest and Tumblr.

Keep up with her releases and events on her website and her newsletter.

Playlist for
The *First* ONE

Gentle On My Mind The Band Perry

Dirt Florida Georgia Line

What Might Have Been Little Texas

What Hurts The Most Rascal Flatts

All My Friends Say Luke Bryan

Bartender Lady Antebellum

Everywhere Tim McGraw

Already Home Ha-Ash with Brandi Carlile

CPSIA information can be obtained
at www.ICGtesting.com
Printed in the USA
JSHW020046160720
6706JS00003B/88